REMEMBERING

Remembering

H.B. Louise

IngramSpark

IngramSpark

First Edition
Editing by Dominic Wakeford

ISBN: 978-1-7362091-4-1 (paperback)
ISBN: 978-1-7362091-5-8 (hardback)
ISBN: 978-1-7362091-2-7 (ebook)

Published by IngramSpark
www.ingramspark.com

Contents

For my family-

Thank you for shaping me into the individual I am today.

Prologue

Caelyn - Three Months Earlier

The rush of cold water was like a tidal wave; crashing into my body while making my limbs fly back. My head hit the headrest hard, and I could feel my vision blur. I know an impact like this will have left me unconscious. I've felt this adrenaline before, and my body warmly accepted the sensation. I vaguely remember the feeling on my legs then my waist, and finally up my arms and chest as the water filled the cabin.

It's the feeling of being submerged in water that my body yearns for. Ever since I was three years old, I would crave the feeling of cold Maine water against my tan skin. David and I grew up around the water so it was only natural, right? My mother used to take us with her to the country club's pool on days that our older sister had school. She would pack up a bag of pool toys, sunblock, and towels before packing us kids in the car. David and I loved to splash around in the kiddy pool and "dive" for our pool treasures. After playing for several hours Mom would dry us off and take us to lunch. This was a ritual we followed for five years. It's how David and I got so close. These memories form the beginning of our unbreakable bond.

When we turned fifteen our father talked with us about scuba diving classes, and we jumped on the opportunity with no hesitation. Since Dad had already taken the classes, it was David and I that took them together. Adrian, our older sister, wanted no part in diving. Besides, the number one rule of diving is always dive with a buddy. Buddy is singular, right? We didn't need her anyway.

The classes were long, but I loved the thought of being away from "home drama." Day after day, our bodies got used to the equipment and warm pool water. However, when it was time to do the real test, it was a cold, fall day in our hometown, Cape Elizabeth, Maine.

I was putting my long, brown hair into a braid when David knocked on the bathroom door. I saw slight anxiousness, but mostly excitement on his face. I, on the other hand, was freaking out. The temperature of the water was around fifty degrees and the air temperature was just above that. It was also our first time diving in the ocean, plus it was checkout day. Checkout day is the final round of tests for new divers wishing to get their licenses. It comprises several tests, completed above and below water, which range in level of difficulty and speed.

David read my anxiety and knew I needed the comfort, so he jumped up on the bathroom counter. He grabbed the toothpaste and squirted some on his index finger as he said something like, "You know, I overheard Mom and Dad talking about us again."

"What did they say this time?" I scoffed.

"They're just glad that we did this together. They're really proud of us for not backing down," he said between scrubs with his finger. He spit into the sink and scrubbed again.

"You and me? Back down? HA! No way. We're in this together, right?" I said, trying to hold back the many concerns flooding my mind. I didn't want to worry my buddy on such an important day.

"Yep. Just you and me, till the end." He rinsed his finger and slid his tall frame off the counter. He stood in front of me and gripped my shoulders. "It'll be fine, Caelyn. I promise. Besides, I'll be right there the entire time. If a shark comes for you, it'll have to eat me too." I'm grateful that he tried to make a joke. He was always the funny twin who somehow managed to make people laugh in grim situations. It was something I tried to learn from him, keyword "tried."

Ending my thoughts, he surprised me with a giant bear hug. My body melted into his, and I felt so small compared to him. We did not compare in height, but we shared the bright green eyes from our mom and sporty build from our dad. The hug ended too quickly, but I was beginning to feel much better. "Ready?" he asked. I grabbed my bag from the ground and nodded my head. *Here goes nothing*, I thought.

In the garage, we learned that Adrian would be staying home as she'd been complaining of a migraine. So, it was my mom, dad, David, and me that would be traveling to our checkout dive. Nerves ran high, but David was mostly excited. I envied his spirit.

We got to the pier an hour later and Mom took a couple pictures of us before we parted ways for the dive. Dad hugged us both and said that he would be waiting on the dock as soon as we were done. Our instructor called us over and took our seats, along with five other divers, to get prepped. The boat ride lasted about twenty minutes, and our driver put out the red and white dive flag when it was time.

Diver after diver jumped off the boat and descended into the choppy water. Then it was our turn. I looked up at David, he put on his mask, and grabbed my hand. "One. Two. Three!" we said in unison as we stepped right foot first into the crisp, unknown water. The water was bitterly cold and it took my breath away. The rush of cold on the uncovered parts of my body left me paralyzed, yet adrenaline coursed through every vein in my body.

We stayed on the surface and waited for our instructor to give us directions as to what we would be doing first. He wanted to test us on clearing our masks of fog, taking off and putting on our weight belts (these keep us weighed down to the bottom), hand signals, and exchanging the octo regulators. We had no problem completing these tests and passed with flying colors.

The dive was cold, but the views made up for the frigid temperature. The deep blue water was filled with colorful coral and fish as far as the eye could see. *What a difference from the pool we had been practicing in*, I thought. David's eyes filled with wonder as we rounded the reef to see the next marine life in our path. We saw Atlantic cod, sea stars, flounder, and lobsters, among others. The experience had topped anything I had ever done, and I think David would agree with me. Although rare, we even spotted a blue shark in the distance. After a while, the water temperature stopped bothering me. David and I followed along with the rest of our class and instructor.

At one point in the dive, David spotted something on the coral and made a motion for me to come see. I slowly approached the spot, trying to not disturb whatever he had found. It was a rockfish that blended in perfectly with its surroundings. We shared a look of amazement and caught up with the rest of the group after a minute of studying the fish. Our dive was coming to an end, and I was dreading the return to the boat. I wanted to stay diving like this forever. I shared a look with David and I could tell he was feeling the same way. I guess it was a twin thing, but I felt I could read his mind in that moment.

We made our ascent to the surface and waited as one diver at a time climbed onto the boat. We took turns rinsing off the salt water and wrapped ourselves in towels to warm up. For the twenty minutes that it would take to return to the pier, I spent half the time writing in my log book and the other half sitting as close as I could to David. I am an innately cold person by nature, so my surroundings were not helping my current situation. Soon the pier came into view, and I got up to gather my flippers, mask, and other equipment. I was stopped short when David grabbed my hand.

"What is it?" I asked clinging to the towel that was around my shoulders.

"I just wanted to tell you how much it means to me that you did this with me, buddy," he said, getting up and nudging my shoulder.

"I love you too," I said, opening my arms and gave him a tight squeeze. I knew this memory of our first dive would hold a special place in my heart.

I threw on my sweatpants and sweatshirt, even though I was still soaked, and grabbed my mesh bag that seemed to be heavier than me. David stepped off the boat first and stuck out his hand for me to grab. I took it and stepped onto the cool concrete. I dropped my bag to readjust it on my shoulder, but David effortlessly took it along with his own.

We found our mom and dad at the end of the pier waiting with coffee cups, and I gladly took one after I gave them both hugs. All Dad wanted to know was how amazing our first "real" dive was. We would tell him something and then he would reference his first and many subsequent dives. It was such easy conversation, and I couldn't keep the smile off my face.

Mom felt that a celebratory dinner was in order for us as soon as we got home. She even told us that she called our grandparents and asked them to come over.

The car ride home would last about an hour and my body was exhausted from the day's efforts, so I decided to take a nap. Before I fell asleep David asked about having our neighbors, the Carters, over for dinner too. I couldn't wait to get home to tell Liam, our best friend, all about it. It didn't take long for me to doze off, listening to the soft hum of the radio and my brother singing along with the lyrics.

But I didn't wake up in the driveway at home. I woke up in a plain white room with a bandage around my torso, a cast on my right arm, and my head throbbing with every blink.

Mom sat in the chair next to my bed and Dad paced, or rather limped, in the other part of the room. Tubes ran from my left arm, and I heard machines beeping around me. I assumed that this was a hospital room, yet I had no idea why I was here. I looked around the room, blinking to focus my eyes on the room, but I only noticed my parents. Where was the rest of my family? I tried to clear my throat to ask, but no words came off my tongue. My mouth felt like sandpaper. It was in that moment that my parents must have heard my failed attempts to talk. Concern and relief filled their expressions, but then a look of hurt replaced them just as quickly.

"Oh, thank God," Dad said rushing to my other side. His calloused hand found my cheek and tears fell from his eyes.

"What happened?" I managed to croak after several attempts; my voice sounded tired and worn. Dad tried to say something but was interrupted by a figure at the door.

"Hello Caelyn, I'm glad to see that you are awake. Mr. and Mrs. Price," the man said, nodding his head in their direction. "Caelyn, my name is Dr. Hynes, and I am your assigned doctor for your recovery. How are you feeling?" he asked. The tall, lanky man, barely filling his white coat, stepped into the room.

"I'm sore, I guess. My head and body aches," I said hesitantly. I was still questioning why I was in this room. I couldn't remember anything after David and I finished our dive. Did we drive home? Did we even make it home? Dr. Hynes seemed more worried about how I felt, when I was worried about my lack of memory and confusion. Also, why did I need a doctor? *I really need some answers right about now,* I thought to myself as I looked from the doctor to my parents.

Dr. Hynes flipped through some papers on his clipboard and paused to speak. "That is to be expected from the injuries you have received. Your right arm is broken just below your elbow, your torso has a gash from where your seatbelt cut into you, and four of your ribs are broken. I want you to take it easy and try not to move a lot at this point. I am hoping the bruising and swelling will go down so we can get you up and walking as soon as you are able. You may feel a little discomfort for the next several weeks, and we will do everything we can to make it better for you."

He flipped through more paperwork after he explained some more instructions for my recovery. However, all I could focus on were the injuries he mentioned. He said something about my seatbelt causing a gash—why couldn't I remember what happened? He began to speak again, no doubt because he saw the confused expression on my face.

"Now to explain your head; it was slammed into the car's window due to the impact of the other car," he spoke clearly and fluently, like someone giving a speech they'd rehearsed for days. "Memory loss can be expected, but by looking at your scans, you might have more confusion than actual memory loss." He paused to let that sink in. "So, I don't think we should be expecting long-term damage to your brain. Can I get you anything? Like more pain medication or water?" he said, pressing something on his hip.

"Maybe some water?" I say.

"I'll have your nurse get that for you right away."

"Thank you." Dr. Hynes started to retreat from the room. "Wait, Dr. Hynes, can I ask you something?" he responded with a nod of his head. "Why can't I remember what happened? Why am I even here? You mentioned a seatbelt and the impact of another car. I'm sorry, I'm just a little confused as to what you mean..." My words trailed off and the room's concerned energy seemed to increase.

Take a deep breath, I thought. *You need to breathe. I'm sure everything will be fine.*

Dr. Hynes walked to my bedside and closed his eyes. When he opened them, there was a look of sorrow etched across his face. The band-aid was about to be ripped off, I could tell.

"I'm sorry to say that you were in a car accident on your way home. Do you remember that your father was driving you, your mother, and your brother, David, back home?"

I shook my head no, confused. I am sure that did happen, but I couldn't remember the exact details and I grew frustrated.

Mom choked on a sob. "I'm sorry," she said trying to compose herself.

Dr. Hynes continued, "At an intersection, about ten minutes from your house, a truck driver had fallen asleep at the wheel and crashed into the back end of the passenger side. Your mother and father, as you can see, are fine and have received minor scratches and injuries. You, on the other hand, were tossed around quite a bit." My mother grabbed my left hand and tears streamed down her face.

"However, I'm sorry to inform you that your brother's side of the car was badly impacted. He was brought here to the hospital, and I tried my best. My whole staff did their best, but we could not save him due to his severe injuries. I am so sorry for your loss. I wish I could have done more." He stood there with his head bowed low, and my mom's head dropped to the bed. "I'm so sorry. I tried everything that I could to save him. His injuries were too extensive." Dr. Hynes didn't smile, nor did he flinch when he said the words. My father came closer to my mom and tried to comfort her. My mind was a mess of memories, and I needed to put the puzzle pieces back together.

I was in an accident. I was awoken by a quick jolt of the car being slammed into the guard rail. Upon impact, my head was resting on the window. Then as something hit the back of the car, my head bounced off the glass and collided with the window again. A sharp pain started below my elbow and I cried out in pain when the seat began to contort because of the morphing car. The hood sparked from the front, and I could barely hear anything. But then, I heard David grunting in pain. I remember seeing blood trailing down his t-shirt, onto his arms. There was a long gash on his forehead and blood continued to cover his t-shirt. I remember looking into his eyes one last time, before they closed forever.

The next two hours were a blur. As my memories flooded my mind, I began to piece together the magnitude of the doctor's words. David was dead. He was gone, forever.

My mother's cries filled the room and the whole hospital floor. My father tried to soothe her and me at the same time, but he was struggling with his own grief. About an hour after the news from the doctor, a nurse came in and offered her condolences. I didn't know what to say in the moment, I was still processing it myself. She gave me some medicine for my pain and asked if I wanted something to eat. *How can anyone eat at a time like this?,* I thought, feeling empty. I declined and tried to just close my eyes. Before I went under from the drugs they had given me, I saw a silhouette in the corner of the room. It was Liam, and I saw the slightest glimmer of a small, kind smile play on his lips.

I was discharged two weeks later, the day of David's funeral, with a little prodding from my parents. They already had to push back the funeral so that I could make it, and did not want to delay it any longer. Around eight o'clock in the morning my parents, Adrian, and I left my cold, depressing hospital room to end up in a cold, depressing funeral home. My mom had brought my black dress from home; the one with the cap sleeves and a high neckline. I was too weak to stand in heels, but I knew my mom wanted me to look my absolute best so I told her to bring them anyway. When we arrived at Miller Funeral Home, my parents directed Adrian and I to go inside as they grabbed some extra things from the trunk of the car. I tugged at the neckline on my dress and followed Adrian's slim frame through the door. As soon as the door shut behind me, Adrian retreated down a long hallway without a word. I tried to call out to her, but I couldn't find the right words. Instead of following her, I decided to walk around.

The inside of the funeral home smelled exactly as I expected: moth balls and flowers, a surprising mixture that wasn't quite as awful as I'd imagined. Yellow and purple orchids were interspersed with a mixture of white flowers all around the rooms. The orchids were my touch because I knew they were David's favorite, even though he'd never admit that to anyone. I didn't know exactly where else to go, but something was pulling me to the back room. Slowly but surely, I walked down the same hallway that Adrian had retreated to. In the back, there was a small kitchen and table with several chairs. I stopped at the door frame when I heard familiar voices. My grandma was talking.

"Adrian, honey you need to eat," her voice sounded firm.

"I'm fine, Grandma. I'm not the one you should be worrying about," Adrian's voice sounded far away when she replied. "I know David was my brother too, but I can't help but think about our relationship. We weren't close like him and Caelyn. It'll be hard now, but I also know it'll be okay eventually. I will always miss him, you know? I just hate that he was the only one to die from the accident..." She trailed off and I knew she was biting her nails. I couldn't help but take that last comment to heart. Should someone else have died? What if the truck hit my side of the car instead? She spoke again, this time short and to the point. "You shouldn't be worrying about me, Grandma."

I thought I was out of tears with the amount I cried at the hospital, but I was wrong. As their conversation came to an end, I found that I couldn't stop them coming. Adrian was right—her and David were never close. He was my twin, but more importantly my best friend. I dream that one day I'll wake up and this will all have been a bad dream. So far that hadn't happened, and I was having a hard time realizing that he was really gone.

"Caelyn, how long have you been standing there?" Adrian came out the door and was startled to see me standing against the wall. Her makeup was running a little and the tip of her nose was red. I jumped and tried to straighten up, but all I managed to do was pull at the stitches on my torso. I winced from the pain.

"Not long, I just needed to rest for a second," I lied.

"Why don't you go sit down? I'll go see what Mom and Dad need help with."

Before she left, she surprised me by pulling me into a stiff hug. I tried to hold back how much I was in pain by gritting my teeth, but she saw my expression when she pulled away.

"Oh my gosh, I'm so sorry. Did I hurt you?" she asked, concern in her voice.

"No, it's okay," I lied again. *I needed to stop the lying before it became a bad habit,* I noted. She looked sad but believed the lie. She left and I decided to walk into the room she had just exited. The whole room stopped speaking and my grandma came over to me.

"Caelyn, you look beautiful darling." Grandma grabbed my hand with both of hers and looked right at me. Her sea green eyes started to well up, so she dropped my hands to dab at them. My grandpa came up to me next and tried to give me a hug. He was gentle, but I couldn't help but flinch at his touch. Since leaving the hospital, the "little discomfort" had increased to "severe discomfort."

"What's wrong?" he asked me.

"Nothing, I'm fine."

There I was, lying to my own grandpa. "Fine, I'm not fine. I am in so much pain, emotionally and physically. Any time someone tries to touch me I feel like they are hitting me with a baseball bat because I'm still so sensitive. I haven't had my medicine yet today, because Mom and Dad got distracted once we got here, which I understand..." I teared up as my breath quickened. I began to twitch as a sense of discomfort overcame my body. "On top of it all, it feels like a hundred degrees in here. I mean come on, why can't a window be opened or something?" I tugged at the neck of dress and pulled at my sleeves. My whole body was on fire, or at least it felt like it. I looked around the room looking for a window but instead, my eyes landed on four different people I didn't see before this moment. Mr. and Mrs. Carter were standing helping my grandma with the food and Evelyn and Liam were sitting at the table. Liam met my eyes, but Evelyn stared at her hands. I couldn't believe that I hadn't seen them before. I mouthed an "I'm sorry" at them before I left the room. I walked as fast as I could to the nearest exit and as soon as the door opened, I felt the immediate brisk Maine air I loved.

With my uninjured arm, I reached down to take off my heels before sitting down on the cold concrete. The tears poured out of me once again as if this was the first time I heard that David was dead. My whole body shook and with every second the pain felt worse. I wanted to rip off the bandage underneath this dress; I wanted to rip off the bulky cast from my right arm; I wanted the pain to stop. I took one of my heels and hurled it into the parking lot while screaming as loud as I could. It angered me that it didn't go very far.

I was about to try again with the other shoe when someone sat next to me.

Through my tears, I saw Liam's dark brown eyes. Concern was etched on his face as he stared at me. I could tell he held back comforting me. Without saying a word, he handed me a small bottled water and motioned for my hand. I opened my palm, and he dropped a white capsule onto it. I stuck it in my mouth, grateful someone knew what I needed. He pushed himself off the concrete step and walked to where my shoe lay.

"While I'm out here, do you plan to throw the other one?" he said, motioning to the heel by me.

I debated his question but slowly shook my head. He came back over to me, careful with each step, probably weighing his next actions. He took the other shoe from me and helped me put them on one at a time. His hands were shaking, and I noticed black and blue bruises on his knuckles.

"What did you do?" I asked quietly. He didn't meet my gaze when he answered.

"I punched my wall," he said flatly and I took in a loud breath. "Don't worry, I didn't break it. My hand I mean. I did put a nice size hole in my bedroom's dry wall though." He stood in front of me and tears filled his eyes. I could tell he wasn't trying to stop them. "Caelyn, I miss him every second of every day. It's not fair what happened, and I keep telling myself that it'll be okay, but it isn't. It's nowhere near okay." He stopped to take a breath, and I started to cry again. "I'm sorry, I just know that I can talk to you about this stuff because you know what I'm feeling."

"Yeah, I know it sucks. The pain in unbearab—" I immediately shut my mouth when I heard someone clear their throat behind me. I turned too quickly to see who needed us.

"Caelyn," my father said, standing in the doorway. "Liam," he then looked at both of us, "the funeral is about to start." Nodding my head, I wiped my eyes with the back of my left hand. Liam offered me his hand, and I graciously accepted. Hand in hand we walked down the hall after my father, back into the stuffy room I just tried to escape from.

"I'll be with you all day," Liam said to me, tightening his grip as we walked toward the big room. Even though his words were kind, all I could think about was the fact that I would be mourning my best friend. Making eye contact with Liam solidified his words somewhere deep within me. I knew he would be true to his word and gave his hand a squeeze before I let go.

The funeral lasted all day and there was a constant flow of people that came to share their condolences. Members from our church brought baked goods, co-workers of my parents brought flowers or care baskets, and even some of our classmates attended. Over half of them came for a few minutes to shake our family's hands and say how sorry they were. Aunts, uncles, and cousins came and stayed most of the day and were even planning on staying for several days after the funeral. Our family friends and neighbors, like the Carters, stayed all day as well.

Throughout the entire day, I found myself searching the room for Liam when I felt overwhelmed. It was no surprise that whenever I made eye contact across the room, I immediately felt calmer. He didn't have to be by my side every second because I felt his comfort through those glances. However, in the moments when I felt like rushing off alone, Liam seemed to sense the uneasiness by appearing next to me. He offered his hands, shoulders, or comforting silence. Along with Liam, my parents and sister were my biggest rocks.

Before the funeral ended, our pastor requested that everyone take a seat in the common area where David lay. This was the time for final words before a small procession would continue to the burial site.

"I'd like to thank you all on behalf of the Price family for coming today and supporting them through this life-changing process. It is because of your compassion and support that they will eventually find peace. On October 28, heaven gained an angel, David Michael Price. At the young age of fifteen, David's life was taken after a horrible accident." There followed a moment of heavy silence. "Any of you that knew David can testify that he was an energetic boy that loved the Lord, his family, and friends," Pastor Johns said as he motioned to our row before continuing. "David enjoyed diving with his sister, school sports, and fishing with his best friend. I have great confidence that David will continue those hobbies beyond the gates of Heaven." He took a long pause and looked over at the casket. "We will love and miss you David, but we know that you are in a better place, now that you are among our Lord and Savior." He opened his bible to a bookmarked page and continued with his speech. "I'd now like to use this time to read one of David's favorite Bible verses from the book of Deuteronomy chapter 31 verse 6. 'Be strong and courageous. Do not be afraid or terrified because of them, for the LORD your God goes with you; he will never leave you nor forsake you.' I believe this speaks volumes, don't you?" he asked the congregation, giving it a moment to sink in.

Many people in the crowd nodded their heads and a few audibly said amen.

"You see, David was a strong young man and had a kind, courageous soul. He was never afraid of what life threw at him because he believed in Jesus Christ and His plan," he paused again to let the room understand what he was saying. Just then, Pastor John began to choke up and turned from the podium. The room felt eerily quiet as Pastor John took a moment to compose himself. "May David find peace through our Lord and Father," he concluded, opening the time up to anyone who had any remaining thoughts to share.

My mother reached for Adrian's and my hand as my father walked up to the podium. He took a deep breath. "I speak for both my wife and myself in thanking each one of you for coming today. I had always imagined my son eulogizing me instead of the other way around..." A noticeable sigh carried round the room before my father went on. "Losing a son is by far the hardest thing I have ever been through. Although impossibly challenging, I believe God's will and grace will help my wife, Beth, our two daughters, Adrian and Caelyn, and I in this grieving and healing process." He took a deeper breath and glanced at us in the front row. Tears streamed down all our faces. "Beth and I were very proud of the young man David had become and what a great brother he was to his sisters. I wish that we had had more time with him to see what type of man he would have grown up to be. I have no doubt in my mind that he would've been amazing. We will miss and love him for as long as we live." My father stood at the podium for a few seconds looking down at his hands. "Now we will be going to the burial site, and with that, all are welcome to join. Thank you all again." He came back to our row, grabbed my mother's hand and began walking to the doors. I was slow at moving, but my dad made sure to walk next to me to offer help if need be.

We had made arrangements so that David would be buried next to my mother's parents in the cemetery. As the small group walked up the hill, a funeral coordinator handed each of us a white rose to place on the casket before David was lowered into the ground.

A few more words and tears were shed before it was time for everyone to place their rose on top of the cherry wood casket. My grandparents went first, followed by Liam and his family, then it was my mother and father's turn, Adrian's, and then finally mine. I placed my rose down with my left hand and then immediately reached into my purse. I felt the bottom of it, finding the one thing I had wanted to give David as a parting gift. I closed my eyes, placing his diving mask on top of the roses. My father came and placed a hand on my shoulder, gently pulling me to him.

I watched the buriers as they lowered the casket deep into the ground. My eyes remained on David's dive mask until I could no longer see the blue and black trim. I remembered the last day I had with him; it was probably one of the best days of my life, while this had to be the worst.

Accepting the fact that I couldn't see the mask anymore, I turned my back to the grave and walked slowly to our car by myself. Halfway down the hill, one of my heels stuck in the ground and caused me to lose my footing. I had no energy left to catch myself so I tripped and fell onto the grass with a thud. I didn't think I could feel any more pain in that moment, but I was wrong. There I laid on the ground as every inch of my body throbbed. I don't recall ever screaming, but I did hear a few shrieks from behind. Or maybe that was me? Before I knew it, my father and Mr. Carter were helping me up and asking me multiple questions. I didn't hear what they were saying over the pain I was feeling in my heart and body. I just gripped at the bandage on my torso, feeling a warm sensation over-coming my chilled body. In one swift motion, my father swooped me into his arms and carried me to the car. He opened the door and gently sat me down with a kiss on the forehead. I saw that his eyes were bloodshot and brimmed with sadness.

The car ride was silent except for the hum of the car's engine and my mother's occasional sniffle. Adrian chose to ride with my grand-parents back to the house. It was around five in the evening, and Mom had arranged for the Carters and my grandparents to come over to eat the dinners we were given. We had so much food we could have been fed for a whole month.

The car was parked and everyone had gotten out but me. "Cae-lyn honey, why don't you go in and get cleaned up so I can give you another pain pill. Then you can eat some dinner," my mom said.

She was holding out one hand for me to take while she held my heels in her other hand. I went on autopilot and accepted her hand. My grandparents' car pulled up behind ours while the Carters pulled into their driveway across the street. Mrs. Carter and Liam walked over with a few dishes in their hands. "Liam, can you help Caelyn upstairs? I'll take what you have there."

I was still running on autopilot as Liam walked behind me, into the house, and up the stairs. In my room, I sat down on my bed and began pulling at my sleeves nervously. I heard a door slam down the hall, which must have been Adrian.

"What can I get you?" he asked me, checking the hallway for the source of the noise.

"Can you get me a t-shirt and a pair of sweatpants? They're on a shelf in my closet." He walked over, disappeared and returned with the clothes.

"Is that okay?" He didn't really have to ask because he knew which outfit was my favorite. I nodded, sucking on my bottom lip.

"Can I have a glass of water too?" I asked staring at the wall, wishing to be left alone.

He nodded his head and retreated out my door. I got up and walked the few steps across the hall and cracked open David's door. The room was dark and musty from being closed for the last two weeks. I squeezed through the small crack I made and turned on the light. Immediately, I noticed that his room smelled exactly like him. Even his bed was made neatly and everything looked like it always did. I went over to his desk and held up a picture frame. The three people smiling would never smile like that again. David was dead, Adrian was hurting, and I would never feel whole again. The longer I stared, I began to taste the saltiness of my tears as they rolled down my cheeks.

The cold, thin frame only made me angrier as the smiles glared back at me. With one fell swoop, I watched the frame leave my hand to only shatter five feet away. I felt the pain in my chest subside, so I picked up the other two frames and threw them too. I went over to his bookshelf and picked up a few books and hurled them at the wall. Emotionally exhausted, I collapsed on the ground. My mind began to comprehend what I'd done. I ruined David's pictures; I ruined David's books, his favorites. It was all my fault. I should have never come in here; it only made me hurt more. I crawled with my left arm over to the mess and started to pick up the glass in a hurry before someone walked in and saw what I had done.

The glass was thin and sharp, but I hurriedly grasped for it anyway. I felt the edges of the glass sink deep into my skin, but the pain didn't bother me. I had to clean up, but I kept thinking his room was too perfect, too put together for the situation. I looked down at my hands and saw blood mixed in with the glass pieces. I screamed and threw the glass out of my hand. I had officially lost all control.

Not even a minute later, Liam was upstairs with my water. I was throwing more books and things off David's desk now. "Caelyn, stop!" he yelled as the glass of water fell from his hand and shattered as it hit the floor. He ran over to me, but I wasn't letting him touch me. "Steve! Beth! Come up here now!" he screamed.

"Get away from me!" I cried.

"Caelyn stop, please let me help you," he reached for me again and his fingers grazed my skin, but I pulled away. As he made his second attempt, my fist collided with his stomach, and a look of complete shock registered on his face. It lasted a few seconds, and he tried again. This time he grabbed my left arm and pulled hard, not accepting defeat. The amount of force from his rough touch caused me to focus on the pain in my body. I had a moment of weakness. His height and strength gave him the advantage as he wrapped his arms around me so that he could subdue me. After my best struggle, I gave into him and sadness replaced the anger as I crumbled into his touch and fell to the floor. His arms were still around me, but this time they were soft and comforting. With that, I felt all the energy leave my bones. My body trembled as the tears came out uncontrollably. "Shh, shh. It's okay," he whispered into my hair as he smoothly rocked back and forth.

How was it going to be okay? All I could think about was how I would never hear my brother's raspy voice in the mornings or smell his shampoo after he showered. I had lost my best friend and in this moment, I had never felt more alone. I wanted him back, but that was a wish that couldn't come true. He was gone forever. Trying to compose myself, I looked through my tear-filled eyes at David's room, but all I saw was the mess I had made. My head fell into Liam's chest as the sobs consumed me once again. At this point, I was gasping for air.

"What's going on?" my father said as he rushed into the room, stepped over the broken water glass, and noticing the redecoration. My mother entered next, followed by Mr. and Mrs. Carter. All eyes were on Liam and me sitting on the floor surrounded by the mess I had made. My father's eyes were full of concern as he stared down at me. "Beth, please get her cleaned up. She's bleeding." My dad's voice sounded broken. My mother hesitantly stepped forward and reached out to me. I flinched and so did she. I held onto Liam for dear life as my mom said something to him. He tried to shift my weight to the side so that he could stand up. I wasn't moving.

"Caelyn come on, let's get you cleaned up and into bed." Liam tried to move me off him again, but I only gripped harder. Choosing a different method, he effortlessly picked me up so we could walk to my bathroom. He gently sat me on the counter and my mom got the first aid supplies out of the closet. He let me hold onto him as she cleaned out my cuts.

"What are we supposed to do?" My father's voice through the open doorway was heard loud and clear.

"She just needs your support right now Steve. This isn't just something she's going to get over in a matter of hours," Mr. Carter said, standing with his arm around his wife's shoulders.

"That's the thing, it's not just my support she needs. It's all of our support." My father must have been gesturing to them. "Especially your son. Liam lost David too." There was a moment of silence. "Liam is like a son to me and Beth, and David considered him a brother. This loss affects your family as much as mine. We will get through it together, I promise."

My mother stood in front of me with a bottle of hydrogen peroxide and gauze. She poured some of the liquid onto my cuts, and I tried to hold back my shrieks.

"I'm almost done, I'm sorry." She finished the cleaning, and Liam stayed through it all, keeping his arm wrapped around my back. Mom wrapped my hand and secured the makeshift bandage with a large piece of tape. "Okay let's get the rest of you cleaned up," she suggested.

Liam, still helping me, followed my mother into my room and sat me down on the bed. He slowly let go of me as she asked him something. He nodded his head and retreated out the door. Panic momentarily set in, but my mother tried to calm me down. "He'll be back. Don't worry. We just need to change you out of these clothes. Okay?"

Once my sweats were on, my mother helped me arrange the pillows on my bed. I needed to be propped up enough so that my arm and torso were comfortable. The doctor warned us that the first few days at home would be rough and painful; I was starting to believe him. Liam returned in about ten minutes with a different set of clothes on, a glass of water, and what looked to be medicine.

"Liam, will you be okay with her for a few minutes? I'm going to be across the hall with Steve and your parents."

"Yeah, we'll be okay."

My mom nodded her head and left the room. Liam stood awkwardly by my bed, not really knowing what to do. I did my best to scoot over and patted the space next to me. He gladly accepted my offer and slid on top of the covers. We sat for a few moments in complete silence, taking in each other's presence. I wasn't sure why, but him being there was so calming to me.

I finally spoke first. "I'm sorry." I wasn't sure what I was most sorry for, it just came out. He took a deep breath and closed his eyes. When Liam's eyelids rose, tears were forming over his brown eyes. I kept talking because this was the second time today I had seen Liam get this emotional. I wanted to get everything off my chest before he could stop me. "I'm sorry for earlier... if I scared you. I can't help these feelings, they're scaring me. I'm sorry for what is to come too. I just feel so lost, so broken. Like I'm not sure what to do next. David would know exactly what to do, you know?" He continued to sit there, listening to me in silence. As I spoke, tears started to fall down his cheeks. Then he went to speak.

"I miss him so much Caelyn. This situation frightens me because I've been feeling things I didn't know I was capable of. There's this horrible anger that just takes over my body. It causes me to lose all control," he said, looking down at his bruised knuckles. "I feel like my chest has an extra weight on it, and it's getting heavier with each coming breath. My head pounds and thinking only makes it worse. I've never felt this way! Why do I feel this way?" He was almost shouting now. "What's wrong with me?" Just then, he turned to face me so quickly that I was momentarily stunned. The hurt and sadness in Liam's eyes was heart-wrenching.

"You lost someone you cared deeply for. I guess with loss your emotions become heightened and make you feel a certain way. I'm not sure, but I do know one thing," I said quietly.

"What's that?"

"I feel the same way. I mean you saw me earlier today. The anger is unlike anything I have ever felt. The sadness is consuming." I debated what I truly wanted to tell him, but the words flowed out before I could stop them. "I know it should have been me. It should have been me and not David." I'd finally admitted my deepest darkest secret that I had been holding on to for the past two weeks. Saying the words out loud solidified my belief in them. It really should have been me. I should have died. David should be among the living, not among the dead. More tears flooded out of me, and I covered my eyes with the palm of my hands.

"What are you talking about?" Liam grasped my wrists, trying to pry them from my eyes. "Caelyn, why would you ever say that?" His brown eyes searched my features with so much concern, like I was a china teacup teetering on the edge of the table.

"If it was me then you wouldn't be feeling these emotions. If it was me then I wouldn't have lashed out and destroyed David's room. If it was me everything would be different. David should be here. Why was it him and not me?" I cried. Something in Liam's expression changed as he looked at me. He wiped my eyes, something he had never done before. He lightly held either side of my face.

"Caelyn," he said softly, "if it was you, I'd be feeling this amount of pain, if not a hell of a lot more. If it was you, I don't think I would be able to see the brighter side, the good at the end of a bad, twisted road. If it was you, yes, things would be a lot different. But if it was you, the difference would be that much harder and more devastating for me. Please, I beg of you, never say it should have been you. I'm not saying it should have been David, please don't think that. He was my best friend and like a brother to me. But in all honesty, I don't even want to begin thinking about if the situation were reversed." He wiped off my tears. "Do you understand me?"

"Yes," my voice was barely audible. I wasn't completely convinced, but in that moment Liam was trying to make me see his point of view. His words were complex and thoughtful, meaning he had been considering everything I said before I brought it up tonight. He was saying he couldn't imagine what it would be like if it was me instead of David. What did that mean? I realized Liam's hands were still on either side of my face.

"Caelyn," he started and then considered his words before continuing. "I need you. I need your comfort, your advice, your company, your friendship, your love, your whole being. I need you. Please don't leave me in the dark. We can get through this together." He leaned forward and brought my forehead to his lips. He gently placed them above my temple and kissed the sensitive spot. Moving about an inch away, from the spot his lips had just touched, he kissed my cheek. "We are in this together because I'm not going anywhere. Promise me. Promise me you won't shut me out." He frantically looked me in the eyes, and a final tear escaped from his.

I looked him straight on, wiped his stray tear with the pad of my thumb, and then laid my head on his shoulder.

"Promise me," he said, his voice sounded tired.

"I promise I'm not going anywhere." With that, he kissed the top of my head and laid his cheek on the crown of my head. I felt his breath grow heavier and even as he fell sound asleep. I was incredibly uncomfortable, but I was afraid to move, knowing I would wake him up. In the last few moments of consciousness, before the pain pills took me under, my mind was racing with Liam's words. He needed me, all of me. I felt a growing sense of love for him and it was just the beginning. He was my support system, my other best friend, and someone I could genuinely say I loved.

That was four years ago this October. The pain of losing my brother comes and goes in waves. I was able to return to the pool water that next summer once the doctors gave me a clean bill of health. No matter the pushing and prodding, I did not go back in the ocean. The ocean only reminded me of everything I had lost the day of the accident.

Now it's the night of Thanksgiving, and I am slowly descending into the dark, cold Maine water. And yet, all I can think about is the day my whole life changed. The day I realized my love for the cold water and the adrenaline it gave my whole body. The pool was as close as I could get to David since I was too afraid of the open water. Still, I'd joined the swim team at the country club and was then recruited for my last two years of the high school team.

My passion for swimming on the high school team led me to Boston University this past August on a swim scholarship. It helped lead me in the direction of falling in love. It helped me tune out every worry in my mind as I competed. Swimming became my life and even made me forget about diving. But why, as I'm getting deeper and deeper, am I thinking about my first dive?

One

Caelyn

"Where is he? He said to meet in front of the dorms, right?" Mom asked, looking around Boston University's campus. One more glance down at my phone to check the time, a brief scan of the sidewalks, and Liam was nowhere in sight.

"Maybe he got held up with some buddies. Don't worry too much, you'll see him sooner or later," Dad said, readjusting a box in his arms. *Where was he?*

"Yeah but I don't really know where I'm going. He promised to help me move in when we last talked over the phone..." I checked for new messages but there was nothing. "That was this morning." I was beginning to worry that he had forgotten all about me. Feeling defeated, I was ready to move in on my own. "Oh well, why don't we go ahead and—" I was caught off guard by someone wrapping their arms around my torso. My box and map fell to the ground as I was picked up and spun around.

"I found you!" Liam's husky voice rang through the commons. He released me down on the ground, and I rubbed my torso, cringing. I shook off the subtle pain and swat him on the arm. A very

1

muscular arm might I add. Had he started working out more? He grinned a genuine smile and looked over to my parents. "Steve and Beth, I am so sorry I'm late. I know we said one-thirty, but my roommate needed help carrying a refrigerator to our room. I'm so glad you found where to go."

"I did go to school here about thirty years ago, son. I think I remember where Danielsen Hall is. I mean, I stayed here as a freshman," my father told Liam matter-of-factly.

"Yes sir, I believe you can find your way around just fine," Liam said laughing to himself. Dad was about to give him more complaints when my mom stopped him.

"Steve, honey, stop giving him such a hard time," Mom swatted his arm like I did to Liam. She returned her focus to the two of us. "Now come over and give me a hug. It's been a long couple of months. Why didn't you come home for the summer?" she asked while giving him her best pouty look.

"Didn't Caelyn tell you I got offered this amazing internship? I couldn't turn it down. But I did call about twice a week to give updates."

He looked over to me with an accusing look while giving my mom a hug. Did he really think that I didn't tell them? Even if I didn't, his mother would have spread the news to my mom. Our parents became best friends the day my parents moved into the neighborhood about twenty years ago, and have been inseparable since.

"Oh, she did, but I would have thought they'd give you a little time off before the school year started back up. That's all... Well never mind that, we'll have plenty of time to catch up later in Caelyn's dorm. Let's find this room, shall we?" Mom asked excitedly.

It took most the afternoon to move my stuff into the dorm. Dad and Liam took several trips while Mom and I made my bed and put my clothes away. When everything was organized on my side of the room, Mom and Dad offered to take us both to dinner.

"Thank you for the offer, Mr. and Mrs. Price, but if it's all right with you, I'd like to take Caelyn to dinner somewhere on campus. You know, a first college dinner that's not ramen noodles or cereal?" he said, looking for my approval. I thought that sounded like a great idea. I love my parents, but I needed this time to separate and get my mind set for next week's classes. After my parents thought this over and asked me what I wanted to do, they agreed to leave and let us eat.

As we walked my parents out of the dorm, my father stopped Liam by the welcome desk and told Mom and I to go ahead. The two of us stepped out into the muggy August air and started to have our own little talk, against my will.

"Does William agree with this?" Mom asked me, stern-faced.

"Does William agree with what, Mom?" she had lost me on this one.

"Caelyn Faith Price, you know what I mean. You told me that you both agreed to try this long-distance thing, but I know how he feels about you hanging out with Liam."

"Just because William doesn't like Liam, doesn't mean I'm going to stop hanging out with him. Come on Mom, he's my best friend." I looked over her shoulder and didn't see Dad and Liam, so we were in the clear to finish this. "Nothing's going to happen with us. I've been dating William for a year and Liam knows how I feel about him. I promise I'll behave, okay?"

"Okay, okay," she said, not sounding too sure of herself. "Just be careful dear. Also, don't forget to call me once your roommate gets here. I was hoping to meet her before we left, but we'll meet her during parents' weekend. Sound good?" I nodded and Mom enveloped me into one of her hugs. Dad appeared with Liam a step behind.

"We're not getting sappy, are we? Because I don't know how I'm going to survive with my baby only two hours from home," my dad said, pretending to dry his eyes.

"Oh, stop it, you big lug. Adrian is home for your office's internship. That's plenty of company!" I said half-jokingly. My dad just laughed and hugged me. We said our farewells and only a couple tears fell when my mom mentioned that she wished David was here with me. Liam and I stood at the edge of the parking lot, waving as their taillights faded into the busy streets. Liam turned to me with a half-smirk plastered on his face.

"You ready for this?"

"Ready for what?" I asked, a little hopeful for an adventure.

"Your first college party, Caelyn."

He stepped into the grass to get back on the sidewalk, and I stumbled after him. *A party? Right now?*

The house was packed with people and it was only nine p.m. on a Wednesday. Liam seemed to know everyone as he led me through the house to the back patio. It was a little overwhelming to hear literally everyone call out to him over the music. He would nod his head in acknowledgment, but he was on a mission. I trailed behind him, trying to wrap my mind around this. Once we reached a set of lawn chairs Liam cleared his throat. A well-built guy pushed his way past three girls to meet up with Liam. The two greeted each other, and Liam turned his attention back to me.

"Caelyn, I'd like you to meet my roommate and best friend, Travis. Travis, this is my best friend from back home, Caelyn." Travis stepped forward and outstretched his unoccupied hand (the other one holding a beer) to shake mine. His grip was firm, and I could see his arm muscles flex as he tightened then loosened his grip.

"It's nice to meet you," I said.

"Likewise. I've heard a lot about you," Travis said, taking a sip from his red cup. "All good things, I swear!" he laughed at Liam's reddening face. I saw that Travis was wearing a plain grey t-shirt that stretched across his broad shoulders, a pair of khaki shorts, and red Polo shoes. He stood about an inch shorter than Liam's 6'2" frame, but beat Liam with his width. He looked to be well over two-hundred pounds.

Liam spoke and brought me out of my daze. *How long was I staring?* From the look on Travis's face it couldn't have been long. "I'll be right back." Liam left me standing there with his friend. I'm all about meeting new people, but I felt a little awkward to be left alone with Travis.

"So, Travis, why'd you pick Boston?" I asked him. He seemed to go along with my small talk.

"Well I was recruited, so to speak, to play football here. I'm an offensive linebacker for the team. So basically I help the other guys look good and protect the important guys—" he stopped talking as I scoffed at his explanation.

"I know what you do," I laughed at his remark.

"Really? Most girls wouldn't know what offensive even means."

"Yeah well, my boyfriend is a football fanatic. He's a Patriots fan and never lets me miss a game. I've picked up quite a bit along the way," I said looking around for Liam. *Where did he go?*

"Your boyfriend's a smart guy," he said before taking a sip. "You should come to our games with Liam! He never misses a game because he knows I'll give him crap for it." He winks at me while I laugh. He downed the rest of his beer in one big gulp. "So, why'd you pick to be a Boston Terrier?"

"Well, my dad always wanted one of his kids to go here so when I got offered a swim scholarship, I couldn't resist. It also helped knowing Liam was here," I said, looking around again for him.

"Oh, so you'll be swimming with Liam then?"

"Yes, she will be," Liam suddenly appeared and handed me a drink. The three of us stood around for a while talking about campus and fun things we should do before classes start.

Travis and Liam took me around the rooms of the house and introduced me to some of their friends. I met several members of the swim team and a handful of Travis's teammates. I hadn't realized how many people Liam knew until tonight. I shouldn't have been surprised, though. He was always very personable when we were kids. Well, he had to be. David and I refused to be the ones to ask other kids to join our beach volleyball games. From day one, that became Liam's job and it worked in his favor at school.

In the past, I was never able to step out of my comfort zone when it came to making new friends or trying new things. I never had to because I always had David and Liam to help me out. They would do the "hard stuff" and I would just follow their lead.

But when David died, I started to change my perspective on life, so to speak. He died so young and hadn't experienced much of life. So, I decided that in honor and remembrance of him, I would live my life in memory of him. I now try new things without blinking an eye, am the first to do something reckless, and try to push myself to make as many friends as I can. I'm still a little reserved in that retrospect, but I'm getting better.

I guess you could say that I'm living in fear of that last day. That last day when everything stops, and I can't do anything else. But I wouldn't say I'm afraid of dying, per se. *Or am I?*

I woke up the next morning with a text and missed call from my mom. I opened her text and it said to call her when I had the chance. I put down my phone, grabbed my shower bag and towel, and made my way down the hall. It was early enough that the bathroom wasn't crowded so I took my time with my shower. After a while I heard another shower turn on, and that was my cue to leave. I really wish I could have gotten a shower in my dorm room, but I'd rather not spend the money for it.

I got dressed and put on my makeup before I called my mom. However, I put the phone on speaker while I was doing my hair.

"Hello," her cheery voice rang through the speaker.

"Hey Mom," I replied.

"Oh Caelyn, how was your first night? Was dinner good? What did you do afterwards?" Her chipper attitude was flipped on even at eight-thirty a.m., and I didn't expect it to waver until she went to bed. Then the cycle would start up again the next morning. I love it about her, but it also makes me envy her.

"It was fun. Liam took me to get a quick bite before we went to this party his friend was having. I got to meet his roommate, Travis, and a couple of my new teammates." I wrapped the pony tail around my already-wavy hair. My hair had just enough of a wave to look like I sprayed it with salt water.

"Sounds like you had a pretty good night. How is his roommate?" she asked me.

"He's really nice! He plays football here and turns out him and Liam have so much in common. He's really funny too." I started to make my bed, placing my multiple pillows in their places.

"So, do you think he'll be someone you'll hang out with or do you think you'll hang out with your teammates?" I heard her gulp on the other line. She must've been drinking coffee and that made me crave it. I looked over at my clock and reminded myself that the coffee shop on campus must be packed at this hour in the morning. I'll go later.

"I don't really know yet. I'm hoping my roommate and I have enough in common that we hang out together. I wonder when she'll get here." I heard myself ramble on because of my nerves. *I really hope she's not crazy.*

"I'm sure she'll be lovely, honey. From the times you've talked, she seems very sweet. As to when she will get there, I have no clue." I hung my towel and shower bag on the hook in the small walk-in closet, then sat down at my desk.

"Yeah, I hope so." I started to grow a little nervous about it now. From the few instances we talked, I figured out that she loves coffee, has a track and field scholarship, and is majoring in sports marketing. *We have two common interest there; we love coffee and we like to run,* I reminded myself. I just hoped she didn't smell bad or dress like some boho hippy.

"Don't be worried. If she's weird you can always switch after your first year. But I doubt that will have to happen anyway. You two will be like peas and carrots!" she joked, referencing her favorite movie.

"Yeah yeah. Oka—" I stopped when I heard people in the hall outside my door. I listened carefully and the knob started to turn.

"Caelyn? What were you saying? Do you have bad connection or somethi—" I cut my mom off.

"She's here, gotta go! Love you," I ended the call before she responded and threw my phone on the bed as a girl about my height entered the room. She carried a box and had three bags strung across her chest. Her hair was shoulder length and dark brown compared to my long, light brown. A woman, who must have been her mom, entered the room after her. They seemed to be arguing about something.

"Bonnie, sweetie, all I meant by it is—" the woman stopped when she noticed me on the other side of the room. Bonnie sat down her box and dropped the heavy bags to the floor. She looked to be a little fatigued, but that's understandable since it was a couple flights up and her bags looked heavy.

"Hi, my name's Caelyn Price, you must be Bonnie. I'm so excited to meet you, finally," I said, putting on what I hoped was a genuine smile. I extended my hand once I crossed the couple steps. She smiled ear to ear.

"Oh, yay you're already here!" she said and instead of shaking my outstretched hand she hugged me. She stepped back, "Sorry, handshakes are so formal. I mean, we'll be living together for the next year or maybe more. Might as well break some of the ice," she said and laughed a little. She seemed totally relaxed in her workout shorts, v-neck tee, and bright Nike tennis shoes. I liked her immediately.

"That's a good way to look at it I guess," I said with a chuckle. However, I did reach my hand out for her mother, "Hi, I'm Caelyn." She smiled and took my hand.

"Nice to meet you Caelyn, my name is Lucille. I'm Bonnie's mother," she replied.

"Nice to meet you too. So, can I help at all?" I asked.

"I like you already," Bonnie said. Then the three of us went down the stairs to retrieve more boxes and Bonnie's suitcases.

The rest of the morning and early afternoon were spent unpacking Bonnie's things. Before Bonnie's mom had to leave, I took them on a little tour of the dorm. Lucille said goodbye to Bonnie around three and left for their home in Virginia. Bonnie and Lucille seemed to be close, but I also found out they butt heads quite a bit. I could tell Bonnie was a little sad that her mom was leaving her.

After their goodbyes were done, we decided to go to the campus coffee shop to sit and talk for a while. "Thanks for your help today, it would've taken us a lot longer if not for you. My mom is a bit of a control freak and would have spent hours setting things out or organizing," she said taking a sip of her latte. I laughed at her comment because I could only imagine. I had only spent a few hours with her mother, but I totally understood what she meant.

"She's not so bad, or at least I didn't notice it," I said, taking a sip of coffee.

"She toned it down, trust me." She laughed at her own joke. "So, when did you get here?"

"Yesterday afternoon. It's about a two-hour drive from home, and my friend, who goes to school here, helped my parents and I unpack."

"Oh, that's nice! My mom worked yesterday and she has work tomorrow, so this morning made the most sense," she took another sip and continued to talk. "My parents are divorced, if you were wondering, so it's just my mom and me. I also have two older brothers, who are both married. One's in the navy and the other is a middle school teacher."

"And you are doing sports marketing, right?" I asked.

"That's the plan anyway, unless I find out I hate it, which is very likely by the way."

More students walked in through the glass doors at the front of the shop. Just as I was about to say something back to Bonnie, two chairs were brought up to our small table.

"Good evening ladies. Are you ready to be amazed, wowed, awed? Whatever you want to call it," Travis looked at me as he said this. He was the first to sit down at the table, and I was confused because I didn't see Liam right away. Bonnie must've been even more confused or surprised that two random guys were sitting with us. Well, they weren't complete strangers to me.

"Who the hell are you?" Bonnie looked at him a little startled. He reached over to shake her hand, jokingly I assume.

"My name is Travis Parker Right. I'm a sophomore at Boston University, and I play football for the Terriers. And since you asked first, I'll ask too. Who the hell are you?" he sassed back as he leaned to the front of the chair.

"I just asked who you were I didn't need details." Wow, Bonnie was a firecracker. It made me smile, but Travis was taken aback.

"I know that." He smiled a goofy grin. "Now, what's your name?"

"Bonnie. I'm Caelyn's roommate. I'm guessing you already know her, right? Or do you always come up and bother strangers?" she asked giving him a pointed look. His mouth opened, I'm guessing to make a smart remark back. Instead, I butted in.

"Yeah I know them both. This is Liam," I said gesturing to my right, "the friend who helped me move in, and Travis is his roommate." The guys nodded along with what I was saying. Bonnie had a smirk on her face as she looked between Liam and me. I should probably nip that idea in the bud before she gets something in her head. I have a boyfriend back home, and Liam and I are good friends. That's it.

"Are you always this cold Bonnie?" Travis asked once he had studied her some more. She scoffed and ran her hand through her hair, messing up the parting.

"No, I guess only to scumbags like you," she said, smirking again.

"Now that's a little hurtful, you don't even know me," he acted upset. To emphasize his hurt, he threw up a hand to his chest. His eyes looked like a puppy after it had been scolded.

"I have a knack for reading people, and trust me, you are a sleazy scumbag." Surprisingly, he smiled at her. *Oh boy.* My jaw tightened as I straightened up in shock by her words. I looked between the three of them and no one's face seemed to react.

"Damn, she's got you pegged, bud. Bonnie, that is impressive," Liam said laughing. "We're sorry for startling you both, but I think we better let this go before it gets worse." Liam patted Travis on the back. "Which I think it will." Travis acted like he wanted to say something back but stopped himself. There was a moment of awkward tension in the group, but Liam broke it—he was always good at reading a situation and acting appropriately. "Can I interest you two in coming with us to a diner just down the road?" We both didn't answer right away. I was waiting to see what Bonnie thought of the offer, but I was sure she contemplated going back to the room. "I promise Travis will be on his best behavior," Liam pleaded. Bonnie shrugged her shoulders, defeated.

"Let's go!"

"How can you get in the water when it's so cold up there? Don't you freeze?" Bonnie asked, exasperated. Liam was explaining the annual swim contest that our hometown has every Thanksgiving. Only college students can participate, for safety reasons really. My parents, along with Liam's, hate the idea of kids swimming in fifty-degree water without a wetsuit. Liam's first time resulted in a broken wrist and a gash above his eyebrow. He swore he didn't want to do it again because he'd finally got back to his normal times for swimming. But he just told his mother and me that, so who knows what he'll end up doing. I looked from him and then to our companions across the table. I could tell they both thought we came from some crazy town.

"Yes, you freeze and it hurts like hell. The sting of the water, your frozen joints rubbing against each other, and the feeling of never being warm again. But everyone does it, it's almost like a rite of passage. Besides, the adrenaline helps you get through the worst of it," Liam answered.

We've been sitting in the diner for three hours just talking and eating off our plates. I can tell Bonnie and Travis were getting along better, but there was still a little tension between them. I couldn't help but wonder if this would become a regular occurrence. I mean, with the four of us hanging out like this. I wouldn't mind doing this every weekend.

The bills got sorted at the counter, and I ran with Bonnie to the bathroom. When I came out Liam was standing by the front door. Our eyes met and my stomach flipped.

Two

Liam

I saw that Caelyn and Bonnie came out of the bathroom and waited for them by the front door. Travis was already out in the car getting it cooled down. The temperature hadn't dropped yet, but I didn't mind it. The heat was better than the brisk, Maine air. Don't get me wrong, I love my hometown and I wouldn't trade it for anything, but moving here was one of the best decisions I'd ever made. Caelyn broke my train of thought when she nudged me in the side.

"You ready?" I gazed into her sea green eyes and no words escaped my lips. I just nodded my head and opened the door.

We made our way to my truck and the three of us jumped in. Travis was sitting to my right and the girls were behind us. The radio was blaring some country song that I didn't know, but it had a good beat to it. I rolled down the windows and the girls got lost singing along with some country singer. The drive to the dorm took about ten minutes and just before turning onto the girls' street I asked Travis to take Bonnie back so I could take Caelyn somewhere.

"Whatever you say buddy. See you back at the apartment," he said, shutting the door after he hopped down. "Let's go, Bonnie. I don't have all night to babysit you. Caelyn, move to the front." Bonnie slammed her door and muttered something under her breath. Travis followed her quick pace, but ran back to the window as I was pulling away. "I'm going to work out in the morning, you joining me?"

"No, I have to take care of some stuff in the morning. I'll go later probably."

"Okay. See ya guys." He ran after Bonnie and I could tell she wasn't super happy to be escorted to her room. Oh well, I wanted this time to show Caelyn one of my favorite places that I knew she'd enjoy too.

"Where are we going?" she said, her excited voice bounced off the walls of the truck.

"It's a surprise," I said looking at her. I couldn't wait to show her this place.

"Ugh, you know I hate surprises Liam. Remember?"

"Yeah I remember." I chuckled thinking back to the memory. I had come back from college one weekend just to surprise her and my parents. A few weeks before, I told her that I had swim practice and that I wouldn't be coming home till Christmas. I knew she would've been upset, but it was worth the lie just to surprise her. I left campus early in the morning and showed up at her house at eight a.m. so that I could spend the morning with her. When her mom let me inside, Caelyn had just gotten back from a run. Beth said I could go up to her room and surprise her.

I was more than excited. I knew at the time how much Caelyn hated surprises, but I thought since I was the surprise it would be okay. Without hesitating, I took the stairs two at a time and found her door at the end of the hall. I took a deep breath and was about to open the door when she came flying out. At the time, she was looking down and obviously wasn't expecting me to be standing there. We slammed right into each other which caught us both off guard.

I tried to regain my footing, but the force of her running into me caused us to totally lose balance. We hit the floor with a loud thud.

"Ow!" she said rubbing her head from the collision with my chin. There was pain on my end too, but I wasn't too focused on that. I was focused on seeing her reaction once she realized who she bumped into.

"Sorry 'bout that," I said trying to move out from under her. However, I was momentarily frozen at the sight of her. She must have been going to take a shower because she only had a towel on. All I could focus on was the feeling of our hearts beating fast against one another, and they were racing. That moment seemed to last forever as I wished for her eyes to notice me. Finally, after what seemed like a lifetime, she met my eyes and the realization that I was home sunk in. She screamed and managed to wrap one arm around my neck. The other held the towel in place. *I am impressed,* I thought.

"You're here," she said into my neck. I could feel that she was smiling against my skin.

"In the flesh," I said holding onto her tighter.

"I missed you so much Liam." She loosened her hold and looked me in the eyes. I couldn't help but notice how jaw-dropping beautiful she was. My eyes scanned her face and stopped on her eyes as they watered. A single tear fell, and I wiped it off her cheek. She looked down from my eyes and realized a towel was her only clothing. Quickly her cheeks flushed the darkest shade of red and as she stumbled with forming words, she fidgeted with the towel. I looked away to give her some privacy.

"I missed you too," I said quietly. She quickly and clumsily got to her feet and began fidgeting with the top of the towel.

"I'm going to—go take a quick shower. Okay? Okay be out in a minute," she said, tripping over her own feet to get to the bathroom.

She closed the door after her, and I stood in the empty hall staring at the door. My mind couldn't stop thinking about how close we were to one another. Maybe it was because I hadn't seen her in four months or because of the moment we just shared, but I couldn't believe how much I meant those words. I had missed her so much and didn't want to leave the next day. I took several deep breaths, but couldn't get my heartrate down until I left her house a few hours later.

What did that mean?

I pulled in front of the secluded river so that the back bed faced the view. Caelyn opened her door and stepped to the ground; I followed suit. We both rounded to the back of my truck, and I lowered the tail bed. Caelyn was lost in thought looking out on the river.

"This is beautiful. How did you end up finding this place?" she asked, leaning against the truck's side. A thick strand of hair escaped her pony tail, and I held my hand in place. I really wanted to fix it.

"Last August I was driving around town and took a wrong turn down that wooded path," I said, pointing back the way we came in. "I hadn't realized it was the wrong turn at the time. I kept driving down the one lane road and found that it opened to this tiny cul-de-sac. It was private and peaceful, you know?" I looked out to the water and took a deep breath. The air smelled of summer and pine. I returned my gaze to her and found her eyes to be closed. She was taking several deep breaths as I had just done. *My gosh, she's beautiful,* I thought. "And I loved the view even more. So, I just kept coming back here when I wanted to be alone or whatever." I quickly finished my explanation and hopped into the back. I didn't want her to see that I was staring. I reached my hand down to help lift Caelyn up. The brief contact of our hands sent a surge of energy up my arm.

"So, you come here a lot then?" She watched me as I laid down a blanket. I took a seat and gestured her to join me.

"Yeah I guess you could say that. It's a good place to think," I said, looking out at the water. I could feel her gaze on me.

"I had one of those at home. Only David and I knew about it..." A small breeze rustled the trees, and I felt her hair brush against my upper arm. I looked over and her eyes were already fixed on mine. "Do you miss him?" She asked randomly. Her voice was soft, just above a whisper.

I thought about her question and a pit formed in my gut. The look on her face and the pain in her eyes confirmed how she felt. I knew it bothered her every day, and I wish I could've done something about it. To be honest, her angst pained me so much that it only increased my hurt over the years. However, I found it was easier for me to hold back my feelings or block them. *Or so you think,* said the voice in the back of my head.

You see, David and I were inseparable. I considered him like my own brother and since Caelyn and him were twins, she was around a lot too. At first, it bothered me that David's sister was always with us when we hung out. But after a while, Caelyn's presence stopped bothering me and she became a part of the trio. You see, Caelyn and David were very close and didn't do much without the other. By that I mean did nothing without each other. That fact alone forged our inseparable bond as best friends. We would swim, run, play outside, and even spend the night together. So basically, where one of us went, the other two followed.

But that all changed the day of the accident, and it scared the hell out of me. I became afraid to hang out with Caelyn because she reminded me so much of her brother. But I cared about her too much to stay away. It took time to be around her again, and I think she felt the same way about me. Right after the accident, we clung to one another for support, but about a month after, the pain was too much. I remember days when I couldn't get out of bed, or call her, or meet her for our scheduled exercise time. Then one day, she stopped calling too.

After weeks of prodding from our parents, Caelyn and I agreed to continue our walks again to get fresh air and exercise. They claimed that since we both weren't eating or sleeping well, a change was needed. In the beginning, most nights ended in crying or yelling. Then, we spent the time together as a quiet break and escape from our dark bedrooms. Finally, we began to share the burden we both felt which allowed for some healing. It was a rough time in our friendship, and we didn't see how we could return to the way things were before the accident.

After that period of loss, grief, and growth, Caelyn and I developed a relationship built on trust, understanding, and compassion. Then, it was my senior year and Caelyn's junior year of high school when I started to feel differently about her. I saw her as more than a friend, but I was afraid of what David would think. I would never know how he felt because he wasn't around to tell me to stay the hell away or to stop being a chicken-shit and ask her out. So, I decided to deny those feelings and went off to college that next year. I've regretted that decision every single day because I missed my chance. She started dating William Jackoby, a law student in Adrian and Evelyn's graduating class, a few months after I left.

"Every day," I answered, placing my hand over hers.

"You know, I think about that day a lot. I had nightmares about it almost every night after you left for school last year. I can't help but wonder what it would be like if he was here. Or even if it was me instead." She looked down at our hands and intertwined our fingers. It was so natural and the spark was undeniable.

"You promised you'd never say that," I said quickly to stop her thoughts. I touched her cheek with my palm and she leaned into my touch.

"You think about it too. I know you, Liam! He was your best friend." Tears started to stream down her face, and I tried to wipe them off, but she flinched.

"If you think that then you don't know me at all," I said, taking my hand back. "I wonder what it would be like if he was here, yes. But never have I wished it was you instead of him!" I said raising my voice. *Why would she think that?* I tried to calm myself before I went on. "I don't know what I would've done if I lost you. That's what I think about." I looked out at the water and Caelyn sniffled beside me. We'd had this conversation several times before and the memories were tough on me. "We've talked about this Caelyn. Why would you bring this up again?"

We sat there in complete silence except for the occasional rustle of trees around us. Not one of us made the first move to speak. I replayed her words in my mind which increased my frustration with her. I was too baffled to discuss this unknown possibility. *Why did she think I wished she would've died instead of David?* Yes, he was my best friend, but Caelyn has always meant the world to me.

I wish I could tell her what I really thought and share the feelings I've held back for years. I wish I could tell her that I would've died that day if she did. I wish I could tell her I loved her and couldn't bear being without her. I wish I could tell her I crave hearing her contagious laugh, seeing her beautiful smile, and touching her soft skin. What's holding me back? Who cares if she has a boyfriend? But that's a lie. *I* cared. It wasn't my place to ruin her relationship, even if he was the wrong guy for her.

"I'm sorry, I'm sorry Liam. I wish I never would've said that. I know you don't think it should've been me," she confessed. "It's just—it's just that I get these massive waves of missing David. But it's not just pain of missing him, it's also anger. Anger that he can't be here with you, with me, living his life. He died so young and didn't get to graduate high school, experience college, start a family." More tears came, but I willed my hand to stay in place. I wanted her to keep talking. Her expression was dark and confused, a look I knew well.

"He talked about this, you know." She looked at me and a small smile played on her lips. "He talked about coming here so that we could all be together. He wanted that taste of freedom so bad." She paused to steady her breathing, before laughing to herself for a minute and smiling, probably thinking about a memory. "He even joked about wanting to be the best man at our wedding. Yeah, that's right. *Our* wedding, how bizarre is that?" she cringed. "For some reason, he never took the hint that that would never happen. But you know how persistent David was when he had an idea," she chuckled softly. "I remember screaming and screaming at him to stop the teasing because it would never happen. I mean come on, you would never like me like that," she laughed through the tears. *What did she say?* She looked me straight in the eyes and continued, "I have to admit, I had a little crush on you when we were younger. And David never let me forget." She looked away.

I tried to keep the utter surprise off my face as what she said sank in. How long ago did she like me? She said when we were younger, but does that mean those feelings were gone? Again, I had to remind myself to stop the wishful thinking. She was in a relationship, of course those feelings were gone now.

"Gosh, he made me so mad, you know?" her voice broke the silence and I was grateful for the subject change.

"Trust me, I know. Remember that one time he took your stuffed rabbit when you were eight?" I started to laugh, thinking of the memory myself.

"I was so mad at him. I couldn't find it for a week and where did it end up? The roof," she said getting riled up. I was dying of laughter at this point and Caelyn was too. "I never figured out how it got up there! Oh, but he did get in trouble," she said, shaking her head.

"Want to know a secret?" She looked at me and nodded. "It was—um, it was my idea. I was also the one that got it up there. David just helped me get it out of your room." I turned away as she started to hit my arm.

"Are you serious? Liam! Gosh I was so mad at him and for the longest time too!" She sat up on her knees and I laid on the bed of the truck, deflecting her hits. "I didn't speak to him for two weeks and you're telling me it was actually you? Gosh, I hate you." I knew she was joking, but she continued to hit me. She started to get a little carried away, and her fist collided with my temple.

"Caelyn, ow." I grabbed her wrist to prevent her from hitting me again. My other hand rubbed my temple subconsciously. This moment seemed oddly familiar, like déjà vu.

"I'm sorry, I'm sorry," she reached over and brushed aside my hand. Her thumb brushed over my temple and her brow creased. "Does it hurt when I touch it?" she asked, her beautiful eyes filled with concern. I saw her irises shimmer with the last remaining light in the sky. The further she leaned over caused some of her hair to frame her face. I shook my head no. I needed her to stop looking at me like that. I didn't want to be responsible for what could happen next.

Her face came closer to mine and she looked me in the eyes. She closed her lids and pursed her lips. They connected with the side of my temple, and her lips lingered a little longer than I expected. They were warm and soft, and I missed them as soon as they left.

"Better?" she asked.

"Much." I noticed that I was still holding her wrist and let go. In that same motion, I sat up and hopped to the ground. I ran my hands through my dark brown hair. It probably looked even messier than before. "It's getting kind of late, we should go back," I said not looking her in the eyes.

"Yeah, I'm getting a little tired." I helped her jump to the ground and went to open her door. After she settled in the truck, I ran around to my side and buckled in.

"Seatbelt," I said, hands tightening on the wheel. Caelyn didn't move or reach for her seatbelt. "Please, Caelyn,"

"I'm going, I'm going." I heard it click. I glanced at her one last time before driving away. She looked to be in her earlier mood. It was my fault too.

I remember the day of the accident like it was yesterday. I woke up to several text messages from David. He was explaining his concerns about Caelyn and how he was afraid she was going to back out of their dive. He wrote that she didn't eat much at breakfast, she looked scared, and she didn't really talk much. Red flags right there. I had to agree that something was wrong, but I knew Caelyn hadn't been a quitter for as long as I could remember. I knew she wouldn't quit that day.

So, after talking with David about it, I texted Caelyn. She seemed to be short through text, but didn't admit to being concerned about the dive. So, I let it go. If she wanted to talk to me, I knew she would.

A couple hours passed and I was stuck helping my dad all morning with his business. It was a Saturday in late October and harvest time. We were clam fishing and cleaning our day's catch so it could be sold to the local restaurants. Around four o'clock that afternoon, I went home and showered as usual. When I came downstairs, my mom was on the phone with Mrs. Price. I sat at the breakfast nook eating an apple as Mom finished up her conversation.

"We would love to be there," my mom said. What was she talking about?

"Be where?" I whispered with my mouth full; my mother shushed me.

"Great, just text me when you get close." She nodded in response to the phone call. "All right. See you later." She disconnected the call, and looked at me with a blank stare. "Why are you looking at me like that?" she said.

"Where are we all going?" I asked.

"The Prices just invited us to dinner tonight Liam." She gave me another strange look. *What was that for?*

"What time?"

"Sometime between seven and seven-thirty, why?" she asked.

"Just wanted to know when I should be ready." I hopped off the stool I was sitting on and ran up the stairs two at a time. Once in my room, I picked up my phone and texted David and Caelyn. I told them I couldn't wait to hear all about the dive and that I would see them soon. I didn't hear anything back from Caelyn, but I did from David.

He said at 5:31 p.m.: *It was amazing Liam! You should've done it with us.*

I responded at 5:46 p.m.: *I wish I could, but this was your thing. Anyway, how was Caelyn? She's not responding to me.*

He said at 5:50 p.m.: *She was a nervous wreck, but she got better. I think it helped knowing I was right there.*

I responded at 6:10 p.m.: *That's good. I want to hear all about it.*

He said at 6:14 p.m.: *Oh, you will, Caelyn just won't shut up about it. She's actually asleep, that's why she isn't responding. Want me to wake her up?*

I responded at 6:15 p.m.: *No no! Let the bear sleep. Haha*

He said at 6:17 p.m.: *Haha you know her so well. See you for dinner?*

I responded at 6:20 p.m.: *Yes!*

That was the last text I sent him. "Yes!"

I ran down the stairs a little after seven, slipping on my tennis shoes. The lights in the kitchen were on, and I heard my mom talking to someone.

"Mom? Are they home yet?" I yelled from the bottom of the stairs. Just then I heard a glass drop and shatter. "Mom!" I ran into the kitchen and a pitcher lay in pieces on the tile floor. My mom's face was streaked with tears. She fell to the ground sobbing. "Dad! Evelyn! Get in here quick!" I yelled and then crouched down to my mother's level. "Mom, what's wrong?"

She didn't answer me. I couldn't figure out for the life of me what was wrong. Was my mom just having a random breakdown? I honestly had no idea what was wrong, but my sister and I were told to get in the car, no questions asked. We did just that. We buckled our seatbelts and waited in silence as my parents got in the front two seats. My mother was still crying and my dad's face was as white as a sheet. He clenched his jaw and unclenched it about twenty times, still not explaining what was going on.

The car ride was brutal. I wanted to know where we were going, and why weren't we going to dinner. That's when it hit me. Something must have happened, and I was terrified to find out what it was.

We turned off the highway on to the stretch of road before the hospital. My mom turned around from her seat. She gave me a weak smile and returned her gaze to the building ahead. *What the hell was going on?*

"Mom, Dad, what is going on? Can you please talk to us? Why are we pulling up to the hospital?" I asked, growing more frustrated. I knew I was raising my voice, but I didn't care. My mother took a few deep breaths before looking at our dad. Evelyn was silent beside me.

"The Prices were in a car accident," she said, calmly holding back tears. "We don't know much, but Steve called and said that both Caelyn and David were in critical condition. It's not looking good, I'm so sorry."

"What?" Evelyn finally spoke. She started tearing up, but I was silent.

"That's all I know, I'm sorry. We're going to sit with them and wait for more news. That's all we can do," she said with more tears. My dad turned into a parking spot and turned off the ignition. I unbuckled fast and opened my door.

"Liam," my dad's voice bellowed into the parking lot. I stopped suddenly and prayed for the tears to stay down. I was freaking out with the news and scared of the unknown. "Son, take a few deep breaths," he said calmly. I listened to his advice and inhaled deeply to calm down. Then tears fell onto my cheeks. I quickly wiped them before my dad spoke again. "I'm sorry."

My mom wrapped me in a hug in the middle of the parking lot. My mind was racing with questions as I tried to understand what was happening. I wanted to know so many things: What happened? Why were they both in critical condition? Would they be okay? When could we see them? Were they in pain? My parents led Evelyn and I into the emergency room doors, and Evelyn froze in place. I grabbed her hand to comfort her, knowing I needed some comfort too. I gave her my most reassuring look, and I knew she tried to give me one in return. As a family, we made our way to the chairs near Mr. and Mrs. Price. My mom gave Beth a big hug as more tears were shed. My dad and Steve also hugged and shared a few words I couldn't quite make out.

We solemnly sat in the lobby for a few minutes before I fully noticed Steve and Beth's injuries. They looked completely torn and battered. Steve's hand was bandaged in thick white gauze and a couple scratches adorned his skin. Beth's arm was in a sling, two white strips held together a gash on her forehead, and she had similar scratches to Steve. They didn't speak of the accident at first, but sat in silence trying to wrap their heads around what had happened. Just then, Steve's parents and Adrian showed up in the emergency room's doorway. They stood looking around as Steve and Beth stood from their chairs and ran over to them. Beth collapsed into her in-law's arms as Steve comforted Adrian. She seemed to be a mess like everyone else.

My parents, Evelyn, and I sat patiently as we awaited our turn to speak with them. We had learned nothing while sitting in the lobby for an hour. But seeing Steve and Beth's injuries assured me that they had to be fine. Now what could be so different about Caelyn and David that they weren't out here? My mind would not stop its constant questioning. I wanted to scream, I was so frustrated. Just before I stood up to find someone who would give me the answers, the Prices returned to their positions next to us.

"Thank you, again, for coming. We are so grateful to have friends like you," Beth said between sobs. My mom moved to comfort her and Beth leaned into her friend. "Sorry, we're still trying to process what happened, but we want to tell you what we know so far." She wiped her stray tears with a crinkled Kleenex. Beth tried to continue, but no more words were forming. Steve spoke for her.

"The doctors are still in surgery with both of them. David's side was hit the worst but Caelyn's seatbelt snapped apart. It caused her to jolt around once the truck hit us. They wouldn't tell us the extent of their injuries, but both seemed to be extreme..." He stopped suddenly. "There was so much blood," he said, shaking his head. He opened his mouth and then closed it. Rubbing the back of his neck he choked out, "I never saw them coming."

"I'm sure it wasn't your fault, Steve," my father whispered. Steve just nodded his head. I sat there and took everything in. My best friends were just in surgery. They would be fine. I kept thinking that a doctor would come out any minute to tell us they were recovering and ready for visitors. But another hour passed and nothing happened. Steve didn't mention the accident again. As a matter of fact, no one talked about anything. The room was silent as we waited for the white swinging doors to open.

Around midnight a man wearing a white coat appeared in the doorway of the waiting room. Our group stood as soon as he started walking our way.

"Steve and Beth Price?" he asked, looking around at the tired faces.

"Yes?" Steve said in response. Beth held his arm tight. I knew for a fact that it was the only thing keeping her upright.

"My name is Dr. Hynes. I've been in surgery with your children, David and Caelyn Price," he said, folding his hands in front. He seemed to be running on little sleep himself. Dr. Hynes looked to be in his mid-fifties with grey hair peeking out from the edge of his blue cap. His eyes masked his feelings, and his face gave nothing away.

"Yes of course, how are they doing? Can we see them?" asked Steve.

"Would you two like to sit down?" He gestured to the seats behind them, but they didn't move a millimeter. I could feel my gut drop deep into my body. Sweat formed on my brow, like it does when I get sick. That's how I felt in that moment, sick. Too sick to hear what I was about to be told.

Knowing that they weren't going to sit down, Dr. Hynes relayed the news. "David arrived first from the scene of the crash. Now, before any decisions were made, we had to take several x-rays to know what we could do to help him. There was a large blood clot on the brain, along with five broken ribs, a broken leg, a sprained wrist, and a punctured lung. We rushed him to surgery as Caelyn was just getting to the hospital. I took my team and rushed David to the OR to see what we could do. After three hours of surgery he had lost too much blood and the clot was preventing the right amount of oxygen and blood from reaching his brain. His organs began to fail, and we tried to resuscitate him many times after his heart finally stopped." He took a moment to gather his words. "I regret to say that we pronounced David Michael Price dead at 11:56 p.m. I am incredibly sorry for your loss. My team and I did everything we could to save him." The air seemed to escape the room.

Beth dropped to the ground and Steve wrapped his arms around her. My mother sat down in the chair and covered her face with her hands. The sobs in the room were too much. I was in so much shock, but I didn't cry. I don't know if it was because the news hadn't sunk in yet or if I was incapable of crying again. Then it hit me.

"What about Caelyn?" My voice cut through the sobs like a diver's body through water. Beth and Steve tried to compose themselves and everyone else looked a little hopeful.

"Caelyn's injuries were not as extreme as David's. However, she broke her right arm, just below the elbow, her torso has a thick and deep gash due to where the seatbelt had sliced into her skin, and has four broken ribs. She also might have a case of memory loss because her injuries show that the left side of her head hit the window when the truck made impact. I won't know the extent of any potential memory loss until she wakes up. Her surgery went well, but she lost a lot of blood. However, she is in recovery as we speak. I can have a nurse show you to her room after this," he said. "I hope it's not too bold for me to say, but you are very lucky that Caelyn and the both of you survived. Not many people can walk away from a crash like that." He nodded to the rest of the room and started to retreat. Before he walked through the swinging doors he said, "I am very sorry about your son. I wish I could've done more for him."

The group's energy was different after that. I don't know how to explain it. All I know is that when they showed us to Caelyn's room, I let out a breath I didn't know I had been holding. We all crowded in her room for about an hour not saying anything. Caelyn's grandparents planned to leave but said they would be back first thing in the morning. I could only imagine how they were dealing with this. It would be so hard to lose a grandson at fifteen, not to mention a brother. My parents stood to leave and motioned for me and Evelyn to come too. Evelyn stood and walked over to them feeling a little awkward. She was never close with David or Caelyn, but she was there in support of Adrian.

"Can I stay? Please. I just want to be here when she wakes up," I pleaded. I didn't want to leave yet. I wanted to make sure she was okay. My mom started to protest but Beth interrupted her.

"Lisa, he's perfectly fine. I'm sure Caelyn would like to see another familiar face," she said placing a hand on my shoulder. My mother hesitated but nodded her approval.

"All right, we'll see you later today. Please call if you need anything at all." She gave everyone in the room a hug and left Steve, Beth, Adrian, and me to wait for Caelyn.

I wasn't able to fall asleep all night since we got the news. We had been allowed to stay up in Caelyn's hospital room until she woke up and the chairs were disgustingly uncomfortable. I waited for her to open her eyes, fidget, or make some kind of sound. Anything. I wanted nothing more than for her to know I was there for her. We both lost an important person, and I felt that we would be able to draw strength from each other, though I knew that would take some time. But I wasn't going anywhere, so time was all we had.

The doctor and nurses made their rounds and checked on Caelyn. They monitored the beeping machines, adjusted her blankets, and checked her vitals. Around four in the morning, Dr. Hynes knocked on the open door and asked to have a moment with Steve and Beth in the hallway. He said something about decisions or options. I wasn't exactly sure what he wanted them for because I was only partway listening. Nothing caught my attention because I was too fixated on one of the most important people in my life. I know I sounded pathetic, but I couldn't help it. There is a saying, "You never truly know what you have until it's gone." Well, I had already lost one best friend. I wasn't about to lose another.

As Beth and Steve left the room, Beth squeezed my hand and gave me a weak smile. Her green eyes were red from the hours of flowing tears, and her nose had been running constantly. They entered the hallway, and I went to sit in the chair by Caelyn. I was so hesitant in my steps, feeling like I was walking on eggshells. The closer I got to her, I saw her injuries from a new perspective. Her torso was wrapped heavily in white gauze. I had no doubt that she would find it itchy. Her right arm, lying on the bed, was in a big cast. Her head was bruised on her left temple and multiple cuts were scattered on her beautiful skin. I noted that her paleness was a new color on her, but the doctors said it was because of the recent blood loss. They assured us that her normal color would return soon. I wanted to wish away all the pain of today and to instead let her relish the thought of this morning. I wanted to sit in David's or her room and listen to countless stories about what the dive was like. But I couldn't.

I looked away from her face because I no longer wanted to see the pain. I dropped to the chair and my head fell into my hands. That's when the tears came, overwhelming me. It poured out of me as if I'd been holding it in for years. I was crying for Steve and Beth, Caelyn, Adrian and myself. I knew it was selfish to be thinking about everything that I lost, because I wasn't the only one who would feel this way. Caelyn had no idea how much her world would change as soon as she opened those beautiful, sea green eyes.

I didn't know how long I sat there, but it seemed like hours. Steve and Beth had been gone for a while talking to the doctors and nurses, and I didn't know when they would return. I had been standing, pacing, sitting with my head in my hands, and finally laying my forehead on the bed, holding Caelyn's warm hand. I rubbed the back of her hand with my thumb and willed myself to look at her face again. I noticed a couple strands of hair out of place and reached to push them behind her ear. Her eyes fluttered open and she looked straight at me. My eyes welled up again, and I tried to push the tears down. *Be strong for her Liam*, I kept telling myself.

"Hey you," I said and hesitantly touched her cheek. She gave me a wimpy grin and leaned into my touch. That small gesture felt electric. She had never done that before.

"Hey," she mouthed. I stared deep into her eyes and looked her over. "Have you been crying?" she whispered. I knew that was all she could get out. I nodded in response. She started to nod off again but not before I heard, "Liam finally shows emotion." She paused and inhaled a breath before saying, "it looks good on you." I was left staring at her sleepy state, wishing she was still talking to me.

As I think back on that day and the imprint it left on me, I wondered why I never told anyone what she said when she woke up. Maybe I wanted to have that moment be just the two of us or maybe it was for other selfish reasons. All I know was that I never told anyone and Caelyn had never brought it up. So that made me feel like she didn't remember.

I pulled into a parking lot by the dorms and turned off the ignition. Caelyn made no move to get out, and I realized that she had fallen asleep. Very carefully I got her out of the truck's passenger side and held her in my arms. I walked with her beautiful, sleepy body all the way down the street and up the stairs to her room. I knocked on her door, trying to not stir her. Her roommate was taking a while to get to the door, and I was afraid I woke her.

"What---," she started to yell as she opened the door. I cut her off.

"Shhh..."

She stepped aside to let us in. I walked Caelyn to her side of the room and gently laid her down on the bed. Her arms slid from around my neck and fell limp beside her. I slipped off her tennis shoes and put them on the floor in front of her bed. Next, very carefully, I took her hair out of the pony tail. Ever since she was little she always complained about getting a headache after sleeping with one in. Lastly, I held her up and slid her under the covers. This time she stirred a little but never fully woke up. I leaned over to kiss her left temple softly and was out of there without saying another word.

Three

Caelyn

I'd been awake since he laid me down on my mattress. But I didn't want him to know because I didn't want to face him again. I let my emotions get the best of me tonight instead of pushing them away like usual. I haven't allowed myself to feel some of those feelings in a long time, but Liam brought them out of me. That scared me, but only because I hated being vulnerable around him. If Liam could hold it in, why couldn't I? My question was interrupted as soon as the door clicked shut behind him.

"Oh, come on, even I could tell you were awake. What gives?" Bonnie was practically jumping up and down on her bed. I heard the frame of her bed creak with every move she made. Since I'd been caught, I rolled over on my side. I didn't know how we became so close in just one day. "Why are you not jumping all over that? I would be eating him up if I were you."

"What are you talking about?" I stifled a yawn and propped another pillow under my head to stay awake.

"Uh, hello? Liam is like a puppy following around his master. He's in love with you Caelyn. Can't you tell?" She looked at me crazily, and I could tell my face showed shock and exasperation.

"Woah, woah, woah! He's not in love with me. Maybe he loves me like a friend or sibling, but he'd never love me in a romantic way. He knows and respects that I have a boyfriend back home and that we're just friends. Got it?" I really thought that over.

Tonight seemed to push the limits of the friendship line I had drawn, but I guess that was partly my fault; I was caught up in the moment. With Liam, that was easy. He made me feel things, and I acted on those with no second thought. It scared me to be honest. But I kept thinking that I loved William and that's that. *Right?*

"Please tell me your boyfriend treats you even better than Liam does. If he does then I'll let this slide." Bonnie looked at me pointedly over the rim of her glasses. I hadn't realized she wore glasses.

"William treats me fine. He's a gentleman, supports me, and is very caring." I tried to think of other things to tell her, but I fell short. What else could I say to get her off my back? "We've been dating for over a year now, he lives in Maine, and he has an internship at my dad's office this year."

"So that means he's older?"

"Yes, he's my sister's age, so twenty-two," I said. We'd just celebrated his birthday at the beginning of summer. I made reservations at one of the fanciest restaurants in town and then we went to a movie. William has never been big on conversation, because he loved the physical aspects of our relationship. Now I know our relationship needed that part, but I still sometimes missed the core strength of communication. I hated to admit that we didn't have that, but it was true. He was and still is not much of a "talk on the phone" type of guy. We don't text a lot either.

Therefore, I value my friendship with Liam so much. Even before the accident, I considered Liam one of my most trustworthy friends and, because of that early bond between us, he continues to be. I wouldn't want to risk that friendship because I'm too afraid of what could go wrong. That's partly why I tried to deny my feelings for him so long ago. Okay, here's a confession, maybe it wasn't that long ago.

"Okay, but why are you not dating Liam? No offense," Bonnie said with a shrug.

"Because we're friends and nothing more. Sure, I did like him a lot when I was younger but that was many years ago. I wanted something to come of it, but by the time I was brave enough to do anything, he was going off to college—."

"You said many years ago, Liam is a sophomore. This had to have just happened, Caelyn." Crap.

"Well, I've gotten over it, William and I started going out as soon as I started my senior year of high school. Besides, Liam d0esn't even think of me in that way." I felt like I needed to defend myself against her accusations. We just met this morning and she was already on my case. Was she always this bold?

"Okay, whatever you say. So, you don't mind if I go after him?" she asked. My eyes opened as wide as they could possibly go. I wasn't pretending to be tired anymore. "I'm kidding Caelyn, don't worry." All I could do was laugh it off. She gave me a look that said we weren't done talking about this. "So, how'd you two meet?"

"My sister knew him from college and set us up on a blind date. I guess we just hit it—."

"No, not William. How'd you meet Liam?" She rested her chin in her palms like a child listening to a story.

"Well, we've known each other since I was born so I don't remember the exact memory..." She laughed as I went on. "My mom and his mom were good friends because they had been neighbors for a few years. He also has an older sister, Evelyn. She's Adrian's age so they became close friends too." Bonnie was listening intently, but looked confused for a moment. "Adrian is my older sister by the way. Evelyn and Adrian kind of did things on their own so I'm not super close with his sister. I actually hung out with the boys more than the girls." I began to think of all the fun things Liam, David, and I used to do: going late night swimming or even helping Mr. Carter with the clam fishing. The more I recalled the memories, the more I remembered David. My somber mood returned, but I continued anyway. "I don't know, our families have always been close. For as long as I can remember, the Carters have always been there."

"So, Liam is your best friend?" Bonnie asked, readjusting her pillows.

"Yeah, he always has been," I smiled softly.

"Then how in the world did you control yourselves? I mean come on, he's good looking, you're gorgeous, you two just look like you belong together. I know, I know it's crazy for me to say this because we just met, but I know love when I see it and you two have it."

"It wasn't always easy though. Yeah Liam and I were best friends, but even when I started to catch feelings for him it got complicated." I looked to the floor.

"Complicated?" she prodded. I had a feeling this would come up, might as well talk about it now.

"Okay, I'll explain. David, Liam, and I were inseparable as soon as any of us could walk. We would have sleepovers in tents in the family room, go on adventures in the woods behind our houses, and race each other for the best swim time. Even though David and I were a year younger in school, Liam never treated us that way. We were like family. So, it would have been weird to like or even date him, you know? He was like a brother to me all those years, and when I started to feel differently towards him, I got scared. But even though I tried extremely hard to deny the feelings, David saw right through me. It was embarrassing not being able to hide anything from my twin brother." My smile quivered as I thought of him.

"Wait, I didn't know you had a twin! Does he go here?" I knew the question was innocent enough, and that Bonnie didn't know what pain it would cause me. No matter who brought it up, the topic always made me emotional. Thinking of David always caused my mood to completely change. I couldn't stop the tears as they slowly fell down my cheeks. Not again. "Shit, I'm sorry Caelyn. Did I say something wrong?" I knew I would have to tell her eventually. I just didn't imagine it being the first night we met.

"No, it's not you. Hum... David died when we were fifteen," I said, barely loud enough for her to hear me. She was silent for a minute and when she spoke, she was quiet.

"What happened?" she choked out.

"My family, minus my older sister Adrian, was in a car accident my freshman year of high school. The doctors said I was lucky to live, but David wasn't so lucky. His side of the car was hit the worst upon impact. The doctors tried everything they could; they just couldn't save him. He died from the extensive trauma." I repeated the explanation I've become familiar with over the years.

"I'm so sorry Caelyn," Bonnie apologized.

"You didn't know," I said, trying to wipe away the tears.

"No, I'm just sorry you had to lose him. I can't even begin to imagine what that would feel like."

"The pain was excruciating at first. I kept seeing him walk through my bedroom door to talk to me, I imagined him at the dinner table, and thought about him all the time. My home became a living nightmare because everywhere I looked, it reminded me of something we had done together. I didn't eat for weeks when I was released from the hospital, and I lost quite a bit of weight. I drained myself of tears the first couple of days, or so I thought, and all I could do was cry when we had his funeral. I felt like someone had ripped out my heart and did a poor job of trying to put it back in." I thought back to those couple of weeks after we lost David. "You know what? Liam never left my side during it all. At first, I didn't want to see him because he too reminded me of David, but the more I thought about it, I thought that he would understand my pain. He lost him too."

I rambled on and on and Bonnie sat there not saying a word. She soaked up the information like a sponge. Not once did she chime in to ask me something; she just nodded her head along with me.

"It was Liam that coaxed me to eat. It was Liam that got me back into running to release my anger and worry. It was Liam that held me at night when the nightmares were too vivid. It was Liam that helped me regain my strength. It was always Liam."

It was six a.m. and I got out of bed without waking Bonnie. Our talk lasted until about two in the morning, and I had already talked myself into a run before everyone was awake. I didn't particularly like running with a lot of people around just because I used the time to think. Liam had been that exception since David died. I secretly liked when we would run together, but we hadn't been able to in a while.

My plan was to run about five miles this morning, but my body was mentally tired from yesterday. So instead I stopped after three miles and headed to the fitness center to lift some weights and do some more leg and core workouts. As I was grabbing a towel to wipe away the sweat on my forehead, I saw Travis. I tried my best to avoid him, but he found his way over to me anyway.

"Early workout?" he said cocking his head.

"Oh yeah, just some running and additional work. You?" I replied.

"Yeah, coaches are checking this area every morning of the week to scout out those putting in the extra work. I guess you could say I like making good impressions." His shirt stretched across his broad shoulders, conforming to his muscles. His hair looked damp from sweat and his skin was flushed.

"Oh, like you did with Bonnie? You consider that a good impression?" I placed my hands on my hips. He chuckled and rubbed the back of his neck.

"I messed up with that one. I am a genuinely nice guy, promise." I stared at him. He threw his hands up defensively. "What? I was just having a little fun."

"She thinks you're an asshole and I don't think her impression of you will change very easily. She's very different than the girls you hook up with..." He looked at me offended. "I'm guessing."

"I'm not looking to hook up with her!"

"Okay, just saying. Well, I guess I'll see you later. Say hi to Liam for me."

"Hey..." he said, running after me. "Why don't you come back with me to the room? You haven't seen it right?" I shook my head and opened my mouth to say no but he kept talking. "We have it set up just like your normal bachelor pad. But it's not a mess like some." I waited to think the offer over. "Besides, I'm sure Liam wouldn't mind if you came over."

"Fine," I reluctantly said after a glance at the wall clock. It read 7:20; he was most likely sleeping anyway.

We walked back making small talk, and I started to understand Travis a little more. He was easy to talk to and, putting aside Bonnie's complaints, he was a nice guy. He seemed quite intelligent, but I don't think he wanted to fully apply himself. I could see how Liam and he hit it off freshman year. Liam can be uptight but loves to have fun; Travis obviously brings out that side of him, and I'm so happy he'd found someone to do that.

He wasn't always so uptight, but after David's death he became more serious. He focused all his energy on making sure everyone around him was fine before worrying about himself. And because he helped take care of me, I don't think he ever had time to heal himself. It worried me, but there weren't a lot of opportunities for me to help him.

Travis opened the door to the apartment building for me and ushered me towards the stairway. "We always take the stairs," he said, but I was confused as to why. There was an elevator, right? "It's a long story."

"Okay," I said knowing it was a story for another time. We walked up the two flights of stairs and exited onto their floor. One hallway branched to the right and another went straight ahead. Travis led the way and, the further we walked, I picked up on the multiple sounds coming from the rooms around me. It wasn't until we reached his door that I heard Liam's raised voice, as if he was upset with someone. Travis took out his key from his basketball shorts and unlocked the door. I hesitated before walking in because I was afraid we'd be interrupting something. Or at least I was interrupting.

Travis walked in and ushered me to follow. I could still hear Liam through the walls from where I was standing. I shook my head a little at Travis. I was uncomfortable walking in to Liam yelling. Travis reached his arm through the frame of the door and grasped my forearm. His grip wasn't too harsh, but I got the message to listen to him and quietly followed. I closed the door behind me and turned to observe their two-bedroom apartment. It wasn't the cleanest place but not as bad as I imagined. The paint seemed to be chipping near the floorboards and the corners of the main living room, and the furniture didn't match. The main room was all I could see, and Liam was nowhere in sight. However, I could still hear him and his voice was only getting louder.

Travis walked to the left side and disappeared through a door. I was left standing in the living room looking like an idiot. I started to walk over to the couch when Travis came back into the room. Liam entered just then and appeared to be on the phone; I could tell he wasn't pleased to be having the conversation. Keeping his head down and listening to the other line, he walked into the kitchen and grabbed a water bottle.

"Who are you to tell me what I can and cannot do with her? I had no idea you were so insecure about us. Or wait, better yet, your own relationship," he said, taking the cap off with his unoccupied hand. His head was still down, so he hadn't seen me sitting just mere feet away.

"He'll be off in a minute," Travis said sitting down next to me, propping his feet up.

"Bullshit, man. I can do what I damn well please. You have no right to tell me I can't see her anymore." He sounded exasperated. "Fine, go ahead and come here. See what good that will do. I know I could just beat your ass anyway." His hand holding the water bottle tensed up, but then released. "Okay, okay, calm down. Caelyn and I are just friends. You don't have to worry about me trying to do anything with her, I'm not interested in her. She's far from my type, anyway." I remained motionless and quiet on the couch. Travis had changed positions and was now interested in the conversation. His eyes widened and he tried to choke something out. Liam's words overpowered them.

"You've got to be kidding me? I don't give a shit what she does! She makes her own damn decisions. She's obviously dating you because she thinks it's right, despite what everyone else has been telling her." He listened to the other line. "Yes I mean every word. She means nothing to me if she continues to make the mistake of being in a relationship with you. In fact, she's an idiot for choosing to go out with you. I already warned her so if she wants to ruin her own life, I'm not going to stop her anymore!" This time his hand clenched too tightly and water poured over his hand onto the tile. "And another thing, how did you get my damn number? I never want to see your number flash across my screen again." He was silent again and his jaw clenched. "Piss off. And if it means anything to you, I won't talk to her again. Like I said, she's idiotic for dating you. It makes her look like an ass." He ended the call and we all sat in silence. No thoughts came to my head. I felt raw from the words that had just cut deep into my flesh.

My eyes began to well up with tears, and I begged them not to fall. Travis cleared his throat beside me. I looked at him, but his gaze was focused in the direction of the kitchen so I looked down at my hands in my lap. They began to feel clammy. *What just happened?*

"Shit," Liam said dropping the bottle and coming to my side in a few strides. He bent down to eye level with me and touched either side of my face with his palms. "Caelyn, I'm sorry. I didn't mean any of that. Please, you need to understand why I said those things, it was that assho—."

"I'm an idiot?" He didn't respond. "I mean nothing to you?" I cried in a pathetic voice. "You think I'm idiotic and I look like an ass?" This time he started to form words, but I cut him off before they escaped his mouth. I was so enraged by what I had just heard. "You know what, it doesn't even matter. I'm pretty sure you're the only asshole in this room," I stood up and walked toward the door. I felt as if Liam had ripped my heart out of my chest and torn it to shreds. I didn't realize my best friend, someone I loved and trusted, was capable of saying such hurtful and ugly words. I knew if I stayed there any longer, I wouldn't be able to think straight. All I wanted to do was leave and clear my head of Liam and the things I'd heard. Liam beat me to the door and blocked it with his body.

"Liam, move." My voice came out small as I looked straight at my feet. I felt my legs shake.

"C," he pleaded, trying to grab one of my hands. I jerked away quickly. I peered up a little and he didn't budge; only stood there looking hurt. *He* looked hurt. How did he think I felt after what I'd just heard?

"Move." This time my voice was stronger, but I didn't dare look him in the eye.

"No," he demanded. "I want you to listen to me, please."

In a split second, all the rage, hurt, and confusion built up and caused my hand to connect with his cheek. He didn't blink once. He didn't seem fazed at all. I immediately felt guilt from slapping him, but this was soon replaced by anger as his words repeated on a cycle in my head. It was like someone hit the repeat button on a bad playlist.

"Damn it Liam, move!" I stared straight into his dark, brown eyes and screamed. "I want out of here now! Now." He still stood there blocking my exit, but I pushed past him. I slid through the tiny opening to escape the suffocating apartment. Once in the hallway I sprinted for the stairs, not even looking for the elevator.

Four

Liam

"Caelyn it's me, again. Please pick up your phone; I really need to talk to you," I pleaded into my cell. "Oh, and by the way this is Liam." I hung up the phone and realized how ridiculous that last part was; she knew it was me. I questioned calling her again but I was interrupted by Travis walking into the living room. I looked in his direction and saw him shaking his damn head. "What is it?"

"If you don't care about her, why have you called her a million times?" he asked. He took a seat on the couch and pulled out one running shoe from under the coffee table. "I mean if I was her, I wouldn't answer, but you didn't ask my opinion," he said with a smirk.

"I've told you this a thousand times since she left, I *need* to talk to her. You know I didn't mean those things I said. I just had to get William off my ass. He's become obsessive." I trailed off, thinking about the phone call I had a few days ago. "Wait, why did you bring her here again?"

It was Travis's turn to squirm in his seat.

"I, uh, saw her at the gym and invited her to see the place. You know, you two being best friends and all, it's funny you never thought about showing her the apartment." He finished tying his left shoe and stood up. Way to turn the topic of conversation onto me again. "I'm going to run with or without you. What will it be?" I reached for my phone and checked the display. No new messages or voicemails had come through in the last few seconds.

"Where are you going?" Travis shouted after me in the quad. His breathing was labored and it came out more like *whe aree goin.* I didn't have time to respond if I was going to make it to the dorms in the next two minutes. I ran into the lobby of Danielson and didn't bother signing in. I took the stairs two at a time and made it to the second floor, looking for room C230. I knew where it was because I took multiple trips carrying up her stuff when she moved in. I stood outside her door and bent over, placing my hands on my knees. It was a lot harder to catch my breath after I ran up those stairs. After a few deep breaths, I knocked on the door, no answer. I knocked a little louder; again nothing.

"Caelyn, please answer the door." I placed my forehead onto the hardwood door and banged it softly against it. I felt like a complete idiot.

"Liam, you look like a complete..." Travis came up to my side, but didn't finish his thought.

"What, no words?" I asked, banging my head again. He didn't respond to my remark. Instead, he too began to knock on the door with his fists.

"Caelyn, if you would so kindly open the door, it would tremendously help Liam's image." He gave me a sideways glance. "People are starting to come out and stare, Caelyn," Travis said, looking around the hall. No one had started to come out. "You know what?

It would also help my image because I'm about to break down this goddamn door. I don't think they'll be very happy with me breaking down another door over here." I stepped back so that my back was flush against the opposite wall. He waited a few seconds and no one came to the door. "I warned you. One. Two. Thre—" Travis lifted up his foot to make contact with the door, but it flew open.

"Stop! Stop!" Bonnie's tiny frame was the only thing that appeared in the doorway. I tried to peer past her to see if Caelyn was there. She was completely shocked to see Travis and his foot mere inches from her. Her eyes looked back and forth from my face to Travis's foot. "Holy shit, you weren't kidding. Caelyn, he was literally going to break down our door." She looked exasperated.

"Can I please talk to her?" I pleaded and tried to push past Bonnie. I wished Travis had broken down the door just so she couldn't block me from coming in.

"Sorry, no can do Liam. She doesn't want to talk to you."

"I almost just broke down your door, I'm not afraid to throw you over my shoulder just so he can see her," Travis said matter-of-factly, coming to my side. I looked between the two of them and Bonnie seemed unaffected while Travis wore a cocky grin. I just wanted to make things right between us. This radio silence from Caelyn was killing me. "What will it be?" Travis asked.

"Goodbye boys," Bonnie slammed the door, and we both flinched.

"Well that could have gone a little better," said Travis after about a minute of silence.

"Shut the hell up," I said sliding onto the floor with my back pressed against the cool, tan wall next to Caelyn's door. I couldn't believe I messed up like this, just when I thought I had her. Just when I thought things might be looking up. I mean, we'd had our moments since she arrived on campus, but we had some great times ahead and I wanted more. If only she could see that.

Travis looked down at me and shook his head, "Don't say I never do anything for you." I gave him an incredulous look. He backed up to the wall across from their door. His fingers mussed his already messy hair. "What the hell man." In a split second his sneaker collided with their door.

Instinctually, my arm flew up to cover my face. My facial expression was priceless while Travis wore the biggest smug grin of his entire life. He dusted off his hands as if they were dirty. I stood up and looked from him to the door that was now lying on the floor; the hinges had ripped right off and the frame was a total splintery mess.

Bonnie appeared in the opening with Caelyn tagging close behind. Caelyn's face was blank; for once she was completely unreadable. Bonnie's, on the other hand, was appalled. Her jaw dropped almost to the tile floor of their common room. She opened and closed her mouth many times, struggling to form words. Her eyebrows came together and she pinched the bridge of her nose.

"I---umh," she started blinking fast and shifting her body weight from one foot to the next. "Caelyn, I—I don't know what to say." She was still looking at the mess on their floor. Her eyes traveled up the door frame and then fell on Travis, who was still standing a few feet away from her. Her dark eyes narrowed and her lips began to curl up. "You," she pointed at Travis, "and you," she jabbed the same finger in my direction, "inside."

"Uh-oh," Travis chuckled, but obeyed. Like a dog, we tucked our tails between our legs and followed her in. Caelyn avoided my eyes and found a spot to stand against their counter in the half kitchen. Bonnie stood in the middle of the room, hands on her hips, while Travis and I took a seat on the futon.

"Can I just say something?" I started to go into a speech, but Bonnie wasn't having it.

"No, you may not just say something," she started, and I opened my mouth to protest. She just held up a hand to quiet me. "I only just met you all, and I've already lived through enough drama to cover my entire high school experience. Now I've heard Caelyn's side," Caelyn squirmed, "and I honestly don't care what your side of the issue is, Liam. But I'm sure Caelyn does, even if she claims she doesn't. So, Travis, because you so kindly broke down our freaking door, you and I are going to the hardware store to buy what we... *you* need to fix it. Right now." She pulled a thin smile that didn't reach her eyes. "Oh, and you're paying."

Travis was frozen for a moment, unable to respond in his usual smartass way. Then, he nodded his head and stood up, giving my shoulder a brisk pat. Bonnie and Travis disappeared through the hole that led to the hallway. That left Caelyn and I sitting here, speechless. All I knew was that I needed to break this tension. I never meant what I said and certainly didn't want to cause this issue between us.

Caelyn pushed herself from the counter and for a second I thought she was coming to sit by me, but she disappeared into her bedroom. I sat on the futon, hands on the back of my neck and hunched over my legs. I was afraid if I got up I would let my emotions get the best of me trying to fix this. I needed to think through what I was going to say. I didn't want to damage our relationship more by begging her to be with me instead of William. I just couldn't do it. I needed to apologize for what I had said; it was that simple.

When I had enough courage, I stood up, and almost ran into someone in the process. My hands reached out to steady that person and myself. My eyes rose and I was inches away from her. Caelyn's eyes were red and a few tears had begun to form. She looked down at my hands that grasped her arms. I let go and both of us took a step back.

"Liam," she started but no other words came out of her mouth. She fidgeted with her hands and then rubbed them on the sides of her shorts. She looked so broken, and I felt even worse for making her feel this way. But I wanted her to talk, I wanted to hear what she was going to say. "Can you just leave?"

That was not at all what I was expecting. It was last thing I wanted to hear.

"Caelyn please, just talk to me," I pleaded, taking her hands. She flinched, but didn't take them away. "We always talk to each other. I need my best friend to talk to me."

"Best friend? If I was your best friend then why did you say those things?" She looked at me and more tears fell. I couldn't see her like this anymore, so I pulled her flush against me. I wrapped my arms around her tiny frame and she broke into huge sobs. She wasn't hugging me back yet, but I tried to calm her down regardless. I rubbed her back and kissed the top of her head before I started to speak.

"I was caught up in the moment, but I need you to know I meant none of the things I said." I let go enough so that I could look her in the eyes. She wasn't looking at me. "Caelyn, look at me." She looked up and took a deep breath. I knew I had to tell her why I acted the way I did. The explanation could help her understand why I said those hurtful words and got so upset on the phone. "William has called me several times since you got to campus, and I'm sure he hasn't told you that. I've ignored every single call until a few days ago. I'm sorry I should have told you, but I didn't know why he kept calling." She was still looking at me so I figured I had her attention. "I answered and right away I knew it couldn't have been about something good. He automatically assumed that there was something going on between us, so he said I needed to stay away from you or else he'd come down here, which is the last thing I wanted. So, in that moment I said those things to get him off my back. They weren't kind, I know they weren't. But what else could I have said to reiterate that nothing is happening between us?" She didn't respond right away, most likely because she was processing. "Caelyn, you mean the world to me, you have to know that. I am a complete asshole. I'll admit that because I deserve the title. A true friend would have never said those things, even if they were under a lot of pressure. I'm so, so sorry. Please forgive me."

"But why would he not trust us?"

That's all she was going to say? I'd completely laid out an apology and she was worried about William not trusting us?

"I don't know. I had to say something, anything to make him stop calling me." She nodded her head slowly. She had her eyes on the ground. "Caelyn, I didn't mean those words, and I never will. Do I support your relationship with that asshole? Hell no I don't, but you already knew that." She laughed. "You can do so much better than William, I swear to you. But if that's who you pick, then who am I to stop you?"

"Okay," she said quietly. She looked like she wanted to say something else, but she stopped herself. Instead of waiting for her to make up her mind, I hugged her tightly again and apologized once more.

"I am so sorry Caelyn, it will never happen again. You mean too much to me." I made sure I maintained eye contact as I said those words. "Are you still mad?"

"Yes," she said, and I began to panic. What else could I say? She must have seen the look of terror on my face. "Look, what you said hurt me, but I know you better than I know myself. If you say it won't happen again then I trust you. If you say you never meant those hurtful things, then I trust you. But it doesn't mean that I'm not hurt."

"I'm sorry, really I am."

"I know you are, so I forgive you," she said.

Could it really be that easy?

"You do?" I asked, shocked.

"Yes, I do, now stop asking me about it. I can still change my mind."

Just like that her usual banter was back, and I knew we would be okay.

"We're still Liam and Caelyn?" I asked.

"Forever and ever," she said, this time hugging me first. I never wanted to let her go, but she broke away. "You need a shower by the way," she said, laughing and holding her nose.

"What, you don't like my manly smell after a run?" I asked inching closer to her.

"Ew, get away from me Liam," she said trying to run away from me, but I grabbed her wrist. This was my opportunity to fully see her today. She was still wearing her pajamas and her hair was a matted mess. I took a fake sniff of her and made a huge show, laughing.

"I could say the same thing about you. Jeez, when was the last time you had a shower?" I asked, fanning my hand in front of my face. She swatted my arm, something she's always done. Gosh I missed her so much these past few days. In that moment, I knew I never wanted to fight with her again.

"I'm so glad I have you around to tell me I look like shit. You're the best," she said, smiling from ear to ear.

"How 'bout this then, I'll run home and shower while you get ready too. Then I'll come back and pick you up?" I asked, making my way slowly to the door.

"Where are we going?" she said, excitement creeping into her voice.

"It's a surprise. I'll be back in twenty-five minutes, be ready." I left and ran down the stairs and the remainder of the way home. All I could think about was how much I loved her, and I didn't know how to stop these feelings. She had to feel the same towards me, right? There was no way she could have forgiven me that quickly otherwise.

The first day of classes came too soon for me because I wasn't really looking forward to school starting. I just wanted to be near Caelyn again. It had been a year since I'd lived next door to her, and I'd missed her so much more than I thought I would. We talked all the time when I was gone my freshman year, but it still didn't feel right.

My schedule didn't look too bad, and Caelyn's was a usual freshman schedule. I looked forward to seeing her at swim practice most days, since we wouldn't see much of one another during classes. I had an easy Monday starting at nine with one of my advanced business classes. Then after lunch, I had an introduction to psychology since I just picked it up as a minor. I loved my business classes because I felt like they were preparing me to run the family fishing business back home. I strictly wanted to focus on the business side, but Dad claimed I should be able to do it all like him. I knew I would enjoy it so much more if I hired workers for the harvest season and then did the rest on my own.

My class had about twenty other business majors, but I kept to myself the first day instead of mingling. After class was over, I stayed after to ask the professor if there were any opportunities for internships this year. I shared that I had one this past summer with the help of my last professor, Dr. Grewson. Dr. Mackaby listened intuitively and said he would get back to me as soon as he heard of anything. I thanked him, left, and hoped I made a good impression.

After I grabbed a sandwich before my next class, I made my way over to the big building that held my psychology class. Students were milling around in the hallways, but I didn't want to sit or stand around. I was looking forward to this class, and grew hopeful that I'd made a wise decision in making this my minor.

As soon as I walked into class, I saw her. She was hunched over in her seat doodling in her notebook. Her wavy brown hair spilled across her shoulders and stray pieces framed her face. She had that nervous twitch with her leg I could have spotted her a mile away. It was crazy to believe that I could pick her out in a sea of hundreds. This class was huge and not many seats were left open after I gawked for a minute or so. The professor walked towards the center of the room, and I walked up the stairs to find a seat in the auditorium. I squeezed past a girl that wore too much perfume and makeup, another girl that smacked her gum way too loud, and a guy that looked half-asleep. I ignored them all and just looked ahead. There was one seat left in the aisle, luckily right next to her. I placed my backpack down and slid into the cold, metal seat.

"I didn't know you were taking this class," I said pulling out my textbook. Caelyn looked up from her notebook and smiled at me. But then the realization hit.

"No way! We have a class together?" She almost screamed, she was so surprised.

"You can never get rid of me," I said, giving her my easy smile while she blushed. Did my eyes deceive me or did I actually see her blush? I was about to say something when our professor started to introduce herself.

This semester was going to be the best, for more reasons than one.

After class was over Caelyn and I walked over to the coffee shop discussing our first day. "So, what do you think of your classes?" I asked her after I ordered our favorites.

"They're good, I guess. I really like my professors so far," she said, taking a seat at a small table. "How did you end up taking a psychology class anyway, Liam?"

"I picked it up as a minor," I admitted. I held my breath as she thought over my choice.

"Wow, really? I had no idea you were interested in that. You're keeping the business major, right? Please tell me you are."

"Of course. Yeah, I love it. I even talked with my professor this morning about being interested in another internship," I said, taking a sip of my black coffee. "I really hope I get the opportunity again, you know? It was an amazing experience and got my mind ready for taking over the family business soon."

"I can only imagine," she paused and held her coffee cup to her lips, looking nervous. "Can I ask you something?" She took a big sip of her caramel macchiato.

"Yes, what's up?"

"Never mind, it's selfish," she said, placing her cup down on the small table. She bit her lip as she looked me in the eyes.

"Caelyn, you can ask me anything and I promise I'll answer, no matter how selfish, stupid, or random it is." I reached across the table and grabbed her hand, giving it a squeeze. I let go and saw Caelyn's cheeks turn red. Did she feel the tingle too?

"Um... okay. Did you ever miss home while you were gone for your internship?" she asked, and I shook my head. "You didn't?"

She sounded disappointed, and I immediately wanted to take it back. But of course, I didn't miss home, I just missed her. I didn't know how to say that to her though. Ever since William got on my back, I was being careful with everything when it came to her.

"I mean, yeah maybe a little. I don't know, I missed my parents and of course seeing you." I could see her mood lighten. "Do you not want me to get another internship?" I asked.

"I didn't say that, Liam. I just asked if you missed home." She stood up, threw away her coffee cup, and started walking towards the door. I gulped down the rest of my coffee and followed her out into the hot Massachusetts sun.

"Caelyn, what's wrong?" I asked catching up to her, "what did I say?"

"Nothing, it's just time to go to practice." I looked down at my phone and practice was supposed to start in twenty minutes.

"Crap, let's go." I took her bag and flung it over my shoulder with my own. We started to jog through the commons.

First day of practice was as I predicted it to be. The guys that were on the team last year returned, and I knew them all. When Caelyn and I walked in they greeted us with a bunch of hooting and hollering. "Carter! Hey, we thought you weren't coming."

"Oh, you wish Wilson. I know you don't want me here just so you can beat my school record." Tony Wilson's pack of friends snickered at my comment. He was probably my least favorite person at this school and it just so happened that I was his too. Last year, my freshman and Tony's junior year, I beat his record that he had been holding since his freshman year. Coach even decided to place me above Tony, and that didn't go down well. Honestly, because of that, I was able to gain the respect of the upper classmen and all the coaches. Tony had never forgiven me and had never been able to beat me in any race since.

"Trying to show off in front of your new girlfriend Carter? What number is this one?" Tony said, trying to recover his image.

"She's not my girlfriend Wilson, and I don't have to impress her. She knows how to give me a run for my own money, and I'm sure she could even beat you." I handed Caelyn her bag and she took it from me, giving me the eye. She wanted me to shut up, but I wasn't going to. I had faith in her that she could beat him.

"Oh really? Why don't we see about that after practice?" he said, disappearing through the door to the pools. Her eyes were already fixed on me when I turned her way.

"Liam, why did you do that? What if I can't beat him?" I could hear her growing mad at me.

"Don't worry, just hurry and change!" I ran into the locker room and stepped out just as Caelyn was.

"Any words of advice?" she asked, rubbing her arms nervously. She looked so innocent and scared and all I wanted to do was grab her and kiss away her fears. I wrapped my arm around her shoulders and squeezed when she leaned into my touch.

"Impress them, which will be no problem for you. You're amazing."

And let me tell you, she did just that.

Caelyn was the fastest girl we had on the team by a long shot. As soon as she dove into the pool for a few warm up laps, you could feel the tension evaporate. When it was time for challenge laps, as we call them, Caelyn showed no nerves and competed at her very best. I loved watching her swim; it was like watching a shark's fin as it broke through the water. When it was time to go up against the older, returning swimmers, she showed even more finesse. Then, she easily beat Lacie Burnes for the back stroke and butterfly records. Lacie wasn't as upset with Caelyn as Tony was with me that first practice. Through the whole practice, I couldn't help but stare in amazement at how good she was. When we were in high school I knew she was talented, but man, she was fantastic now. I looked across the pool and met Caelyn's eyes and gave her a big smile that showed my approval.

Practice went just as well for me as I, yet again, beat Tony. I also beat Brad Fisher, a new contending swimmer for a top position. I hadn't been in the pool for about two weeks and the chlorine was warmly welcomed by my body. As I swam, I tried to focus on working just as hard as Caelyn so she could see that I was improving too. I still knew that I could beat her, but she wasn't far behind. At the end of practice Coach called me off to the side.

"Liam, how was your summer? Did you swim a lot?" he asked me as I took off my cap and dried off.

"You know Coach, actually not a lot. Can you tell?" I was beginning to get a little worried.

"Are you kidding me? You continue to surprise me Carter, your times are even faster and if it's possible, your form looks the best it's ever been," he said, giving me an approving nod.

"Thanks Coach, that means a lot." I figured he was done talking but he brought up something very random.

"So, what do you think of the new freshman, Caelyn Price? Did you get a chance to watch her? She's quite the impressive swimmer," he motioned towards her with his clipboard. Caelyn was standing off the side of the pool with a group of girls; she looked to be enjoying herself. One of the girls said something that made the group laugh and gosh, she looked as beautiful as ever. "Know who I'm talking about Liam?" Coach interrupted my thoughts.

"Yeah, I know her, really well actually. Caelyn and I come from the same home town. Believe it or not, she just started swimming competitively her last two years of high school, but she's always been a natural sir," I said to him. "Can I ask you something, Coach? What do you think of her?"

Coach scoffed. "What do I think? I think she's amazing and we're lucky to have her on this team. She will be a great contender and asset during our season. I'm thinking of having her swim back and butterfly. What do you think?"

I knew those were her best strokes and her favorites. "I think that sounds perfect sir," I said smiling.

"But don't worry Liam, you'll always be one of our greatest swimmers here," he added as he walked away. I just barely got out a thank you before he exited the pool area.

I started to make my way over to Caelyn when I saw Tony talking to her. Oh shit, what does that tool have to say to her?

"Are you ready or not?" he asked her.

"Look, I don't think you really want to race me," she said trying to get out of the bet.

"You're probably not even that good then," he laughed and started to walk away. *Did he even watch her today?* I was about to speak up when Caelyn corrected him.

"Oh, no I'm good. I'm just afraid you might cry if a girl beats you, Tony," she said putting her cap back on. "Are you ready or not?" She fired his own words back at him. I couldn't have been more proud of her. She looked around the pool and met my eyes. Her features began to soften as I grinned at her.

"Let's go Cassie," he said, deliberately getting her name wrong and smirking knowingly. He asked one of his friends to count them off while he and Caelyn stepped up on the dive blocks. He put his googles over his eyes and looked over at Caelyn.

"One. Two," Mark said.

"It's Caelyn by the way," she said just as Mark called out three. Caelyn perfectly flew off the block leaving Tony frazzled. She managed to dismount a second before Tony and I knew she had an advantage. Right away I started rooting for Caelyn and many of our teammates followed suit. At the end of the first lap Caelyn was leading, but by the beginning of the second lap Tony took the lead. This went back and forth between the two of them. At the other end of the pool, I saw that they were about to do their final kick turn, and I noticed that Caelyn led by a stroke. She used her famous kick turn that she routinely employed when she wanted to get a better lead.

The room grew silent as they were neck and neck in the last stretch. Tony made the mistake to check out his opponent and it caused him to falter. Caelyn pushed forward and was in the lead by two strokes. She passed the flags and in three strokes she touched the wall. She stood up by the side of the pool as Tony touched the wall.

"Damn it," he said, slapping his hand on the water as Caelyn wiped her face off. The smile plastered across it was undeniable, and I knew she was proud of herself. Heck, I was proud of her. I went over to the side of the pool and grabbed her hands to pull her out.

"Did you see that? I haven't swum like that since season last year." She was talking a mile a minute and the others around us were too. They were obviously impressed with the show they just witnessed. If anyone questioned her before, surely they couldn't now. The room tensed up as Tony got out of the pool, but no one was looking at him. They were looking towards the door. Coach stood there, arms crossed, leaning against the wall.

"Might I say, that was quite the show," he clapped his hands and started to retreat out the door. "Caelyn, welcome aboard," he said and then followed up with, "Wilson, I expect you to spend extra time in the pool this year."

Tony's face scrunched up and he began to snarl. I grabbed Caelyn's hand and started to leave the room, but the group of girls from earlier stopped us. They surrounded Caelyn and couldn't stop talking about how good she was. Her cheeks grew a deep shade of red, like they always do when she is paid a compliment.

"Thanks guys, I really appreciate it," she said to each of them.

"A group of us are going to get some pizza, you want to join?" Lacie asked as everyone began to quiet down. Caelyn looked to me for my approval. After our class, we'd made plans to go to dinner so that we could work on our psychology homework, but I just nodded my head.

"Go, I'll be fine," I said walking away, but before I could get very far, she grabbed my arm and gave me a quick hug. As soon as she touched me, she was gone. However, I still caught a slight glimpse of a blush forming on her cheeks.

"Yeah sure, let's go," she said grabbing her stuff. Lacie and a few other girls gave me a small wave goodbye as I left the rec area. I was hoping Travis was done with practice so he and I could get some food. One quick glance at my phone and I had a message already waiting for me, but it was from my mom. It said: *Call me.*

She picked up after two rings. "Hey Mom, what's up?"

"Oh, honey hi. I just wanted to call and ask how your first day of school and practice was," she said. I knew she missed having me at home since I was her baby, so I was used to her calling me, wanting to talk. For the remainder of the walk to my apartment I explained to her about my business class, mentioned that Caelyn and I had a class together, and told her all about practice. I said that Coach intended to put me as one of the top positions again and that Caelyn would also be in the same boat. She wasn't surprised by that news.

"You two have always been my little fishes." I could hear her smile through the phone. "Well honey, I'll let you go, I have to start making dinner." We ended the call and I walked into the apartment. Travis sat, still in his football clothes, on the couch in the common room. I set my bag down on the ground by the door and opened the fridge. I grabbed two waters and sat on the couch, handing Travis one. He was being oddly quiet tonight. We sat there for about an hour, not saying much when I got up to get a shower. As much as I loved the chlorinated water, I wanted it off my skin. When I was done, I walked out into the common room just as Travis walked out of his room.

"Hey, I ordered us a couple pizzas, hope you're hungry," he said grabbing another water from the fridge.

"Starving, thanks." I sat on the couch again not bothering with the little homework my professors gave me today. There was a knock at the door and Travis went to answer it, money in hand, thinking the pizza delivery guy was here. Instead, there stood Lacie Burnes. I didn't even know she knew where I lived this year.

"Hey, can I talk to Liam?" she asked Travis. He motioned for her to come on in, and I stood up. Memories flooded my brain when she stepped through the apartment door. This wasn't the first time Lacie came to "talk" to me. She used to come over a lot last year to work on homework, but we ended up fooling around instead. It sounds awful, but I never really felt anything more than a friendship with her. All I wanted was for someone to help me keep my mind off Caelyn back in Cape Elizabeth. She was happy with William, and I wanted to feel something too.

"What's up Lacie?" she looked around our apartment with a blank face. It wasn't messy so I didn't know what she was thinking. Travis could sense she wanted us to be alone, so he walked into his room and closed his door. A few seconds later I could hear the faint hum of his TV through the walls. I didn't know why he was being so unusually quiet tonight. She took a seat on our couch and patted the cushion next to her. I sat down on the other one, so she scooted toward me.

"So, I was thinking maybe we should do some homework," she said moving in closer to me. Before I could say anything, her lips connected with mine. Like an old habit, I kissed her back and my hand found the small of her back, pulling her to me. Her fingers ran through my wet hair and she started to deepen our kiss. I felt nothing, but not because she was a bad kisser or anything. She knew what she was doing; I just never felt the excitement you feel when you're in love.

I thought she was pretty, some would argue beautiful. She had short dark, brown hair that was always down and her eyes were the color of chocolate. She had the perfect hourglass figure and she was short, but not too short. I knew she liked me and at one point I guess I might have developed some feelings too, but my eyes were never truly for her. Every time I looked into her eyes, they weren't sea green. She didn't have long hair that I wanted to run my hands through. She was just a pretty girl that I liked to hang out and mess around with.

After about twenty minutes Lacie ended up sitting on my lap and her shirt laid on the cushion next to us. I broke away and immediately regretted ever letting Travis welcome her in. She wasn't the girl I wanted to be kissing. That girl had a boyfriend that lived two hours away, and it just so happened that he hated me.

"What's wrong?" she asked me, looking worried. She tried to kiss my neck as her hands roamed down my chest. I pushed her off my lap and stood up, running my fingers through my messy hair. This was all wrong. I let out a deep breath. I felt so sick that I couldn't even look at her.

"Lacie, this isn't fair to you," I claimed.

"What isn't fair, Liam?" She stood up and came over to me. She pressed herself against me and wrapped her arms around my neck. "We're just messing around," she said forcing her lips to mine, but I pushed her away again. She didn't miss a beat and grabbed me again. "Come on, what's wrong with you? You used to love this." She ran her hand down my chest stopping low. I felt the sudden urge that I wanted to be sick. Her touch was making my stomach hurt.

"Don't you want more than just someone to mess around with? Like an actual relationship?" I asked, pushing her away from me and handing her shirt to her.

"Yeah of course, but I know you don't want that," she said, holding her shirt to her chest. "I'm willing to let go of that so that we can do this," she whined.

"Well what if I told you I don't want to do this anymore?" I looked her in the eyes. I needed to let her know I was serious about this. She looked hurt for about a second and then took on a hopeful expression.

"So, does that mean you're ready for an actual relationship then?" She moved towards me, smiling.

"Yes," she kept moving toward me and I took a step back, "but not with you. I'm sorry."

"Oh okay, I get it," she said, putting her shirt on fast. As she walked to the door she said, over her shoulder, "Whatever Liam." I didn't move when the door slammed; I didn't even flinch.

"What was that about?" Travis said as he came out of his room.

"I told her I didn't want to fool around with her anymore," I admitted, sitting down on the couch. I felt sicker than before.

"Why? She's so hot! How often do you have a girl like that be okay with just messing around and not being in a committed relationship? Never," he answered his own question, not even skipping a beat. "What's going on with you, man?"

"I want a relationship. I want to be committed to one single person and have them be committed to me," I said as I sat forward.

Travis thought over my words for a second. "With Caelyn?" he asked matter-of-factly. The question was simple and as soon as I heard her name my heart pulled against my chest. I didn't answer him. "What are you waiting for, Liam? Go over there and tell her how you feel, admit you love her right now. Want me to get my video camera so that you can show this moment at your wedding and to your kids?"

"You're an asshole, you know that?" I stood up and started walking to my room. "Just because I want a relationship with her, doesn't mean I love her, Travis." I lied.

"It's obvious," he said answering the door to get the pizzas. I slammed my door, no longer hungry. I laid on my bed wishing I could fall asleep early and be done with this night. After hours of tossing and turning, I couldn't fall asleep. I replayed what Travis said over and over. *Is it that obvious to everyone except me?* I decided to get up and move around because I wasn't falling asleep anytime soon. I paced my room, thinking back on a raw memory.

It was about two weeks before the accident and David had texted me to come over. I walked across the street and opened the front door, something we always did as kids. Our parents agreed on an open-door policy because we were always coming and going. I took their stairs two at a time and walked into David's room after I glanced across the hall and saw Caelyn's door closed.

"Hey what's up?" David said, spinning around in his chair. He threw the small ball that was in his hands and missed the makeshift basket he had attached by the door.

"Still not very good at that I see," I laughed, picking up the ball and dunking it in one try.

"Not all of us are good at everything Liam," he said, missing the basket again. "Hey so I was thinking, maybe we could have my mom drive us to go see the new Terminator movie in town?" he suggested.

"Yeah sure, sounds great," I said stuffing my hands in my jean pockets. I looked around the room and back out to Caelyn's closed door. "So, where's Caelyn? Why is her door closed?" I asked calmly, or so I thought. He didn't answer me right away and I looked from the door to his blank face. "What'd I say?"

"Nothing," he started to shake his head, but I had to coax him.

"No, tell me."

"What's going on with you and my sister?"

Oh shit, I'd been caught. But how? I hadn't told anyone how I felt about her. I automatically went on the defensive.

"What are you talking about? With Caelyn?" He shook his head and looked at me wide eyed. "Oh, my gosh nothing. David, really? She's like my sister." I hated lying to him, but I was afraid how he'd react if he knew the truth. I tried to brush it off and made another basket in the meantime. *Could he really see through my lies?*

"Oh, come on Liam, I know you better than I know myself. I can tell something has changed. Maybe not with her, but definitely with you," he said. "I don't know what it is exactly, but I see a difference in how you look at her, talk to her, and talk about her. You even started wearing jeans this past month," he pointed at my outfit. "Dude, I know when something is up with you, especially when it concerns a girl."

After all he said, I was stuck on one comment. *She didn't feel what I felt?* I knew I should feel nothing after that one thought, but still I was hurt. What was wrong with me? Shouldn't I be able to talk to David about this? I immediately answered my own thought because this was Caelyn we were talking about. David's twin sister. His twin and my best friend.

I sat down on his bed and ran my fingers through my hair, then down my face. I couldn't believe he knew. "What do you think?"

"All I'm going to say is this, I know you like her and know you have for a while. She's my sister so I need to say this too: you break her heart, I break you. If you love her, then let it be only her because I want her to be with the best guy who will treat her right. You could be that guy Liam," he said calmly. "But it's none of my business because this is between you and her. Now, if or when you decide to tell her, that's your decision. Hell, you don't even have to tell her. But don't let her pass you by if you truly want to be with her. She's too good of a catch." He was dead serious. David always spoke so highly of Caelyn, and he knew exactly what made her special. "Here's a promise Liam. I won't be the one to mention it ever again. It's up to you to decide what to do."

"Thanks," was all I could say. I was speechless.

"Just don't be a chicken-shit, because you'll regret it for the rest of your life." He clapped me on the shoulder and we went into town to see the movie. I honestly don't remember much about it, but David said it was really great. On the way home, David's mom picked up Caelyn from the mall. She went with some girls from school to shop for their Christmas dance dresses. She rode in the front seat and David and I were behind her. I expected David to make some face at me on the way home, but he did no such thing. He didn't even punch me in the arm like he usually did when a girl I liked was around. He kept to his word and never mentioned it for those two weeks.

Then he was gone forever. When he died, I thought my secret crush on Caelyn died too. Boy was I wrong.

Five

Caelyn

When William called Liam, he became extremely protective or controlling. He'd started calling me twice a day, once when I woke up and then after he finished his internship for the day. At first, I loved the extra attention, but then it became annoying and a chore to talk to him. He wouldn't really have anything interesting to say and always talked about himself. He never asked how school was going or if I was having a fun time. Nothing like that at all. It was always about him, but I didn't think much of it at first.

Since William and I started dating, I felt like we never fully developed a deep connection. I think I had been looking for someone that would push me out of my comfort zone and give me attention. To be honest, I thought I was looking for someone to fill the void when Liam left for Boston. William landed in my lap at the perfect time, and I felt it was a no brainer to go out with someone who was nothing like me, older, and more experienced in the dating realm.

Then, the longer we dated, I saw that we were no longer compatible. However, at that point in the relationship, I didn't know what to do because I was scared to let go and say goodbye. I was scared to lose another person in my life because I was thinking irrationally or immaturely. What if William and I had more to our story? What if I was reading too much into the small bumps in the road and ruining a good thing in my life? I knew deep down I wasn't reading into anything, but I still didn't know how to end things with William. Also, to be truthful, I was scared how he'd react, so I stayed. I knew it wasn't healthy, but I did love him and figured we could grow together.

So, when I was at school, I tried to look past the bad and focus on the good. I didn't know any better.

One day, William called when I was on my way to the gym. Somehow the topic of BU's ball came up in our conversation. He insisted that he was coming, but I didn't want to force him to attend; it really wasn't his scene, and I didn't want him to come and ruin my night. Besides, he had just gotten out of college and had his fill of balls and school functions. Even though I protested, he still insisted that he would be coming and we made plans to have him stay at my dorm that night too. I was a little hesitant on that last part, but he kept pressing the issue so I just agreed. This was one of the many red flags I recognized, but chose not to act on because I thought he was trying to make an effort.

When I thought about William, I found myself comparing him and Liam. Every time I did this, I realized my relationship with Liam was completely different than mine with Will. With Liam, conversation flowed easier and I was never put in uncomfortable positions. Liam was always understanding and wanted to see me thrive. Recently I'd noticed him looking at me more and more. But unlike other guys caught in the act, he never looked away embarrassed. He would simply smile or wink in my direction which usually made my stomach flip. Then, of course, my cheeks would blush. It was always the cheeks that gave me away.

In other revelations, I decided that I want to spend every spare moment I had with Liam. Sometimes I even chose to hang out with him over Bonnie which I told myself I would never do. But I couldn't help it, Liam made me laugh and smile. I'd craved that feeling for a while now and knew William wouldn't be able to give that to me. However, I didn't want to throw away our relationship because of the many unknowns that would come from us breaking up. So, I found myself in a tough situation. And what better way to confuse myself even more, than to think about both possibilities and what each had to offer. I mean, I was a worrier and wanted to think over every angle.

I first started noticing a change in my relationship with Liam last year when he came home to surprise me. William and I were on a break for two weeks, and I warmly welcomed Liam when he came home. He seemed different too; clingier and protective, but in a good way. From that day on, every time my phone's screen flashed his name, or the home line rang, or even when I saw his car in the drive, my insides fluttered and my heart raced.

Trust me, these feelings didn't just appear overnight. I'd always had a special place in my heart for him because he was my first love. When I was younger, I imagined getting married and having a family with him. When I daydreamed about my future, Liam was a part of that dream. David caught on quickly because, let's face it, we had a special connection. David teased me so bad but never in front of Liam, for which I was grateful. Once we started high school, the teasing got worse because I had started to deny the feelings I had for Liam. But then freshman year started, the accident happened, and then everything changed.

A few weeks after David died, my feelings for Liam started to come back. Okay let's be honest, they never truly went away, but I no longer suppressed them. And from there, they only increased because of how close Liam and I were. Although the feelings were there, I pushed them to the background because I didn't have room in my heart to love anyone then. We were both too consumed by our own grief to pursue the possibility of us. Hell, I didn't even know if he felt the same way. The timing was confusing, and I couldn't bear the thought of losing Liam if something went wrong. So, with that in mind, I pushed my feelings aside and looked to Liam for support and nothing else.

I always welcomed these old memories because it helped me remember that time in my life; the good and bad about my brother, my family, my relationship with Liam, and who I used to be. The worst thing I could have ever done was block these thoughts from my memory. If I would have allowed myself to break and love Liam then, I don't think I would have healed after David's death. Truthfully, I felt if I replaced the pain and hurt with love and happiness, I would forget my brother and the pain that came from losing him.

Nonetheless, a part of me still wondered what it would be like to end things with William and pursue my feelings for Liam. Would it be the right choice?

I was on my way to an early morning swim practice and a memory with Liam, Adrian, and Evelyn flooded my mind. It was the one-year anniversary of David's death, and the four of us had promised to visit his grave. We showed up to his tomb in layers of clothing and blankets because the nightly temperatures in northern Maine dropped significantly in October. We took turns telling stories of the most prominent things David missed that year. We talked about school drama, family get-togethers that ended in screaming matches, and random events we wished he could have witnessed. By the end of the night, the four of us were crying. This memory held a special place in my heart because we laid out our feelings and supported one another. Surprisingly, Evelyn felt David's loss strongly that night. It was hard for me to realize that she was close with him because I never remembered them being particularly friendly. Despite what I might've thought, David impacted everyone he met. Everyone loved David and he loved everyone back. I envied his ability to touch people's lives. He was so sweet and genuine. I just hated that he was taken from us so soon.

It was that night, with the four of us huddled around his tombstone, that Evelyn shared a secret with us. She told us that her and David had shared their first kiss together. Things finally started to click when I remembered the two of them together. It was young love, but nothing too serious. They were awkward around each other because they were unsure of their feelings and how that would impact the relationship between our families. I felt sorry for Evelyn and wished I had known. The news was a shock which then made me angry because that was something David neglected to tell me. I don't even think he told Liam either.

Through the early morning fog back on campus I saw a familiar figure standing outside the indoor pool facility.

"Morning," Liam said, opening the door for me and following me inside.

"Morning," I squeaked as I ran into the locker room. I hurriedly changed into my suit and walked out to the pool. Coach stood by the diving blocks holding a whistle and clipboard. This sight was completely new to me, and I could feel my nerves pick up.

At exactly 6:15 a.m. Coach blew his whistle and bellowed roll call. Afterwards he explained that a new type of relay had been added to the meets as a new experiment this year.

"The relay will consist of one male and one female swimmer and each will be required to swim a two-hundred meter medley. For those of you that are not quite awake yet this fine morning, that means fifty meters of the fly, breast, back, and free. You and your partner need to decide who will start and who will finish. Be very smart in your theory because you want to be strategic. You never know who you will face." I could feel my teammates squirming in their own skin. "I have strategically selected four duos to compete for the two duo spots BU will have this season. Today's practice will show me who is prepared to fight for such an honor. Like I said, this has not been done before." He looked among the scared and anxious faces.

"This is going to be awesome," Liam said, squeezing my hand. The tingling sensation traveled from my palm to my shoulder.

"First duo," Coach glanced at his clipboard, "Wilson and Burnes." Tony and Lacie emerged from the group and clasped hands in a loud clap. "Second duo, Fisher and Dots." Brad, a transfer sophomore, and Grace, a junior, stepped forward. They were an odd duo, but both strong swimmers. "Third duo, Gilles and Hamilton." Seth was a new member to the swim team but was a senior and Sarah was a freshman like myself. Coach looked over his clipboard briefly before announcing the last duo. I held my breath, praying my name was called. "Fourth and final duo, Carter and Price."

"Yes!" Liam raised his hands up for a double high five. Our hands clapped loudly and our grins were unmistakable. I was beyond happy that I'd been given this opportunity to compete for a spot. I knew Coach had made a great decision in putting us together by the look he gave us when he announced our names.

"Everyone else, start treading. The four duos, you have two minutes to plan your lineup. We will complete this at least three times today and the two duos with the fastest times will be our competitors. Now start strategizing," he demanded, starting his stopwatch.

"You have to swim last," Liam immediately whispered to me.

"What? Why?" I asked full of panic.

"You're perfect at closing out relays. Besides, if I can go first I can try and give you a bigger lead because I have the best two-hundred meter medley time. Well, besides you."

He had a good point. Liam's medley was one of the fastest on the team, but I was the fastest girl swimmer we had. I liked the idea of his plan, but it still made me nervous knowing I had to finish it out for us.

"Okay fine."

"You're the best one here Caelyn. Coach knew we'd be a force to reckon with. That's why he paired us together. We'll be unstoppable." Liam gripped my shoulders to thoroughly get his message into my head. I nodded and sucked on my bottom lip.

"I'm a little nervous," I admitted. "That's a lot of intense swimming for me Liam." I motioned toward my side where I was injured during the wreck. Liam's face filled with concern.

"Just breathe and if it hurts, we stop and drop out. It's that simple," he said matter-of-factly. "It's not worth the risk, got it? Your health matters more."

"Okay," I agreed reluctantly. We would never drop out.

"Swimmers, take your place on the block." Coach blew his whistle letting us know our time was up. Liam took his place along with Lacie, Brad, and Sarah. I knew he could finish this many seconds before his competitors, which would be perfect for me in case I needed a bigger lead. All other thoughts but the relay escaped my mind. Coach's whistle rang loud and clear and the four of them leapt off the block. By the end of the first fifty-meter fly, Liam was keeping his word about giving me any extra advantage he could. Then, he was blowing everyone away when it came to the breast stroke. I started to grow nervous as soon as the back stroke started because I knew that was Liam's weakest stroke. Brad and Lacie had gained a little bit of distance but were still behind a few strokes. The last fifty-meter free began when Liam kick turned.

I stepped up to the block and put on my goggles, waiting for Liam to touch this wall, being careful not to disqualify us. Liam reached the flags and in three strokes he touched the wall, way before the other competitors. I leapt off over Liam and dove into the pool. The fly was by far one of my favorite strokes because it came naturally to me. During my medley, I tried my best to block out all fears and nerves because I had to give everything to this. I wanted Liam to see that I could do it. I wanted to finish us out strong. When I did my second-to-last kick turn, beginning the fifty-meter free, I could barely make out Liam's shouts above me. He was encouraging me, saying I could do this. Those words helped me push to the end and I used my famous kick turn and swam my heart out to the finish line.

My fingertips grazed the wall and I stood up. I looked left and right and saw no one else at the wall. I took off the googles and saw a look on Liam's face I had rarely ever seen. His eyes were wide with excitement and he had the biggest grin on his face. He was no longer shouting, just looking at me with pure amazement. Coach called out my time and the other swimmers reached the wall around the same time. Liam helped me out of the pool and spun me around like he did the first day I moved here. I cringed as my side pulled uncomfortably. He must have noticed because he put me down carefully. He put his hand over mine on my torso, trying to apologize with his actions.

"You did it. See, I told you you could." The look of pure pride was displayed in his dark brown eyes. "Our time was fantastic all thanks to you. 4:45:07. What got into you? I've never seen you swim like that."

"I don't know, I just really wanted to win," I explained, a little out of breath. The pain in my torso began to subside. I felt warm just from the looks Liam gave me; if he looked at me like that for the rest of my life, I would be complete and utterly content. "I had a good partner," I said, nudging him in the stomach and feeling his abs tense under my brief touch. I wondered if he was experiencing the warmth and tingling sensation I was. I automatically felt guilty because I was the one in a relationship.

"Okay okay, our fastest team as of now is Carter and Price, followed by Wilson and Burnes, then Fisher and Dots, and in last place, Gilles and Hamilton. If you want to change anything up, now is the time. We start the next relay in a few minutes."

Coach walked over to the other edge of the pool and gave instructions to the rest of the team. Liam and I agreed that we were going to keep the same game plan, but try even harder for a faster time. After that second race, we were still in the top position and had even managed to improve our time by seven seconds. That was huge. I could feel my muscles in my body begin to ache when I stepped out of the pool before the third and final race.

"What's wrong?" Liam was right there when anything was amiss, but I didn't want to tell him I was feeling achy. We had one last race to do, and I desperately wanted to secure one of the duo spots.

"Nothing, I'm fine," I said, fibbing just a little.

"Bullshit, what's wrong? Did I bother your torso when I picked you up?" He lightly poked at my side and I barely cringed, but Liam was quick on his feet. "Oh no, shit, it's my fault."

"No, it's not, I just think it's my muscles. I haven't swum like this in a long time. We have one last race so I'll be fine."

Coach blew his whistle which meant it was time for Liam to take his position on the block. His time slowed down by a second which I expected because the two-hundred meter medley was not easy to do back to back. Even though his time slowed down a second, our competitors were nowhere in sight. Lacie and Tony had even switched places in the relay, and Tony still couldn't catch up to Liam.

It was my turn to take the block. I hoped and prayed the pain would subside as soon as I started to swim. The first hundred meters were alright, but on the start of my one-fifty-meter stretch, I could feel the pain increase. Blocking out as much as I could, I charged forward and finished the free with Lacie nowhere near me. When I came up to the wall, it was hard to hide the tears forming in my eyes from the amount of pain I felt. Liam was by my side in a matter of seconds. I looked around the pool and noticed all eyes on me. I glanced toward the opposite side of the pool and my other three competitors were just starting their last twenty-five meters. How was I able to finish so quickly?

I got out of the pool and Liam offered me a towel. I grabbed and wrapped it around my shoulders, swaying a little bit in the process. Liam grabbed my towel and pulled me to a standing position, but my body suddenly felt incredibly heavy. I dropped to the ground.

"Caelyn, what's wrong?"

Liam was on my level as soon as I hit the floor. It was hard to find which Liam was talking to me because I saw at least two of them. I blinked trying to clear my head, afraid I was causing a scene.

"Nothing, how was that? I'm not really sure how that was possible." I stood up quickly and the room started to spin once again. Liam's muscular arm wrapped around my waist to keep me from falling.

"You are insane, literally a mad woman. That last medley was the fastest one you've ever done, 2:17:06. What got into you? Did you even know you were doing it? I mean seriously Caelyn, it was faster than some of mine." He was shaking his head, trying to figure out how I did that last medley. Trust me, I was in shock myself. "Our collective time was 4:23:59; which is crazy. Everyone else is around the five-minute marker." He was rambling which I knew meant he was pretty excited.

Coach seemed impressed by what he had seen today, especially with Liam and me. I had to agree that Liam and I blew the rest of our competitors out of the water. With the last race done, Coach called off practice early for half the team and asked the duos to stay a little longer.

"Today I have seen many of you test your personal limits to fight for this spot on the team. I was extremely impressed with all of you, but one particular duo..." Coach turned his body to where Liam and I stood. "Carter, Price, I don't know what I saw today from the both of you, but I loved it. You're in the clear and have rightfully earned this position on the team. I'm looking forward to this season with the both of you. Congratulations, you are dismissed for today." Liam and I said thank you and wished our other teammates good luck. I wasn't certain what Coach was going to do for the second duo because they were all equal in strength and speed.

I hurried into the locker room and hit the shower to get the chlorine off my skin. I wasn't sure what happened earlier, but I was feeling a little better despite the tight feeling in my torso. I changed into shorts and a t-shirt and threw my knotting hair into a bun on top of my head. In one swift motion, I grabbed my bag and walked out of the locker room into the main lobby. A few stray teammates remained and wished me congratulations, and I thanked them while looking for Liam. Feeling defeated, I walked out and started the five-minute walk to my dorm.

"What happened today?" I turned around and literally jumped two feet in the air. My hand flew to my chest as I tried to catch my breath.

"Don't do that, you know how much I hate to be snuck up on."

"Answer my question." Liam didn't seem to be joking around. Still being the gentleman he was, he quickly took my bag from my shoulder and looped it over his neck with his own. "Oh, and I'm not accepting 'nothing' as an answer."

There was no hiding from this.

"By the end of the second relay I was feeling my muscles ache, which I thought was normal because my torso always acts up after

I swim heavily; you know this. I blocked most of the achy feeling until it became extremely painful as I got into the one-fifty-meter marker of my turn. I didn't want to stop because I knew how much this spot on the team meant to you. Plus, I didn't want to worry you. I know how distracted you can get when you worry about something."

"Why didn't you stop though?" Liam asked incredulously. "I told you it would be okay!"

"And disappoint you? And Coach too? No thank you," I said as he signed his name on the visitor's clipboard in Danielson Hall. We took the stairs slowly as I finished my explanation. "So, then I gave it everything I had. I finished, got a little lightheaded, but it's okay because we got the spot Liam. We really got it." I paused, key in hand. "Aren't you excited?"

"Caelyn, I'm beyond excited. You were so amazing today, I felt like I was watching a turning point in your career today. Like it was just so incredible that I could watch you and be with you through it all. We really have a chance to be something great with this." I saw an idea spark in his eyes. *This is exactly why I couldn't stop,* I thought. "Like if this duo does well, then it could join as a heat in the Olympics in a few years. Then, maybe we could even join a national team and try for a spot." He was daydreaming, but this was something he'd always aspired to. I hated to tell him it wouldn't come true, that we had careers and jobs to start. He seemed to be coming down from his high when a realization hit. "But when you are feeling this way—I..."

"That was after we raced twice, we'll only have to do it once every meet. Maybe twice at special meets," I pointed out, opening the door to my room. I honestly didn't know how often we would have to swim it, but I wanted to ease his worries.

Bonnie had already left for her eight a.m. class and had plans to go home for the weekend. My room felt entirely too quiet; I already missed her spunky yet reassuring attitude. Taking a seat on the futon in the common room, I thought about what I wanted to do with my day off.

"That means nothing, Caelyn, we can turn down the spot. I don't want to risk an injury on top of your existing one," he said, motioning to my torso. He was referring to the scar that decorated my olive skin from the top of my ribs to right above my hip. I subconsciously reached for it, and flinched at how sore it felt.

"Look I promise I'll be okay." I tried to reassure Liam the best I could, but he was still a little hesitant.

"Fine, but you know I'd be just as satisfied if you said you couldn't risk it." He went to grab something from the other room. I heard rummaging and then his head poked around the doorway. "Where's your heating pad?"

Heating pad? For who? "Under my bed."

He disappeared and came out with my heating pad and comforter. He plugged the pad into the wall and spread out the comforter on the futon. "What are you doing?"

"Movie day? Just like old times," he said, walking into my bathroom. What was he doing now?

"Don't you have class?" I yelled after him. I thought he had a twelve o'clock today.

"Yeah, I'm just not going. Here you go." He held out his hand and dropped two Advil into my palm and handed me a glass of water. Gosh, he was the best. The best, best friend that is, nothing more. "What do you want to watch?" I thought about it for a second and gave him a look like he should know. "I know, I know." Liam turned out the lights and moved the heating pad onto my torso. "Comfortable?"

"Very much so, thank you." I was warm and cozy as the music progressed to the opening of the first Harry Potter movie, one of our favorites.

When we were younger Liam's mom would always fix up their family room with pillows and blankets and we'd all sit down to watch the whole series. It was one of my absolute favorite things to do. I felt completely at ease sitting next to Liam, but I had a nagging thought in the back of my mind. David would surely enjoy this if he were here. Liam put his arm around my shoulder and gave it a quick squeeze guessing my thoughts; something he was impeccable at.

"I know," was all he said.

Six

Liam

As soon as the second movie started Caelyn was fast asleep on the futon, and I was no longer looking at the screen. I couldn't help but watch Caelyn as she slept so soundly. She had no creases in her brow, no scrunched-up nose, and yet the smile I loved still played on her lips. Oh, how I wanted to kiss those lips. I wondered what it would be like. Would it feel different? Would we be different because of it? What if these feelings I had ruined everything we had been building since the very first day we met?

Caelyn stirred a little in her sleep and caused some of her hair to fall from the knot on her head. The comforter had also fallen off her shoulders. Trying not to wake her, I reached across to readjust the comforter. That's when I saw the light pink line decorating her torso just under the hem of her shirt. I dared a closer look as I brought the hem up a few inches just above her belly button. Caelyn's breathing appeared to be even which meant I wasn't disturbing her.

The scar was thin toward her hip and then gradually got thicker the further it went up. I had seen it many times before this when we had gone swimming in the pool after the accident, but I had never been so curious. I had the sudden urge to run my fingers across it. Slowly my hand was above her torso and one of my fingers began to trace the pink scar. It felt soft and even with her skin, but the feel of the scar was a little different from the actual skin on her stomach.

How could this cause her so much pain? Why was it that, even four years after the accident, Caelyn was constantly reminded of that terrible day? When the pain comes back, she remembers losing David and there wasn't anything I, or anyone else, could do. My fingers continued tracing the scar, but I immediately felt guilty for intruding on a private part of her. She had never let me see it this close. Stopping, I reached for the comforter and covered her shoulders.

Caelyn stirred one last time before my eye lids felt too heavy for me to keep open. She shifted her body weight over towards me and rested her head on my shoulder and laid one arm across my lower waist. The warmth I felt was undeniable, and I never wanted this moment to end. I heard the movie softly recede into the background as I gave into sleep.

"Hey, a group of us are going to the Chi Phi's mixer tonight, you wanna join us?" Travis asked in between reps on the weight bench. I was spotting him even though he didn't really need my help. I thought about his question and at first I thought why not, but then I had second thoughts.

"I don't know man. Can I think about it?" He placed the bar above his head and sat up. Sweat dripped from his forehead onto his gray t-shirt. He pinched his eyebrows together.

"What's to think about? Lacie will be there."

I rolled my eyes. "You know I ended that Travis." I walked over to the leg press and took a seat, adjusting the machine to the desired weight. Slowly I started the reps as I pushed out the air in my chest.

"Fine, then Sydnee will be there." My eyes bugged out of their sockets. Sydnee was a junior sorority girl that I had met last year at Chi Phi's fall mixer. She was pretty cute with long, wavy blonde hair and blue eyes. I remembered the first time we ever met; she was wearing short shorts and a tight, low cut red shirt. By the time one of the guys introduced me to her, she'd had a couple beers and I'd only had one. I was more of a social drinker back then, and now that I was competing more rigorously in swim I tried to stop.

Anyway, by the end of the night we ended up back at her place and things escalated quickly. I ended things abruptly because I couldn't follow through with what she wanted from me. I didn't feel that I was there with her, like my mind was somewhere else. Somewhere else, meaning back home with a girl that had a boyfriend. Sydnee seemed upset when I made up a lame excuse as to why I had to leave, but didn't question me. We had gotten together a couple times after that, but only at parties when she was completely wasted, and I felt lonely.

I hated admitting that because it made me feel like shit. I knew it was my own fault, but I couldn't help it. I never bothered correcting Travis on his assumptions when I got with these girls because he suspected me to be this great guy who always had ladies trailing after me.

"That's not happening either," I said, relaxing my legs after my final rep. I was getting irritated that he even brought up this subject.

"Fine man, I don't know if Caelyn will be there so I was just trying to think of some other girls that would automatically jump at the opportunity you gave them. I know there are more options if you're not interested in those two. Let me think. What was that other girl's name?" I knew exactly who he was talking about and my stomach already started forming knots. Do not go there, Travis.

"Don't," I warned.

"Julie? No that's not it, Jessica?" He pondered for a little longer, only making me more pissed off. "Jamie?"

"Jennifer," I regretfully admitted. In the first few months of college my freshman year there was a junior girl that was taking one of my core classes. She was constantly flirting with me and trying to make a move. So, one night, Travis convinced me to go with him to some early Halloween party at one of the fraternities with some of his football buddies. I hadn't been able to make it home for the exact anniversary of David's death and so I had been really upset for about a week. Travis, trying to be a good friend, thought it would be a good idea to get me completely drunk at this party to take my mind off home. He didn't know why I was so upset that week because I wasn't completely ready to share that deep of a secret with a guy I had only known for a few months.

Long story short, this Jennifer girl was at the party dressed in some slutty costume which looked really good with her long, tanned legs. She had her hair in two braids and she was wearing a lot of makeup. She found me out back sitting in one of the lawn chairs by myself and took that opportunity to literally attack me. At one point her skimpy outfit was on the grass and she tried pushing herself on me even more. I was already drunk off my ass, but I wasn't letting anything happen because I knew I'd regret it right away. I didn't want my first time to be with some wasted girl I didn't know very well. Especially outside on a lawn chair at a fraternity Halloween party. Then the next thing I knew I was crying, and Jennifer couldn't run away fast enough.

That whole night I slept in the bathroom because I couldn't stop throwing up. Every few hours Travis would come in and bring me some water, but he didn't harass me about Jennifer. I guess he could tell there was something bigger going on. Well, because I was so drunk, I ended up spilling everything about my life in Cape Elizabeth, including David, to Travis between the hurling episodes. He sat and listened, but didn't say much. I didn't expect him to anyway because, let's face it, we're guys and sentimental crap goes right over our heads. But ever since then, he's been a lot different with me and our friendship grew deeper that night. I never expected I'd find someone like David again, yet Travis surprised me and we've been best friends ever since.

"I'm just joking around man, I'm sorry." He must have realized what night that was too, just like I had. I shrugged my shoulders and took a long drink from my water bottle.

"Don't worry about it," I mumbled. Travis's eyes flickered back behind me and I saw a tiny glimpse of something, but it was too quick. I turned around and saw Caelyn and Bonnie walk into the rec center. They showed their ID's and made their way to the elliptical and treadmill. Caelyn had headphones in, and met my eyes before she stepped onto the gym equipment. Her cheeks turned a deep rose color as she averted her gaze.

"You're drooling," Travis said. I was still staring at Caelyn even though she had started her workout. "This is disgusting. Come on, let's get back to work," he grumbled.

An hour later, Travis and I were finishing up some running interval exercises when Bonnie and Caelyn looked to be done too. Bonnie's first track meet was coming up so she had been coming to the gym any chance she could to help prepare for the meet. Caelyn, just wanting extra exercise ahead of our first swim meet, came with her. Travis brought his shirt up to wipe his face because he always forgot to bring a sweat towel. I could tell the girls were staring at him and probably everyone else in the rec center was too. Travis loved showing off his six-pack every chance he got and I'll admit, it was annoying.

"Hey guys, we were planning on stopping by the diner for some breakfast, you want to come?" Bonnie asked. Bonnie ended up being one of Caelyn's best friends here, and I'd begun to consider her a friend too. She was always with Caelyn unless she had track or class. As soon as Travis heard Bonnie's question he automatically spoke for the both of us, but tried to make it sound laid back.

"Yeah, I don't think we have any other plans this morning, sounds good." For extra measure, he brought up the hem of his shirt to wipe his already dry face. I saw Caelyn roll her eyes, and I knew she was unaffected by his attempts of showing off. Bonnie on the other hand showed the perfect poker face.

"Okay, we were thinking of leaving in about two minutes," she said nonchalantly. "Will you both be ready by then?"

Not skipping a beat, Travis answered for the both of us. "We can leave right now, Bon."

My expression must have given away my surprise, because Caelyn snickered beside me. I straightened up and kept my mouth shut until Bonnie and Travis were a few feet in front of Caelyn and me.

"Bon? Did I hear that right?" I whispered into her ear. She shivered after the last word left my mouth, and I realized that I was right up next to her ear. I quickly moved to the side and Caelyn caught up with my question.

She laughed nervously before she answered. "Yeah, I thought that's what I heard too," she returned to her normal self as she spoke again. "I don't even call her that! When did they get on nickname basis? And how? That's the real question, Liam." Travis said something and Bonnie's head fell back as she laughed.

"We better get to the bottom of this and fix whatever is going on. I don't want our little group getting weird," I said calmly, trying to play off my own feelings towards Caelyn. I briefly saw Caelyn's facial expression darken, but only briefly.

We were near the diner and Travis had mentioned the party to the girls. Bonnie and Caelyn didn't quite agree to go, but they didn't say no either. I was secretly hoping Caelyn wasn't going so I could have an excuse not to go too.

I opened the door to the diner and Bonnie and Travis walked in. Caelyn was still standing on the sidewalk looking at her phone. Her shoulders slumped forward and her arms looked flushed. This was something I had picked up on a couple years ago—when Caelyn starts to get worked up her forearms get a little red and the hairs on her arms stand straight up.

"What's wrong?" I asked, closing the door a little. She looked up from her phone and shook her head. I stepped toward her and she shook her head harder while putting her hands up.

"It's okay, I just have to make a phone call." I didn't move toward her or walk toward the door of the diner either. She didn't look okay, but I didn't want to pry. "Really, Liam, I just have to call someone really quick. I'll be in in a minute."

"Okay, I'll go ahead and order for you if you want?"

"Perfect." Her smile didn't reach her eyes, but it was close.

I walked into the diner and found Travis and Bonnie sitting at our usual table. They both had coffee sitting in front of them, and as soon as I sat down our server had a cup of black coffee in front of me. Just what I loved. I took a long sip and tried to listen to Travis and Bonnie's conversation. They were arguing about something no doubt, but I kept checking through the window for Caelyn.

"Liam, where's Caelyn?" Bonnie stopped her argument. She was looking around the diner, towards the bathroom and then checking the front door.

"Outside on the phone," I said, taking another sip of my coffee. Bonnie's eyebrows shot up.

"With who?" she asked.

"I don't know, she wouldn't say." I shrugged my shoulders and looked out the window again. Caelyn was holding her side as she paced the sidewalk.

"Shit," Bonnie grabbed her bag and asked Travis to scoot over.

"What's wrong?" he asked, not moving. She let out a large sigh.

"Nothing," she said, trying to push Travis aside. He didn't even slide on the booth's seat.

"Well then I can't let you out until you tell me what's wrong." He smiled lazily. "So what's wrong?"

"It's that asshole," she said quietly.

"You're going to have to specify or speak louder Bon, I'm not as young as you darlin'."

"First, don't call me that ever again. Second, I said 'that asshole'. You know, her boyfriend? He's been calling her nonstop for a week now and he won't stop picking a fight. He always makes Caelyn feel worthless, and I'm starting to get tired of it. I've already told him to back off, but that didn't stop him from calling again."

"Let her up," I demanded. I threw a ten-dollar bill on the table as we all stood up from the booth. Caelyn walked in to see us standing at the table.

"Are we leaving?" Caelyn stuttered. She looked caught off guard and her eyes seemed a little red.

"We were coming to check on you," Bonnie muttered.

"Why? I was just talking to my mom. Did you—oh okay, you told them." She shook her head slowly, before taking a deep breath and walking toward the table. She motioned for all of us to sit down. "Honestly guys, I was talking to my mom. About the other thing, don't worry about it, I've got it under control, I promise." She looked into my eyes on that last part.

"Why do you look so upset then?" I had to ask.

"My mom had texted me early this morning asking what I was going to do about this coming October. A few of the bigger businesses that my dad works with have decided to donate a memorial in honor of my brother. She was giving me dates on when she wanted me home," she explained. "I'm not wanting to go home alone this year," she said hesitantly. I wrapped my arm around her shoulder. I still felt terrible that I wasn't there last year.

"You know I'll be right by your side," I squeezed her shoulder. She smiled softly and looked at me. She looked a little relieved.

"Travis and Bonnie, I know you never met David and you haven't even met my family, but I feel like we're all so close. With that being said, my mom had mentioned that I could invite the two of you. You could stay with us at my house. Well, that's if you'd like to come for the presentation of the memorial and all. Bonnie, you can stay with me in my room. Travis, you can have my brother's old room."

"Or you can stay with my family," I interrupted. I didn't really like the sound of Travis staying in David's old room, and I also didn't like that he would be so close to Caelyn and Bonnie while I was across the street.

"Or that, whatever you are most comfortable with." Caelyn looked a little sad, but I could also tell she was anxious about inviting them to such an important event. My mind was still spinning about who was donating this for David. "I don't want to make you two feel like you have to come, but I would love it if you were there to support us through this," she said, motioning to me.

"I'm in," Bonnie and Travis said almost simultaneously.

"Really?" Her eyes lit up with excitement.

"Of course, you're my best friend. I would love to." Bonnie reached across the table and grabbed Caelyn's hand. "I am honored you invited me."

"Me too," Travis said. I was waiting for him to show a little bit of sentiment, but I could tell he was struggling to find the right words. "When is it?" he asked instead.

"October 27th-November 1st," she told us.

Seven

Caelyn

The first two months of college had gone by too quickly. I was doing great in school and swim was going better than ever. I still struggled with the pain in my torso, but it hadn't been bad recently. It tended to be better if I didn't concentrate on it, but that was hard some days. That being said, I tried to focus all my energy into planning what our group was doing for the formal. My group consisted of Bonnie, Travis, Liam and their dates, and William and me. We had planned on keeping the night laid back and casual because it really wasn't that big of a deal.

As the weeks went by and we got closer to the formal, my first swim meet was just around the corner. Trying to get my mind off it, Bonnie had suggested shopping because she didn't have a dress yet. She was off in the dressing room as I sat in the waiting room of the boutique.

"Why aren't you trying anything on?" Bonnie yelled through the fabric sheet that separated us. I was just planning on wearing one of the dresses I already had and agreed to come for moral support.

"Because I have a dress," I admitted.

"Caelyn no offense, I've looked in your closet and you don't have anything." She laughed to herself, and I smiled. Her spunky attitude and unvarnished honesty had grown on me. She slid the curtain back and shyly asked, "What do you think?"

The dress looked amazing on her and was perfect for the occasion. It was long and emerald green which looked stunning on Bonnie's skin tone. It clung perfectly to her curves and had a plunging neck line. I was sure she loved it, but I wanted to reassure her too.

"I love it," I said, moving closer to get a better look. "It fits you great, but make sure you have tall enough heels so you don't have to hem it. Other than that, it's perfect."

"You think I should get it? Maybe another store has a better one." She was worrying too much about this dress.

Bonnie was going with a guy from her economics class who I had never met. She told me that I didn't have anything to worry about because they were strictly friends. She never talked about him or anything, so it was very random when she brought it up last week. I was growing very suspicious about the situation.

"You're not going anywhere else because you are buying this dress. Plus, you have nothing to worry about because you said this guy wasn't your type," she blushed and started closing the curtain. I knew she was hiding something from me, but I didn't pry. Just then, my phone started to ring.

"Hello," I said in a sing-song voice.

"Hey C, where are you guys?" Liam used the nickname David and he used to call me when we were kids. I liked that he was starting to use it more; it made my heart warm.

"Some boutique downtown, why?" I asked, confused.

"Bonnie asked Travis and me to come in and meet you guys, something about making sure we had the appropriate clothes for the formal?" He cleared his throat, and I could hear Travis's muffled voice through the receiver.

"She thinks we'll look bad and she doesn't want us to embarrass her," I heard Travis say in the background.

Bonnie opened the curtain with the dress in hand and whispered something to me as Travis was answering me. "Hold on Travis, Bonnie is trying to tell me something." I covered the microphone.

"Actually, I lied before. Travis is my date," she bit her lip and continued, "the guy from my econ class doesn't exist. Please don't be mad."

I was sure my eyes were bugging, but I didn't care. I couldn't get over how shocked I was that Travis and Bonnie were each other's dates. Liam had talked with me about asking someone from the swim team to go with him, but he hadn't asked her yet. My phone started to beep and I looked at the screen. My chest tightened and my stomach did a nauseous flip.

"Hey, call Bonnie if you need directions to the boutique, William is on the other line," I said as I switched calls. I took a deep breath and answered as cheerfully as I could. "Hey baby," I walked past the counter to the front of the store and then out the door.

"Hey, I've got bad news," he said tiredly.

"What's wrong? What happened?" I could feel my palms start to sweat, and could tell my forearms were heating up.

"I won't be able to make it down to Boston for the formal next week, your dad is having Adrian and I accompany him to this conference for a few days," he paused. I could hear some typing on the other line before he continued, "Look, I'm sorry. I know this was going to be the first time we would see each other, but I can't get out of it. Do you hate me?"

"Of course not, if it's work-related then that's fine. I understand. Besides, it must be a big deal if my dad wants you both there." In that moment, I was upset but a little relieved. "When did he decide on this? I called him at the beginning of the week, and he didn't mention it." I didn't want to beg for details but I was curious. It wasn't like my dad to go to a conference in the fall, especially this last minute.

William stumbled around for words and finally choked out, "He just said something to us today, there might be a few others going too." I didn't know my dad had more than two interns, either. "Hey look, I got to get back to work, I'll call you later this week."

Later this week?

"Why not tonight or tomorrow?" I had to ask. I didn't want to be a super-needy girlfriend, but I felt like we hadn't talked in a while. I was wondering if something was wrong.

"Your dad has us working long hours on this new case. I don't have time to call and talk about nonsense every day," he said, annoyance in his voice. "Is that okay with you?"

"I was just asking, William. I wasn't starting a fight," I said calmly. Though I was hurt, I didn't want to fight with him today.

"Yeah okay, well I should go," he said flatly.

"Okay, I love you," I said, hoping for him to answer. The line dropped, and I was left staring at my phone outside of the boutique. I prayed for the tears to stay down and tried to take a few deep breaths. I hated that every time we talked, there was always something he accused me of. I decided to stop my pity party and walked back into the boutique to find Bonnie.

"Is everything okay?" Bonnie looked concerned.

"Yeah, why wouldn't it be?"

Bonnie looked like she wanted to say something but kept her mouth shut. She paid the lady at the counter for her formal dress, and we walked down the sidewalk to another store.

"I know you said that you had a dress in mind, but I saw this dress in here the other day and I couldn't help but think of you." Bonnie opened the door for me and walked straight to the counter. I looked around as she talked with the owner of the store. The dresses were chic and too formal to me, but I had already seen a handful that I would have liked to wear. Was I even going to go anymore? "Hey, the boys are in the back trying on suits if you want to go help them," Bonnie suggested. I complied.

I didn't see the boys right away, but I heard Travis complain about wearing a tie. I took a seat outside one of the dressing rooms and waited for them to come out.

"Why do I have to wear a suit? They're all so constricting," Travis opened the curtain and stepped out. He had on a dark gray suit that fit him extremely well. The jacket hugged his biceps just enough and the pants were a good length. "What do you think?"

"I think it looks good on you. It'll match Bonnie's dress perfectly." I gave a genuine smile, and he smiled back at me. He reminded me of a little kid when their parents promised them ice cream.

"What about me?" I hadn't realized that Liam had opened his curtain as well. He stood in the opening of his dressing room with a black suit and a dark purple bow tie untied around his neck. His white shirt was unbuttoned at the top and I could see his olive skin peeking through. My eyes traveled to check out the rest of him. I noticed that the suit jacket fit him perfectly and the pants hugged him just right. I had to admit he looked really handsome in a suit. I also noticed that his hair wasn't as messy as usual. However, his dark brown eyes were unmistakable.

"Very handsome," I admitted, standing up and walking to stand in front of him. I motioned to his bowtie and he nodded. I took the two sides in my hands and started to tie it. I could feel his breath on the top of my head and tried hard not to blush. Our proximity made that nearly impossible. I finished tightening his bowtie and took a step back to marvel at the sight of him. As I looked him up and down, he was undeniably attractive. Again, I had to stop thinking of him like that because I had a boyfriend. *Well, a boyfriend that never wanted to talk to me anymore,* I thought. *And a boyfriend that didn't say he loved me earlier.*

Liam stared into my eyes, and I felt the room heat up. I couldn't stop myself from staring back, but Bonnie brought my attention back to the task at hand.

"Caelyn, there's a dress in that dressing room there," she said, walking over to Travis and inspecting his suit.

"I told you I have a dress," I whined.

"Just try it on," she rolled her eyes at me while I reluctantly went into the dressing room. I immediately stopped as I laid eyes on the most beautiful dress I had ever seen. It was a deep shade of purple and appeared to have a tight silhouette. There was a beaded belt right across the torso that didn't continue to the back. Looking at it more, I saw that the back was beautiful too. It was a deep v that ended right below the small of my back. The front was the complete opposite of Bonnie's dress with a high neck line. The dress looked soft, and I was growing more and more excited to try it on. I continued to stare at the dress as Bonnie peaked her head through the sheet.

"Travis and I are going to find him some dress shoes in the other room, call me if you need my help." She winked at me and closed the curtain after her. I started to undress and slid the dress on feet first. The dress easily slid over my hips, and I tried to zip the lower half of the dress before I tied the top, but I was struggling. I held the top of the dress and pulled back the curtain slowly. Liam was looking down at his hands as he sat, still in his suit, in the waiting area.

"Will you help me tie the top and zip the bottom? Please." Liam looked up, and I could have sworn I saw his eyes bug out of his skull. He slowly walked over, taking his time examining the dress. I turned around and pulled my hair to the side. His hands found the zipper and zipped up the skirt slowly. The air seemed to be sucked out of the room because I couldn't take a breath. His fingers traced the edge of the dress where the zipper stopped and then trailed up my back and grazed my fingers to take the ties from my hands. Slowly he tied a bow at my neck and his hand rested where my neck and shoulder met. I could feel his hands tremble while my entire body tingled with electricity.

"What do you think?" I said breathlessly. I turned around slowly, trying to keep my eyes on him. We were close enough that I could pick out the scar above his eyebrow. He had gotten it in last year's Thanksgiving swim contest. His brown eyes were staring into mine, and I wanted to melt from the look he was giving me.

"You are absolutely breathtaking," he said, choking for air. "See? I can't breathe." Liam laughed under his breath. He reached up towards my face and tucked a loose strand of hair behind my ear. His palm rested on my cheek, and I felt myself automatically lean into his touch. "I—I..." Liam's words stopped forming in his mouth. His brown eyes were full of mixed emotions, which I had a hard time reading. In this moment, I focused on the sound of my breathing and the spark my cheek felt from his touch. He cleared his throat, "You should get this dress; William will love it. Really."

Just like that our moment was over and Liam's hand returned to his side. My mood transformed from overwhelmed to disappointed. William was not coming anymore. The more I thought about it, I realized I was more relieved than anything, but still wasn't happy about how he treated the situation earlier. Maybe, just maybe I was more disappointed with the fact that I could no longer feel Liam's gentle touch.

"About that," I averted my eyes to the beaded belt, "he has to attend a conference with my dad and Adrian so he won't be able to make it." I picked at the gems on the belt before admitting, "I don't even know why I tried this on, I'm not going anymore."

Liam didn't respond right away, but when he did he was quiet. "You could go with me?"

I was taken aback when the suggestion came out of his mouth. He was smiling his nervous grin and gripping the back of his neck. That was a look I was familiar with.

"Don't you have a date?" I asked. "If you do, I wouldn't let you cancel your plans just so you can take me. I will not let you do that." I shook my head back and forth, not wanting to ruin his night. I didn't want him to feel bad because my date bailed. He took the step that separated us and softly placed his hands on my shoulders. My stomach churned anxiously, something it had stopped doing with the mention of William's name.

"I don't have a date yet. I was waiting until the last minute because I didn't have anyone in mind to take." Admitting that must have made him feel weak so he quickly added, "I mean plenty of girls would go with me, but I just wasn't interested."

"Are you sure? I don't want you to feel obligated to go with me." I tried to ignore his last comment about a lot of girls wanting to go with him. I wasn't allowed to get jealous.

"Why else do you think I have on a dark purple bowtie that just so happens to match your dress perfectly?" I thought over his words. Then I started to get curious at how much of a coincidence that was. "It was Bonnie's idea; I had no idea that William wasn't able to come. Also, I'm really sorry he won't be here because I know how much it meant to you. If you ask me, that's a total dick move for him to cancel like that. But that's enough talk of him. I know we can make the best of it, C," he reassured me. His hands ran down my biceps and then to my hands. "So, what do you say? Will you accompany me to the ball, Ms. Price?"

"I would love to," I smiled simply. I felt incredibly happy that Liam was going with me. Just then, breaking up our little moment,

Bonnie walked in with a slumped-over Travis. As soon as Travis walked in, he looked at me and straightened up.

"Damn," he whispered.

"Watch it man," Liam grew defensive. The tips of his ears got red which was a sign he was getting irritated. There was a moment between the two of them that was fleeting, but I caught it.

"No, he's right. Damn Caelyn, that fits you perfectly," Bonnie smiled ear to ear and started dancing a happy jig. "I'm so good, I knew it would look great on you," she smirked, holding her head high. I ran my hands down the front of the dress, admiring the soft fabric and how it clung to my figure. I really loved this dress.

"Yeah yeah, it's a winner Bon. Thank you so much." I gave her a quick hug before entering the dressing room to change back into my shorts and t-shirt.

Eight

Liam

I sat on the edge of my mattress holding my phone between my fingers, awaiting a message from Caelyn telling me when to pick her and Bonnie up. Honestly, I surprised myself by asking her to go with me. Bonnie had originally put the idea in my head, but when Caelyn told me that her asshole of a boyfriend couldn't even make it down to see her, it made my decision easy. Bonnie had even gone out of her way to pick out a bowtie that matched Caelyn's dress perfectly, even without knowing that William was going to cancel at the last minute. It was perfect, and a great sign for me.

Travis peaked his head around the frame of my door, "You ready man?" He looked to be cleaned up nicely, and I knew the girls would appreciate it. I guess he noticed that I was ready because he walked in and handed me a box with a flower.

"What's this?" I asked, surveying the white rose. He held onto an identical box too, but his accent color was different. His flower had an emerald green wrist band and mine was purple.

"I thought the girls would like these," he said matter-of-factly. I must have been staring at him with an incredulous look on my face. "What? I've learned a few things from my mother. One, girls love flowers and two, never wear the same underwear two days in a row."

"You're ridiculous, but very smart for doing this." My phone buzzed then and Caelyn's name lit up on my screen. I tried to ignore the knot in my stomach at the sight of her name. The message read: *We're ready when you are :).*

"The girls are ready," I said, standing up from my bed. I smoothed down my jacket and followed Travis out to the main living area.

"Dude, I haven't been to a formal since my senior prom, and I hated my senior prom. It was not enjoyable," he shivered, remembering the memory.

"I'm sure this will be better." I thought back to my senior prom just about two years ago. The memory brought back so many mixed emotions. I had asked Caelyn to go with me, and she bought a gorgeous, blue dress. She even made an appointment to get her nails and hair done. Just like Travis, I ordered flowers and made a reservation at the nicest restaurant in Cape Elizabeth.

I had gotten ready and my mom and I were about to walk out the door when our home phone rang. I figured it was Mrs. Price calling to see where we were. My mom kept nodding her head and finally said that I would understand.

"Caelyn has been vomiting for the past two hours and can't move from the bathroom floor without getting sick again," she said, looking at me with sympathy in her eyes. "I'm sorry Liam, Caelyn insisted that she could go, but Beth isn't having it. She's too weak." Without another word, I ran upstairs and changed out of my suit and into a pair of basketball shorts and a t-shirt. I went into our kitchen and found my mom and dad standing around the counter about to start dinner.

"Stop what you're doing," I demanded, and both my parents looked at me confused. "I want you two to take my reservation at the restaurant. It's too late to call and cancel. It's at six-thirty with a view of the harbor. Please go and enjoy it," I pleaded with them.

"I don't understand, what about prom son?" my father asked shocked.

"If Caelyn can't go, I'm not going either. I only wanted to go with her anyway," I said and my mother shook her head. My mom knew why I didn't want to go with anyone else, but I doubt my dad had caught on quite yet. Before my mom had an opportunity to speak I chimed in again, "Please go, I'm not going to use it. If you need me, I'll be over at Caelyn's." I turned from the kitchen and walked toward the front door.

"Liam!" my father called from the kitchen.

"What?" I yelled back. I didn't want him to argue with me. This was the right thing to do. This was what my heart wanted me to do; be with the girl I cared so much about.

"Take this to her," my dad handed me a sack full of saltine crackers, green apples, and chicken noodle soup. Well, that was fast. "Hope she feels better," he winked at me, and I went on my way.

I knew he understood exactly what I was feeling. I ran across the street with her flower in hand and rang the doorbell. Beth appeared in the doorway a few moments later.

"Liam, what are you doing? Shouldn't you be on your way to prom?" she looked very confused, but a small smile played on her lips. Beth knew, I knew she knew. Everyone but Caelyn knew how I felt.

"I couldn't imagine myself going without Caelyn, so I thought that I'd come on over and keep her company," I admitted stepping through the frame. I peered my head up the stairs and didn't hear anything, so I looked behind Beth towards the kitchen and family room.

"She's upstairs hon," she said, grabbing the food from my hands, but I kept the flower. I nodded my head once and took the stairs two at a time. I stopped just outside of her doorway, afraid of what I would see. I turned into the frame and saw her immediately. She was sat up in bed like the time I kept her company after David's funeral. I instantly started sweating, remembering and reliving that moment. I took a deep breath and walked in anyway.

She looked pale lying in her mound of green sheets. Her hair was pulled back into a curly bun and her makeup was smeared with sweat. I walked closer to the side of her bed and saw that a wet cloth had slipped off her forehead. I absentmindedly reached for it which caused her to stir a little.

"What are you doing?" she slurred, obviously confused. She tried to sit up a little more, but her body was too weak. I pushed back her shoulders slightly. I wanted her to stay where she was. There was no use trying to get up because she would probably just get sick again.

"If you aren't going to prom then neither am I." I went into the bathroom and dampened the cloth. I returned and put it back on her forehead. "Better?" I asked her. She had a tear that had escaped her eye, and I reached for it.

"I'm sorr—" she began but I interrupted her.

"Shh, it's okay. What movie do you want to watch?" I asked pushing back a few hairs from her face.

"I just want to sleep. Will you come and sit with me?"

She looked so sad and weak, but also adorable and vulnerable. Of course, I would sit with her, that's what I was there for. I went to the other side of the bed and sat on top of the covers. She moved closer, I put my arm around her and she snuggled up perfectly into my side. For the next hour, I studied her features as she slept. Sometime in the night I had dozed off, but woke up to Caelyn moving around. She ran into the bathroom and I followed. She heaved several times into the toilet as I sat beside her, holding her stray hairs back. This was a routine we fell into for the entire night. Beth and Steve came up and tried to give her some of the apple slices and crackers I had brought, but she was either asleep or too busy vomiting to care about food.

Around three in the morning I helped take off her runny makeup and removed the many bobby pins in her hair. At six her fever broke and she finally kept some food down. Meanwhile, once I knew she would be okay, I went home to shower and grab a fresh set of clothes. I hopped in the shower and about five minutes later I was out getting dressed into clean shorts and a t-shirt. My mom was up and standing in the hallway once she heard me moving around.

"How's she doing?" she asked sleepily. She moved to stand in my doorway with her robe and slippers, her hair matted on one side.

"She was up all night vomiting, but finally kept some crackers and apple slices down this morning. I just came home to get a shower before going back over there," I said, running my hands through my hair. "Mom, when I got there I had the worst flashback to the day of David's funeral. She was sitting in bed, minus the casts and bruises, and had been crying." I collapsed on my bed. I didn't want to get worked up this early, especially if I was going back over to see Caelyn. But I couldn't help it; I couldn't shake the memory from my head. "I felt this knot in my stomach and couldn't will myself to go in." I took a deep breath, and she sat next to me on the edge of my bed.

"How'd you go in?" she asked calmly.

"I knew she needed me. I knew that I could help her feel better," I admitted.

"Liam, what are you doing?" she asked me.

"I don't know." I didn't want her to speak the words that were on the tip of her tongue. I didn't know what they would mean for Caelyn and me. I didn't know what to do since I would be leaving for college in a few months. All in all, I knew that I was too scared to talk about this out loud.

"You love her, don't you?"

It was a simple question, but I felt my entire body grow cold and clammy. She looked at me with concern and felt my forehead. "You're burning up Liam." I could barely reach my trashcan quickly enough. I heaved multiple times into the bin and my mom just rubbed my back. It was such a simple gesture, but it broke me. I laid on my bathroom floor for the rest of the morning, sleeping and vomiting in turns. Around noon Caelyn was standing in the doorway of my bedroom.

Travis and I stood outside the girl's dorm waiting for them to come down. Travis kept fidgeting with the cuffs of his jacket. I could tell that he was more than a little nervous. It was something I had never seen before.

"You look fine bud," I said, clapping the back of his shoulder. His shoulders felt rigid and didn't budge when I tried to lighten the mood. My hand reached back to rub the back of my neck, and I felt the muscles in my arm pull from the amount of swimming I'd done in the past week. Travis's mood worried me. He didn't have his normal, easy banter and I was dying to figure out why. "What's up with you?"

"Do you know how nervous I am about tonight? I feel like this is a chance to show Bonnie that I'm not just some tool. I'm different. I don't want her to see me that way, Liam. I don't know why, but I have this feeling that I need to prove her wrong. I want her to have a good time tonight, you know?"

He was rambling on and on about how he wanted her to be happy, all the while hinting that he wanted to be the reason for it. The more he talked, the more I realized tonight needed to go perfectly for Caelyn. She deserved a night away from the William drama as well as the stress from the upcoming swim meet. She deserved to be happy and carefree, and I wanted to make that happen.

Minutes went by and we were still lost in our own thoughts about the night. Bonnie and Caelyn walked out of Danielsen Hall, and I saw Travis straighten up. The tension was still present, but it wasn't awkward. He stepped forward offering the flower to Bonnie and said something to make her laugh. I was happy for them and wished that tonight could be everything they wanted.

Then, my eyes found Caelyn's, and I was completely blown away. She looked absolutely beautiful, and I had to hold back every instinct in my body to not run up and kiss her. I felt time stand still as she walked towards me. I just kept looking her up and down, soaking in every bit of her and tonight. Her light brown hair was pulled up and out of her face into a low, curly bun. She wore a pair of diamond studded earrings, and her makeup was heavier than usual but still beautiful and natural.

Next, my eyes traveled down the length of her body. The high collar of the purple dress sat perfectly against her skin. The dress's torso hugged her middle perfectly and showed off every curve of her hips. As my eyes traveled down to the ground, I noticed that she was a few inches taller from her heels. Heels and Caelyn really don't mix well, or at least they didn't use to. My eyes traveled up to her face again, stopping briefly to admire her figure one last time. Well, at least one last time for a minute or two.

She closed the gap between the two of us, and I got a good look in her eyes. She had perfectly accented her makeup to make her green eyes pop even more than usual. Her irises sparkled in the last of the sunlight, and I could see every emotion play through them. She was happy, but seemed nervous and even a little sad. I stopped gazing into her eyes for a moment to grab the flower that was meant to be on her wrist. My hands reached for hers, and I slid the band onto it. She smiled down at our hands.

"You look absolutely beautiful," I said leaning in to kiss her fore-head. She leaned into my kiss; she actually leaned in. When I moved away her eyes were closed and whatever sadness I saw earlier had been erased.

"Thank you, Liam," she said. I offered her my arm and she took it willingly. "You don't look too bad yourself."

I was beginning to realize that she was confident in walking in heels now, something I had never seen before. Caelyn had always been the one to ditch her shoes at dinner and carry them out of the restaurant when our families dined out together. She was always the girl that made David give her a piggyback ride from the beach—not wanting her sandy feet to rub against her sandals. Had she really changed that much since I went to school?

Travis and Bonnie walked a few paces in front of us and seemed to be getting along for the time being. I really hoped everything worked out for them tonight; I had never seen Travis this worried about a girl before. Who knew a spunky, outgoing girl like Bonnie had such a big effect on a tough, macho man like Travis? It amazed me to watch them banter back and forth; it was such a refreshing thing to see since Travis hadn't had a girlfriend in a while.

After the seven-minute walk, we arrived at the building. The girls couldn't contain their excitement as we walked through the highly decorated lobby, which opened into a huge conference room. It was dimly lit with fairy lights and candles on every table. The room was huge, but the hundreds of people there made the room feel small. Bonnie and Caelyn led the way into the dark room, and Travis and I followed behind.

"Let's go Travis," Bonnie said after hearing a favorite song, but he didn't budge. She started to frown and let go of his arm. When he saw her expression, he immediately grabbed her hand and pulled her toward the crowd. She perked up, and as soon as they reached the dance floor she started to sway her hips back and forth.

"I'm not much of a dancer, but how about we go and give it a try?" Caelyn's voice broke my focus on Travis and Bonnie. I looked Caelyn in the eyes as she said, "I mean, we didn't really give your senior prom a chance." The smallest of smiles crept across her lips, and I couldn't contain my excitement. She remembered. Just then, I thought that this was an opportunity to be even closer to Caelyn without having to worry about who saw us. We only knew a few people here and half of them weren't going to be paying attention to us.

"Let's go," I said. I wrapped my arm around her waist and walked toward the outside of the floor. Another song came on that Caelyn immediately recognized. Her body loosened and moved with the beat. "You know this song?" I screamed into her ear.

"Yeah, Bonnie made a playlist full of this stuff," she said, shrugging her shoulders as we pushed our way through groups of people to find Bonnie and Travis. They didn't seem to notice us, but I didn't care. I just wanted to dance and enjoy my time with Caelyn, and I had a feeling it was mutual.

Caelyn reached one hand behind my neck and pulled me closer. She moved her hips in a way I've never seen before. Then her hands found mine. "Loosen up Liam, we're just having some fun," she yelled into my ear.

Without another word, I felt my body release its tension. It seemed to me that a trend had developed within the order of songs. It began with about five faster songs, three mid-paced ones, and then finally two slower songs. I wasn't complaining; I had never had so much fun, felt so intimate, and so connected with another person. Some of the time Caelyn and I were just being goofy and screaming at the top of our lungs to Katy Perry or P!nk. Then minutes later we were grinding, leaving no space between us. Then her hand was around my neck and my hand was on her waist, keeping us close for the slower songs.

A little while into the dance, we took a break to get a drink. Bonnie and Caelyn sat at the table while Travis and I went to get drinks. They seemed to be getting hot and a little tired, but you could tell they wanted to dance more. We noticed that the DJ was yet to play a slow song you could really dance to, so we decided to rest our feet in the meantime. Caelyn bent over to take off her heels and started rubbing her feet. She saw me watching so she stopped and gave me an unreadable look.

About two songs later, a slow one came on and people on the dance floor started partnering up. I stood up and reached out my hand. "May I have this dance?"

"Of course," Caelyn took my hand and kept hold of it as we walked to the floor. I felt my hand tingle with her touch. Every part of tonight had been perfect, and I was dying to show her how much I truly cared about her. I was nervous, but had made up my mind that I needed to do something. I didn't want to sit back on the sidelines anymore. This was something I'd contemplated for a long time, and I knew my decision was risky and probably not appropriate. I just knew I was willing to chance it.

Her hands were clasped behind my neck and my hands rested lightly on her waist. My eyes connected with hers, and I got sucked into the sea green color I loved so much. After a few seconds into the song, I took a chance and tightened my hold and pulled her closer to me. She reacted naturally and leaned into my touch, resting her head on my shoulder. We stayed perfectly content for the whole song.

Without missing a beat, another slow song played. This song, "I'll Be", was a little more upbeat so I took her hand and twirled her around. She giggled softly to herself after the second turn, and I craved the closeness between us again. I pulled her against me and she tightened her hand on my shoulder.

While listening to the lyrics I realized how this song was a perfect representation of how I felt about her. I wanted to always be the person she could come to. I wanted to be that shoulder to cry on. I wanted to love her and care for her no matter what. I wanted to be her person she could always count on.

The song was coming to an end and without wasting another minute I pulled away from her slightly. I looked down into her eyes and then down to her lips. I saw her lips part slightly and that was my sign. I gently lowered my head and kissed her softly. I pulled away and gazed into her eyes—they showed complete shock but no anger. Seeing that she wasn't angry, I leaned in again, this time more forcefully. My left hand pulled her waist toward me and my right hand cupped her cheek. I felt a little resistance at first, but she realized I wasn't going to stop. Then to my surprise, she kissed me back. She actually kissed me back. Her lips parted slightly, and I pushed my tongue past them. She grabbed ahold of the front and back of my shirt as our kiss deepened.

When she kissed me back, I felt my whole world stop. This was it, I was finally kissing the girl of my dreams. I was finally kissing the girl that I never thought I had a chance with. And the best part was, she was kissing me back with as much passion as I was exerting. My entire body was on fire as our kiss intensified. Then, all the sudden, it abruptly stopped. Caelyn pulled away from me and her eyes got big. Tears started to fill those beautiful green eyes, and I became scared. Why had I pushed this? I had made so much progress with her tonight and I ruined it all. The risk I took wasn't the right one. *How could I have been so stupid?*

"Caelyn, I'm—" I tried to reach for her hands to pull her back to me. To apologize. To do anything that would fix what I had done. Instead, her hand connected with my cheek, hard. She took a step back from me, and her right hand rose to her lips. She touched those lips that were touching mine only a few seconds ago. She took one last look at my exasperated face and quickly hurried out of the banquet hall. I was left staring at the back of her purple dress as she made her way out of the room. The pain of seeing her retreating figure was greater than anything, at that moment.

Nine

Caelyn

I ran out of that banquet hall as fast as my feet would allow. I thought I heard someone scream my name as I left, but there was no way I was turning around. The doors flew open, and I was met by a cool breeze. I wrapped my arms around myself and started making my way to the dorms, away from the ball, away from Liam.

Liam had kissed me. He kissed me and I kissed him back. And this wasn't just an average kiss; it was passionate, sweet, and full of emotion from both ends. But then I stopped it and slapped him across his face; his adorable, kind face. I couldn't believe the nights' events. *Did I actually slap him?* My emotions must have caused me to act out, but I felt so confused. I liked the kiss. Correction, I loved the kiss. I felt things when he pulled me close and kissed me, that I haven't felt in a long time. But I shouldn't have loved it and I knew I was wrong. I messed up big time and all I could think about was William. *How would he react when I told him?*

As I walked outside, thoughts raced through my mind. Maybe I overreacted with the slap. I know I could have handled that situation differently and I should have. But some part of me still thought

I did the right thing. I am in a relationship with William. I should have never let Liam kiss me. *But slap him?* I questioned. Then, a small part of me thought that I needed to kiss Liam. I felt so much clarity when his lips met mine. I had these undeniable feelings for my best friend that I couldn't shake and the kiss proved just that. I wanted to turn around and apologize to Liam because I was afraid I'd ruined everything between us.

I pushed through the quad as my emotions turned over the evening. I loved everything about tonight. Liam had made me feel cherished and special which was something I never felt when I was with William. I felt safe, and I had more fun with him than anyone else. Did these conflicting feelings truly appear because Liam kissed me or had they been present the whole time? Why was I trying to fight for my relationship with William when I clearly had feelings for Liam?

My thoughts were interrupted by a loud commotion off to my right. I slowed my pace to see what was causing the scene. I squinted through the dark quad and could barely make out what I saw—three large men crowding around one another. They all seemed quite plastered by the way they were rambling and staggering across the walkways. I held my head up, but tried to discretely pass them. Unfortunately, I was already seen.

"Heyou," one of the men slurred. I kept my focus forward and made my strides more confident. Something about how those words came out sent a major red flag to my brain. The men walked in my general direction but I kept my pace fast, hoping I could outrun them. This situation was making me feel uncomfortable, but I knew I shouldn't show how I truly felt. *Caelyn you can't run. Keep walking. Head up.*

"He said, heyou," the other guy slurred his words, but they held a little more force than the last guy's. I pretended to not hear them and kept walking. Their legs were much longer than mine, and I could sense their steps behind me. My feet were aching from keeping my heels on for so long at the formal. I was barefoot now because I had forgotten my shoes at the table when I ran off. Maybe I could make a run for it? I was only a few minutes away from my dorm building, and I didn't have my phone to call for help. Just then, I regretted leaving the ball in such a rush that I forgot the necessities. I tried to keep walking, paying no attention to the three men. But soon enough one guy caught up to me and grabbed my arm with a tight grip. I couldn't run now.

"Are you just going to ignore them?" This guy seemed to be in his right mind compared to the others. He was much taller and broader than I was, and my stomach dropped fearing what was about to happen. I must have not said anything because his grip tightened even more. He gave it a little pull. I was close to his face now, and he lowered his head. "I said, are you just going to ignore them?" I could smell the alcohol on his breath. Fear was coursing through my body, and I began to sweat. I closed my eyes and swallowed hard. I needed to speak up and answer him.

"No—no, no I'm not," I stammered trying to break out of his vice grip. I looked frightened around the quad but couldn't see anyone through the darkness. I strongly debated screaming right there, but I was terrified of what would happen if I made a noise. These men were so much bigger than me and with the influence of alcohol they could do anything. I tried to think of anything else to get away, but I was coming up with nothing. I was beyond terrified.

The other men came closer around me and the guy loosened his grip—just a tad. "You know, you have a pretty face and from what I can see a nice body too." I think everyone in a two-mile radius heard me gulp. I checked around again for any sign of life and saw no one. The leader reached for the pieces of hair that had fallen out of my low bun. I flinched back and his hand shot and wrapped around my neck. I struggled to catch my breath and began hyperventilating. The shock of his actions left me frozen in my spot. "You don't have to make this hard," he said, his other hand running down my side until it rested just above my hip. His fingers were placed on my scar, and it made me feel sick to my stomach. I tried to move away from him once more, but his grip tightened around my neck. I coughed, trying to get air. The other two men grabbed my arms in a matter of seconds, and I was paralyzed with fear. "This should only hurt a little," the leader said in a sinister voice. I looked fearfully among my attackers and wondered what I could do to get out of this situation. I tried to squirm, but I was unable to move. The closer the leader got to my face, the more I could smell the alcohol on his breath. I wanted to gag, to scream, to cry but my fear silenced me. The feeling of fear left my mind when I felt his hand gather up the materials of my dress, and I lost all composure.

"Help! Help me! Someone please—" I screamed as loud as I could, and tried kicking my legs in front of me, striking where he lived. He let go of my neck and the other two men staggered back. I saw my chance and bolted past the leader. Tears fell down my cheeks as I continued to scream for help. "Help me! Please!" I didn't think I would make it out of the situation unless I ran for my life.

Suddenly a pair of hands were on my shoulders tugging me back. The force was great enough to knock me to the ground. My head hit the concrete first and the rest of my body came with it. My vision started to spin, and I saw stars above. I blinked to adjust my vision, but the stars were all I could see. I felt useless as I tried, and failed, to regain my composure.

The man took as much strength as he could muster and kicked me in the torso. I clenched my teeth and reached for my stomach. The wind was knocked out of me, but I managed to cry out in agony as I registered the excruciating pain. Hopefully someone could hear my cries and save me if I couldn't run away. The leader's voice was clear above me even though I couldn't see him.

"You little bitch, I'm going to make sure this hurts a lot." His hands gripped the fabric at my feet and he started to pull it up toward my hips.

I struggled as best as I could, but my vision was taking too long to adapt. I cried and thrashed about to get him off me. I knew that if I did nothing he would rape me. I had to give everything I had to protect myself; I was alone in this.

The skirt of my dress was around my hips, and the man appeared right above me. I felt his cold and clammy hands on my thighs as the other two men grasped my hands above my head. I felt defenseless and regretted leaving the ball in my emotional state. No matter what I tried, I couldn't escape.

"Please no, no, no," I cried harder, facing the fact that there was nothing I could do now. My makeup was running down the sides of my face as I cried imagining what would happen next. I dreaded his touch on my body and his hands were inching upwards along my thighs. My body shivered with every sob and his grin was sickening.

"You bitch," he said, sliding his hands up higher. I thought I would throw up. Then, all the sudden, his slimy touch was gone. I no longer felt his body weight pressed against me. Through my tears, I saw his burly figure lying on the ground by my feet. A darkly dressed figure stood over him throwing punch after punch, hitting the drunk man in his face. Then, the pressure was lifted from my arms as my two captors were knocked onto their asses next to me. I heard a shriek, but I didn't know who it belonged to. Was it my own?

A new set of hands were around me, but they were gentle. I still couldn't help but flinch at the touch of them. "Caelyn, get up, now!" A girl's voice was the source of the sound. She was pulling my dress down to cover my bare legs, clearly trying to help me. I couldn't help but try and get away from her. I was scared this was part of my captor's plan.

My eyes had yet to adjust from being thrown to the ground. I tried to sit up by myself, but my torso ached with pain. I winced and cried out again. "Caelyn, come on! We have to get you out of here." I blinked as fast as I could; trying to see who was talking to me. The blackness was replaced by a blurred Bonnie. My best friend was right in front of me and trying to save me. I started to cry more, relieved that someone had come to my rescue. She tried to help me up as more people came into the quad. She adjusted the hem of my dress, but it didn't erase the feeling of disgust. The man had come so close to raping me, and I'd been powerless to stop him.

The sirens were mere yards away and a few officers ran to our aid. My vision finally cleared, and I saw two nicely dressed men with spots of blood on their white shirts standing over three unconscious men. These familiar men turned around toward me, and I slowly began to recognize them. Travis and Liam looked at one another to make sure they were both okay and then glanced over towards me. Travis breathed a sigh of relief and leaned over placing his hands on his knees; he seemed to be in pain. With his hands on his knees, he leaned over and threw up the contents of his stomach. Without thinking about his friend, Liam ran over to me and grasped me in a hug. The tears came all at once and we were both standing there sobbing.

I tried to ignore the pain in my head and torso as best as I could, so that he could hold me. His hand grabbed the back of my head and pulled it to his chest while his other arm clutched my shoulders. My adrenaline was racing, but the pain I still felt was excruciating. I cried harder against his chest, piecing together the events of tonight.

"Liam, you're hurting me," I choked out. He let go quickly and moved back. He assessed my appearance, and I saw him grimace. Did I look that bad?

The police hurried to cuff the three men on the ground, reading them their rights as they started to come to. An officer made his way to me and began to ask multiple questions. My eyes kept glancing over to the sidewalk where the man had assaulted me. I felt my stomach wretch and I heaved and heaved until my stomach was emptied in its entirety. Bonnie was there in moments, rubbing my back and whispering soothing words. After I felt well enough, I returned to answer the remaining questions the officer had. Someone I didn't know had brought me a bottled water to wash out my mouth.

We had caused quite the scene in the quad and several people were standing around and staring. I heard the murmurs, and they only made me feel dirtier. I tried to block their comments and questions as I talked to the officers. I had no reason to feel dirty. I was the victim.

After about an hour of questioning, when the officer saw that I was having a hard time keeping myself upright, he said, "I think I have everything we need Caelyn. Can I have your number so that I can call you if I need any more information?" I nodded wrapping Liam's jacket around my shoulders. "Is there anyone that can take you home and watch you for tonight?" he asked, concern in his voice.

"Yes officer, she has me," Liam appeared next to me, attentive and ready. My stomach tightened at the sound of his voice. Oh Liam. I wanted his arms around me, I wanted to feel safe again, I wanted to go back to the moment before I slapped him. I tried to smile at him but failed.

"Great, then I'll let you take her home so she can get some rest." He started to walk away before turning to Travis, "You need to go to the hospital, son. You don't look too good." Travis was doubled over by a tree, holding onto his side. He had been refusing care since the paramedics arrived on scene, blabbering about football season.

"I'll go with him," Bonnie offered quickly. "Liam, get Caelyn cleaned up." Travis reluctantly climbed into the back of the ambulance and Bonnie followed him. The doors closed, and I was left staring at the red and blue flashing lights as they exited the quad and rounded the street.

The events passed by quickly from the moment the cops arrived at the scene to when they were wrapping up. My head was spinning with what had happened. I had almost been raped on my way home tonight after I'd stormed out of a dance because my best friend kissed me. Maybe the best and the worst part of it was that I liked the kiss.

Liam spoke to the officers on the scene before walking over to me. I grew very nervous and unsure about what to say. I was afraid to be alone with him after everything that had happened tonight. Even though I wanted him to hug me tight, I was afraid of anyone touching me after what had happened. My skin was crawling, I felt dirty, and I couldn't stop shaking. Liam walked over to me slowly, and I wrapped my arms around my waist tighter. He stopped a few feet in front of me. "Will you be alright to walk to my apartment?" he asked, genuinely concerned. His eyes searched my body and then rested on my eyes. Even through the dark I could make out the concern in his beautiful, deep brown eyes.

"Why not my dorm?" I asked with a shaky breath.

"Bonnie won't be back for a few hours since she's going with Travis to the ER," he paused. "Plus, I'd rather keep you company instead of leaving you alone. You heard the officer," he fidgeted and rubbed the back of his neck. "Please just let me stay with you. Please don't fight me on this one," he painfully pleaded with me. My only response was a nod of the head.

We walked the short distance to Liam's apartment building in complete silence. He stayed near me while also keeping his distance. He carried my shoes and clutch which he must've grabbed from the formal. A few hours before, he had given me his jacket, and I pulled it tight around myself. As my adrenaline was beginning to fade, I felt a faint ache in my torso from where my assailant kicked me. I gripped my sides tighter hoping to stop the pain. Liam followed me up the stairs as I took them one at a time. At each landing, I had to stop to catch my breath, but Liam was there waiting if I needed him. We made it safely to his room, and he unlocked it for me.

I entered the room slowly, still clinging to my sides. I gripped so tightly I was afraid I was hurting myself, but I couldn't stop. I still felt the man's hands on my body as I laid on the ground helpless and in gut-wrenching pain. I tried to clear my head of the facts, but I couldn't dismiss the memory. I walked to the couch and sat down. I could hear Liam bustling around in the kitchen, but I wasn't sure what he was doing. A few minutes later, he sat two mugs in front of me.

"Hey, don't cry," he knelt to my level. His hand fidgeted, but rethought about wiping away my tears. "Caelyn, talk to me," he begged. I looked up from my hands, and my tear-filled eyes met his. One look in those eyes, and I completely crumbled.

"I'm sorry." My sobs were heavy, and I couldn't seem to catch my breath. I admired his restraint, but he couldn't take it any longer as he wrapped me in his arms. I flinched when he first touched me, but when his touch didn't hurt or make my skin crawl, I leaned into him. His hands ran from the back of my neck to my back. I felt every hair stand up on my body.

"Shh," he cooed as he comforted me. I wrapped my arms around him tighter. My body shivered uncontrollably as he continued to hold me. After what felt like an eternity, I began to calm down. Liam had been rubbing my back and trying everything he knew to calm me down. "How about you get a shower and then you can get some rest?" he suggested still rubbing my back.

"I don't think anything can wash away the feeling of that man's touch." I shuddered and the tears began to prickle.

"Would it be worth a shot? I know it'll help you feel a little better."

With a little extra prodding from Liam, I decided to take a scalding hot shower. I had him help me take out the pins from my hair and unzip my dress. His hands shook the entire time he helped me, afraid that with one touch I wouldn't let him near me again. The weird thing was that his touch was comfortable and safe, even after what had happened tonight. I knew I was safe as soon as his arms wrapped around me.

The hot water helped rinse my body of my assailant's toxic touch. I scrubbed at my skin to erase the man's hands and washed my hair twice to get the smell of alcohol out of it. I towel dried off and looked in the mirror at my bare image. The outline of bruises had already started to form on my stomach from where I'd been kicked. I ran my fingers across a few of the spots and cringed at how sensitive they felt already. I quickly wrapped the towel around myself and opened the bathroom door. The bathroom door was directly connected to Liam's bedroom and he was sitting on the edge of the bed. I suddenly stopped feeling scared. I felt insecure with just a towel wrapped around myself. My hair was damp and left down to cover my shoulders.

"I'm sorry, did I scare you?" Liam asked quietly. He looked so upset with himself. He fidgeted when I didn't answer right away. "Look, I have some clothes that you can change into, and I left some tea on the bedside table. You take my bed and I'm going to go take the couch." He stood up slowly and walked over to the door. "I, uh, also called your mom and dad to let them know about tonight. They are freaking out, but I told them you were safe with me and to call again in the morning. I hope that was okay, and I didn't overstep my boundaries." The words that came out of his mouth didn't register with my brain. I just stared at his retreating figure and before I knew it I blurted out...

"Wait, Liam!" I said urgently. He stopped and turned around with the door handle in hand. "Will you please just sit with me like we used to? I really can't be alone right now." I didn't want to sound pathetic, but I also couldn't bear to be alone. Liam let go of the handle and shook his head. He went to his dresser and grabbed the clothes that sat on top.

"Here, change into these," he said, trying not to meet my eyes. I'm not sure if I said thank you or not because I was too concerned by Liam not looking at me. I walked back into the bathroom and shut the door halfway. I quickly changed into the sweatpants and shirt that he had picked out for me. I came back out and found him setting up a makeshift cot at the foot of the bed.

"What are you doing?" I asked sadly.

"I'm making my bed," he asked confused. He stopped fussing with the blanket and looked at me.

"I was kind of hoping that you would sit up here for a bit, or at least until I fall asleep. Please Liam?" I was desperate at this point, but I didn't care. Liam was the only one that could help these feelings go away. I was pleading with my eyes, and I saw his shoulders slump.

"Alright," he agreed after a few moments of silence. I walked over to the side of the bed that he already set up for me. When I was sitting, Liam turned off the light and walked to the other side of the bed. He climbed up and settled under the sheets. I scooted closer to him and rested my head on his shoulder carefully. I was testing the waters because I knew he was too scared to touch me first. His left arm wrapped around my back, and I snuggled up closer to him. A few tears escaped my eyes, but I tried to wipe them away before he noticed. "Caelyn?"

"Hmm?" I kept my eyes closed and focused on the steady rhythm of his breathing.

"I was terrified tonight. I feel like this was all my fault." He paused. "If I didn't... kiss you, then you wouldn't have run out of the ball. Then you wouldn't have been put in that vulnerable situation. I feel personally responsible for what happened. And, the thing is, every time I touch you I feel like such an ass. I should've run after you faster. I ran, I promise I did. But I felt that I had ruined everything between us." He spoke fluently, though I could tell he was fighting to maintain his composure. "After you left I ran to get Travis and Bonnie because I was afraid you wouldn't want me around. But as we were walking, because Bonnie couldn't run with her heels at first, I heard you scream and did the only thing I could do. I ran to help you. Your screams are still playing in my brain." His composure began to crack. "Then as I got closer I saw you on the ground, and I grabbed the guy that was on top of you, and I hit him. I hit him and I hit him and I wanted to do so much more." He was starting to tear up so he stopped talking. I felt him take a shaky breath and then knew his own tears had begun to fall. I wrapped my arms around his waist. "If I didn't get there in time, I would never be able to forgive myself." The words came out broken between the sobs. "Hell, if I would've seen him rape yo--."

"Shh," I said, sitting up and looking at him. "But Liam, you did get there. I don't know what would have happened if you didn't make it, but you did. You were there. You saved me," I cupped my hand on his cheek. My hand instantly felt warm.

"How are you touching me right now?" The question sounded so innocent coming from his lips.

"You make me feel safe; as if nothing ever happened." Liam's hand rose to mine and grabbed it without pushing it away. "When you aren't near me, my mind is caught up in its own thoughts. Liam, I've never been with a man like that before. I was completely terrified that my first time would have been with a drunken rapist. But you came and saved me. You truly saved me." I leaned forward and rested my forehead on his. Our hands were still joined on his cheek. "I just need you here with me," I begged. I wanted to forget. I wanted to block out the memory of tonight.

"I'm not going anywhere, Caelyn." He made sure he moved back to make eye contact with me when he said those words. I focused on his brown eyes in the dark room. They showed concern and care, and I acted on the moment. I leaned forward slowly until my nose met his. I felt his hot breath on my lips and his body trembled. "C," he whispered. I stopped so close to his lips, waiting. I'm not sure if I was waiting for myself or approval from him, and I'm not sure which one came first. We both moved the few centimeters until our lips touched and were locked. His lips were comforting and their touch on mine was unmistakably electric.

The intensity was slow at first as his hands ran behind my neck and then through my hair. My hands stayed on his cheek and his chest. He pulled back slightly, and I already missed his lips. I craved for their comfort, for their fullness, for their tingle. I closed the gap, this time with more urgency and desire. He responded quickly and our lips parted, welcoming the deeper kiss. Every part of my body was on fire and I never wanted it to stop, afraid of facing my other thoughts.

Liam wrapped one arm around my upper back and the other around my torso. He lowered my back flush onto the mattress while continuing to kiss me. His hands traveled to my sides and hips and then one came to my stomach. The pressure was just enough that it pushed on my new bruising. I cringed and pulled away. I bit my lip, trying not to make a noise. "What happened? Did I hurt you?" Liam searched my face and his hands left my stomach. Without saying a word, I grabbed the hem of my t-shirt and pulled it up just above my ribs. His eyes traveled to my stomach and he took in a sharp breath when he saw the bruising. "What happened?" His fingers lightly traced the forming bruises.

"One of the men got angry that I wasn't going along with it so he kicked me." My voice broke and the tears came back again; I didn't know how to make them stop. Liam stared at me in shock and then looked at the bruises on my torso. He pulled the t-shirt he gave me down until it covered them. He adjusted the pillow so that it laid right under my head, before scooting so that his face was inches from my own.

"Shh," he said, calming me. He reached over and rubbed circles on my back. My eyelids got heavier and heavier, and I was almost pulled completely under by sleep's spell when I heard him say, "I'm sorry I kissed you, but I'm actually not sorry." He took a deep breath and continued in a whisper, "I will protect you forever C. I'll never let anything bad happen to you."

I awoke in the middle of the night screaming and flinging my arms around the bed. Then, the fear increased when I saw no one next to me. Again, I began to relive what had happened to me. Just then, Liam's figure appeared seconds after I screamed and his cellphone was in his hand.

"What's wrong?" he asked, his voice full of concern.

"Where'd you go? I thought you said you would stay with me." I knew I sounded pathetic, but fear had taken over my right mind. I looked around the room for my assailant. My nightmare had been so real that I still felt the drunken man's hands on me.

"I was calling my mom and Bonnie," he said quickly. "I'm sorry, I needed to check in on Travis, and I really needed to talk to my mom." He sounded disappointed in himself that he wasn't with me.

"It's fine, it's fine." I reassured him, still wary that the man was hiding in Liam's room. Abruptly I said, "I need another shower. I can still feel his hands on me." I shuddered when I mentioned him. I looked away from Liam and rushed into the bathroom. Closing the door behind me, I let out a big breath and turned the water as hot as it could get.

Ten

Liam

The library had been eerily quiet when I got there around four a.m. to cram for my exam. I had been up early the day before preparing for today's swim meet and fell asleep studying when I finally had the time to sit down. I only woke up when I heard Caelyn scream in the room next to me. Since the accident, I insisted she stay at our apartment, unless Bonnie swore to call me every time Caelyn had another nightmare. I didn't like to be clingy, but I had made a promise, not only to Caelyn, but to her parents to keep an eye on her.

Last week I got a concerned phone call from Caelyn's dad. He was afraid this would break Caelyn and was unsure if she should stay in Boston. Her attack was three weeks ago now and she was trying her best to return to normal. Well, her new normal at least. She was struggling, but her school therapist insisted that she maintain routine. I also assured him that I wouldn't let Caelyn out of my sight. I was as concerned for her well-being as much as he was, and I couldn't imagine another prick touching her. He said I was a good man, and told me to call him if I needed anything. So far, I hadn't needed to but Caelyn's nightmares were seemingly getting worse. I wasn't sure when they were going to stop, and I didn't know how much more I could take.

Steve called me again at the beginning of the week asking for updates. I assured him that we would make it through these last few days and then, soon enough, we would be home for David's memorial. After the incident, Caelyn had asked her parents not to rush down here, telling them she felt safe as long as I was near her. So, they respected her wishes but still called every day, morning and night, to check in on her.

As for school life, Caelyn's teachers and our coach had been informed the week after her assault. Her therapist suggested she take a week off all activities including school and swim. This was only precautionary so that she could relax and recover. She didn't need anything else to stress her body and mental state.

When Caelyn woke me up around two-thirty this morning, I immediately shot up from the kitchen table and ran to my bedroom. She was covered in sweat and couldn't stop shaking. I tried to comfort her, but she pulled away from me. This was another thing that had started since that night. I backed away and successfully reminded her who I was and convinced her to take a shower. After complaining that she didn't want to go back to bed, I suggested we get out and go to the library. It was an excuse for her to get some fresh air, and it allowed me to be in a quiet environment to study. We made sure to grab our things for the day and left my apartment.

As I sat trying to study for my last midterm before fall break, all I could do was look over at Caelyn. She had fallen asleep across the table. Her head lay on her sweatshirt, that was on top of the table, and her hair was slightly damp from her shower. Her breaths were even as if she were in a deep, peaceful sleep. I wondered how long that was going to last.

I hated seeing her like this: always scared to go to bed, constantly exhausted, and extremely paranoid and jumpy. I feared that a dropped book or a noisy car horn would set her off and cause her to spiral backwards. She had already made great strides since her attack. At the beginning, she would only let me touch her when she wanted to be cared for. Then it became a known fact that she did not want to be touched. I knew this only because Bonnie had called me over to their dorm room late in the night because Caelyn was hysterical. I ran over there and as soon as I tried to calm Caelyn down, she lost it even more. That must have been the hardest part of it all. I couldn't hug her or hold her or even rub her back to calm her down. She was so sensitive and swore every touch reminded her of her assailants.

I attempted studying once more. Thankfully, I could block my thoughts of Caelyn for a few hours while I crammed. This business exam was the last one I had to take before my swim meet and before Caelyn, Travis, Bonnie, and I left for Cape Elizabeth. I couldn't wait to see my family and take a break from school. It couldn't come soon enough for me. Although I welcomed the thought of a vacation, I was ready to face today's challenges and anything else this weekend brought me.

I reached across the table and gently shook Caelyn's arm. Her sleepy eyes met mine and my heart pounded in my chest. She looked around confused at her surroundings and a look of panic overcame her features.

"Shh, Caelyn. It's all right. I just wanted to let you know it's almost time for my exam." I kept my hand on her forearm, and she didn't pull away just yet. She took a deep breath and I could see her shoulders relax. I loved being near her these past few weeks, but with everything going on, we still hadn't discussed the kiss. Or both kisses for that matter. I knew she felt a little guilty because she was still technically dating William. However, when I brought him up lately she would only shrug her shoulders and change the subject. I hoped they would be over soon, but that was me being selfish.

"Want to go get some food?" she asked as we walked out of the library. That was literally the best question to come out of her mouth all day. She smiled softly, awaiting my answer. She knew I wouldn't deny her suggestion. She knew me too well.

"Where to? I have an hour."

We walked to the coffee shop that was closest to the building where my exam was. We walked in, and I had her order first. She got a plain coffee and a bagel. This had become her staple here on campus whenever she needed a little pick-me-up or a good breakfast. I ordered after her and got a black, dark roast coffee with room for cream. I also ordered a breakfast sandwich. As soon as I reached into my back pocket for my card, Caelyn's slim arm reached from behind me to pay the barista.

"This one's on me, trust me," she smiled at me, and I didn't argue. I knew she felt bad for these past few weeks. Though I'd assured her she hadn't been a burden, no matter what I said, she never believed me. I loved taking care of her these past few weeks—I promised her parents and her that I would. Sure, sometimes I didn't get enough sleep, but I knew this was the least that I could do since I still blamed myself for the whole incident. I tried to refrain from telling Caelyn that because I knew it bothered her.

For the next forty-five minutes, we sat talking about anything but the attack and how she was feeling. We talked and laughed about the meet this afternoon. Both of us were anxious, but ready to show Tony how our duo was doing since we couldn't race last week. We also discussed the weekend and what the specific plans were. Bonnie would be staying with Caelyn, and Travis would be staying with me. We planned a time to leave that evening so we could sleep in our own beds for an extra night. I was beyond ready for that part.

I had almost lost track of the time because of our easy-going conversation. She wasn't crying or jumpy, she was just Caelyn. She laughed at my stupid jokes and/or comments and even threw in a few of her own. I missed this, the ease and familiarity of our chats. I jumped up from the table, with ten minutes until my exam, and thanked her for breakfast.

"You're the best," I yelled as I walked towards the door. "See you in two hours for the meet." I thought I heard her say she couldn't wait, but I wasn't for sure.

I ran to my exam and took a seat at the front of the class. The front never intimidated me; it only made me feel like I belonged there. I wanted to feel comfortable before my exam. I grabbed my pencil from my book bag and waited for the professor to pass out the packet of papers.

"How'd it go, hon?" my mom's voice rang over the receiver. She called me on my walk to the pool.

"I think it went okay," I said.

"Don't be so passive Liam," she sighed and laughed. I chuckled as well. She knew me so well.

"I think I aced it, Mom," I admitted.

"That's my boy." I could tell she was smiling through the phone. Her voice was soothing and comforting, something I welcomed. "Anyway, I just wanted to call and get a gauge for when you and your friends will be coming home."

"We're leaving here tonight so that we can have the whole day tomorrow around the Cape to show Bonnie and Travis. Then the next day is for David. We'll be careful I promise." I already answered my mother's next question.

"Okay good. I just want you to be safe..." she trailed off on the other line. There was a moment's hesitation before she spoke again. "Send my love to Caelyn. We can't wait to see you all."

We said our goodbyes just as the rec center came into view. I hurriedly ran into the locker room and changed into my suit. Just as I was about to grab my cap and googles from my locker, the door slammed shut. I jerked my hand back quickly. *What the hell?*

"Shit, what gives?" I asked, a little pissed off. Tony stood off to the side of my locker door with his body leaned against the others. His hand was still pressed on my locker door.

"Just wanted to wish you luck in today's race. I've heard Caelyn's had a rough couple of weeks and she hasn't been to practice for a while. Care to elaborate?" he pried.

"It's none of your damn business Wilson," I said evenly.

Again, he pushed me more. "I heard something about sexual assault? Like rape?" I clenched my teeth together hard. The muscles in my jaw moved slightly, and Tony noticed them move too. However, he did not flinch. "Come on Carter, why don't you share with me how tragic this is for you, knowing that she's carrying another man's baby?"

"Wilson, get out of my way," I said, trying to keep my cool.

"Carter, just tell me."

"Move, Wilson."

"Come on, jus—" Before he could say anything more, I grabbed his arm quickly and twisted it around so that I held him in a rear wrist lock. He grimaced at the pain but I didn't let go yet. I positioned my mouth incredibly close to his ear so that he heard me loud and clear.

"I never want to hear that you were responsible for spreading around those rumors. If you are responsible, you can only begin to imagine what I would do to you." I was seething. "Also, leave Caelyn and me alone. No matter if you have a good or a bad day today, we'd still beat your ass any day of the week." I flung his wrist down. The look on his face was priceless and I wished I had taken a picture. Without giving him another second of my attention, I walked out of the locker room.

My blood was boiling and the stifling air around the pool didn't help. Random people were walking to the stands and my teammates were warming up or gathering around the dive blocks. I saw Caelyn keeping to herself over on the side. She was biting her lip which proved to me that she was nervous. I stayed away, hoping my bad mood wouldn't rub off on her. I was up next to warm up in the pool, but before I could mount the block Coach clapped his hand on my bare back.

"You ready for today Carter?" he asked looking out at the pool. I had a feeling he was going to ask more questions.

"I'm ready Coach," I admitted wholeheartedly.

"Good, good. How is Price doing? I know she's had a rough past couple of weeks." He looked antsy when he made that last comment.

"She's having a better day today, Coach. It's been tough, but she's ready for the meet. Believe me when I say that she'll block everything out except the pool and the clock for the next few hours."

Caelyn was always good at separating life away from competitions so that she had a clear head for the race. She couldn't race if something was on her mind in high school. Therefore, our old coach always told her to think about three things: herself, the pool, and the clock. But the thing about Caelyn was that she never thought about herself. That meant she focused on the pool and the clock. So far, it worked like a charm for her.

"I'm glad to hear that." Coach nodded and blew his whistle, showing that time was almost up. "You're a good man, Liam. Now get warmed up."

To everyone's surprise, Caelyn swam her personal best at today's meet. With everything going on, I was unsure how that was possible. After two weeks off practice, she swam for the first time last night. She wanted to loosen up the day before the meet and claimed it would help clear her head. I was happy I didn't protest because she was on fire. She beat her competitors in both the butterfly and backstroke by seconds. She was stone faced almost the whole meet, but that all changed when it was my time to take the block. Then, her face lit up when I exited the water after my first race. She looked proud, and I thought I even caught a glimpse of something else in her expression.

"Have any pointers for me, Coach C?" I asked, rubbing the water off my face with my hand.

She thought about my question for a moment as her cheeks grew rosy. I loved how her cheeks reddened just from me saying C. It reminded me of that close encounter we shared, and my own cheeks blushed at the memory.

"Well, how about you start swimming well?" she joked back. This was something our team joked about constantly. Coach would ask us to try a little harder at practices and everyone would always say, *oh you actually want us to be good?*

"Oh, my bad. I forgot," I nudged her as I walked back to the block before my next race.

This time I pushed myself a little more just to show Caelyn I could be better. I received a reassuring nod and smile after I touched the wall after my final lap. When I got out of the water, she was back to wearing a stony expression. We only had a few more races until our biggest race all season. This was our first meet together and our first time ever swimming in the same relay. I knew we would be fine, but I grew more and more anxious as the meet progressed.

We took our positions against the three competing duos on the blocks. I noted I was competing against three other girls, and momentarily thought I had it in the bag. The buzzer sounded and we leapt into the water. The water felt cool against my skin as I pierced through my lane. I focused solely on my strokes and the rhythm of my breathing. This allowed me to zone in on the task at hand. We had to win.

I approached the last two laps and was almost a full lap ahead of the girls when my leg got a cramp. I slowed down ever so slightly, trying to work through the pain. My competitors gained a little time on me, but I didn't let it happen again. I passed the flags and touched the wall in three strokes. Caelyn dove in over me. Moments later I was out of the pool as the other three men entered the pool. She had a good lead on them but her weakest stroke was coming up. I gritted my teeth as she completed her kick turn into the breast stroke. Surprisingly, she continued her previous stroke's momentum and swam strong. I cheered her name along with the rest of our teammates. No one cheered for Tony, and I smiled at the thought.

It was down to the wire now as two competitors neared Caelyn's position. She was on the last stretch and she used her special kick turn to give her an extra nudge. Thankfully, it put her back in the lead. She swam harder and faster, not knowing where the other three opponents stood. About halfway down the last stretch, she was neck and neck with the guy in the adjacent lane. Our coach screamed louder than me, which surprised some of our teammates standing nearby. I couldn't watch any longer; this last lap was going in slow motion. I peeked one eye open just as she touched the wall first. I jumped up and down excitedly while the whole team erupted in a loud uproar. She emerged from the water and took off her goggles to look at the clock. Our names appeared in the first-place spot.

Her grin was unmistakable, and it made my heart soar. I wrapped her in my arms and lifted her slightly off the ground as she squealed. I let her down and her face was flushed with color. No words were spoken because our eyes did all the talking. As soon as I let go, the rest of our teammates came to congratulate the both of us. Even Lacie put aside any remaining hard feelings and congratulated us. However, during awards later, Tony avoided all eye contact. All in all, Caelyn and I walked away with three individual first-place awards and the team took first place overall.

Once the awards finished, we hurried to gather our things and shower before hitting the road. My plan was to shower in the locker room and then run to my apartment to grab my duffle bag that I packed the night before. Afterwards, Travis and I would drive over to Caelyn and Bonnie's dorm to grab their stuff. Then the four of us would hit the road for Cape Elizabeth. We figured we would arrive at the Cape by nine p.m. if we stayed on my schedule.

As I waited for Caelyn to shower, I sent messages to Bonnie and Travis as well as my parents about our departure and arrival time. I liked being punctual—always have and always will. My body was already exhausted from today's swim meet and exam, and yet I still needed to drive for two hours. I prayed I would be able to stay awake for the drive home. Just then, Caelyn walked out of the locker room, hair up in a wet bun. She looked pretty chipper. I, on the other hand, was struggling not to fall asleep. I smiled softly at her and took her swim bag.

"You don't look too good," she said warily. "Liam, we literally just won one of our biggest swim meets of the season." She was running high with adrenaline from the win. I couldn't help but laugh at her.

"You do know that I had an exam this morning, swam in three races, and haven't gotten a solid night of sleep in three weeks, right?" I didn't mean to sound harsh, but it came off a little too abrasive. I was afraid how she would react to that.

"No, I know. I'm sorry. I know that's all my fault Liam." She looked down at the ground, but reached up to touch my arm. "I so appreciate everything you've done for me. I really can't thank you enough. You've been so amazing to me." She smiled, and I smiled back in response. Gosh I loved her smile. She made me so proud today. How could someone go through all the things she had and still look ahead? I knew how—she was the strongest person I had ever met.

"That's what friends are for, right?" the words hurt leaving my lips, but I couldn't think of anything else to say. It was such a friend zoning line, but she did technically still have a boyfriend. Thinking of William made me realize I hadn't noticed him calling recently. I wondered what had happened or if things didn't look great for their relationship. For now, I pushed the thoughts aside because I wasn't sure if that was a safe topic to discuss. I liked the Caelyn who came back today. I missed her and prayed she stayed around for a while.

Fortunately, I made it through the drive back to Cape Elizabeth with my three passengers. The girls had fallen asleep in the back while we were talking about Caelyn and my childhood. Many of the stories included David, but they were great memories. Regardless, there were many moments where I felt the familiar pang of grief in my chest when someone brought up his name. But hey, this weekend was about him so I needed to get used to saying his name without breaking down. The first few anniversaries were extremely emotional and comprised of hours of crying. Every year got easier, but the memories were always hard to talk about because he wasn't here to give his two cents. He would have loved to correct our stories or exaggerate some detail.

As soon as we pulled into the driveway, Steve and Beth came outside to welcome us. They were surprised to see two sleeping girls in the back of the truck. Silently, Travis and I got out of the car, and I introduced them.

"Nice to meet you, son. We're very glad you could join us this weekend," Steve said as he shook Travis's hand. Beth on the other hand just sniffled and gave him a big hug. "Caelyn said the meet went well today?" Steve said, directing his attention to me.

"More than just well Steve. She got three first-place awards, even one in our duo. You should be very proud; I know I am," I said happily.

"I'm glad to hear that Liam. I also know that you had your own first-place awards, congratulations." I nodded my head. "So anyways, I'm sure today was pretty busy for all of you. Why don't you guys go get some sleep before tomorrow? I can already tell the girls are pretty exhausted," he laughed and checked the time on his watch.

"They were out thirty minutes into the drive, sir," Travis said laughing.

"Travis, please call me Steve. 'Sir' makes me sound so old," Steve assured him.

Travis responded, "Yes sir... I mean, of course Steve."

"I think we're all pretty tired from the sound of it. We'll take the girls upstairs and then head over to my house, sound good?"

"Of course, thanks boys," Beth smiled, and the two of them grabbed the girls' bags.

I went around the truck to Caelyn's side and took her in my arms. She leaned into my touch and readjusted her head into the nape of my neck. The loose strands of hair tickled my neck, but I tried to ignore the feeling. Travis followed with Bonnie up the stairs to Caelyn's room at the end of the hall. Her room was just as I remembered it. It was a light blue color and everything seemed to be in its place. Her bed was neatly made, and I unsuccessfully tried to move the many pillows. Caelyn stirred in my arms and mumbled something before falling back asleep. I placed Caelyn down on her side of the bed and took her shoes off. Next, I very carefully undid her bun and her hair fell in a mess around her shoulders. She took a deep breath, and her face showed a content smile.

I started to reach down to kiss her forehead, but I got nervous. Travis and Bonnie were also in the room, but he was busy helping her get into the covers. And yet, I still felt weird. Instead, I opted to brush away her loose strands of hair while giving her one long lasting look. I told myself I would see her tomorrow.

I found it incredibly hard to leave her tonight because I was so used to being with her these past few weeks. I was going to miss checking on her in the middle of the night, comforting her after a nightmare, or waking up to her making breakfast. I know I gave it a bad rap, but it really wasn't that miserable. Caelyn's well-being was a top priority to me, and that would never be completely miserable.

As every day went on, I continued to develop deeper and deeper feelings for her. I knew this wasn't just some brief attraction. This was something so much more, and I didn't want to fully admit it to myself. I couldn't because she was in a relationship. Every time I thought about it, my stomach clenched up so tight that I couldn't think straight. Travis and I retreated down the steps and over to my house. My parents were waiting to greet us, but I knew they were tired. My dad must have been working long hours, as usual, and Mom usually shares his exhaustion. We said our goodnights and walked upstairs.

"I think I understand now," Travis said quietly.

"What do you understand?" I asked confused.

"Caelyn," he clarified. "I've never fully understood the two of you, but I get it now."

"It's complicated, Travis. I'm not sure you do."

"Let me explain then," he began to interrupt me. "You lost your best friend when you were a sophomore and she lost that same person when she was a freshman. I remember the story, and I know how important he was to you. I remember hearing that pain in your voice as you talked about everything you lost when he died. He sounded like the guy everyone wanted to be." He paused for a second, thinking over his words. "But I just now realized something, Liam. You didn't just lose David, you lost Caelyn and any opportunity you had to date her." His words stung more than they should have. He decided to dig in a bit more, "See, the timeline of your liking her never made sense to me. You have loved her for years, and you're too scared to tell her. You lost the opportunity because David died and you never wanted to cross that line. Now it's too late, so you say. Am I right?"

"You don't understand. She's in a relationship," I said defeated. "She'll never like me like that now. I lost my chance."

"You didn't lose anything," he said and closed the guest room door. I was left standing in the hallway, dumbfounded by my best friend's words.

I woke up around seven the next morning and knew Travis was still out cold. I quickly changed into a pair of joggers and threw on a t-shirt. After fastening the laces at the end of the hallway, I ran down the stairs and out the door without a notice. I knew Travis would behave himself, and besides, I wasn't going to be very long.

I began a steady jog towards one of my favorite places so I could clear my head. Travis's words still rang in my ears this morning, but I willed the thoughts to stay down for a few minutes. I passed the main strip of town in no time because Cape Elizabeth wasn't very big. I rounded the corner of the lighthouse and saw the water immediately; it looked absolutely beautiful. It was a beautiful October morning, and the brisk Maine air was just what I needed to clear my head. I neared the lighthouse for a little break before I made my way home, and that's when I saw her.

Her back was to me as she sat on our bench overlooking the water. It was the bench David, Caelyn and I rested on in the middle of every run. Her hair was braided down her back, and she was wearing ear warmers to protect her from the wind. I realized just then that it was a bit chillier than I had originally thought. To my surprise, I didn't have many articles of clothing to keep warm, but the sight of her set my body on fire.

She didn't hear me come up from behind, or if she did she didn't show it. I sat on the other end and we stayed there peacefully for a few minutes just looking out at the water. The sun was shining bright on the ocean and the lighthouse stood tall with a few seagulls circling it. I closed my eyes and took a deep breath. The air filled deep within my lungs.

When I opened my eyes, Caelyn was staring at me. I was caught off guard at first, but I didn't stray my own gaze. Her green eyes mirrored the sea this morning, and I was incapable of reading their expression.

"William isn't going to be home this weekend," she said squinting back out onto the water. "Adrian won't be either. Something came up that my dad needed to go to for work, but he didn't think it was right to leave now, you know? So, he's sending the two of them. I don't know why it's acceptable for Adrian to go and miss this weekend, but whatever."

I let her words sink in and waited for her to say anything else. She didn't.

"Are you okay?" I asked her, concerned. It was all I could say without making a rude comment about William

"I wish Adrian was going to be home. But between you and me," she lowered her voice, "I'm glad William isn't going to be. I haven't seen him since I left for school, and I still don't want to see him. It doesn't feel right anymore."

"I get that, I guess." I had a feeling she wanted to tell me something else so I waited patiently.

"Do you think I'm doing the wrong thing, being with him?" she asked innocently.

"I do," I said without hesitating. *Liam, what the hell,* I thought. So much for keeping my mouth shut and emotions in control. "He's not right for you. Maybe I just haven't noticed, but your boyfriend should be calling you every day, especially given what you've been through. He should want to check up on you, talk to you, anything. Now, I haven't seen him calling you or anything lately. No boyfriend should neglect you, no matter how busy they claim to be." I could feel my blood start to boil. Finally, this was the moment I could tell her how I felt. I could tell her that she deserved so much more. She deserved someone that would love her and want to spend every waking minute with her. She deserved someone who loved talking to her and making her laugh. She deserved someone like me.

"It was my dad who told me that he wasn't going to be here. He didn't even tell me." Caelyn sounded upset, and I was afraid the tears would start. I scooted over to her side of the bench and wrapped my arm around her shoulders. She leaned into me, and my body immediately felt warmer. She rested her head on my shoulder as I kissed her hairline.

"Honestly, I know you're technically still dating him, but you aren't really, C. This relationship seems one-sided. Maybe you have feelings for him and he doesn't reciprocate or it's the other way around," I said hopefully. "To be honest with you, I'm not sure and you shouldn't feel obligated to explain it to me. You just deserve someone so much better." She didn't move or correct me. "In my opinion, at least."

What she said next broke my heart.

"We never should have kissed Liam."

I froze, unable to form words. I knew I never should have kissed her, but it felt so right and natural to me. Technically it was wrong, but if I could do it again I would. Her words made me upset, and the hope that we would be together some day came to a standstill.

"It confuses me Liam. That's all. I'm confused, but I can't be. No matter how right you are about William and me, I'm still technically with him. I've been away from him for so long, you know? I can't push my loneliness onto you just because I haven't seen my boyfriend in months. Please understand that this situation is not easy for me." She paused to take a deep breath. I kept my eyes on the water. "I mean, come on, you and me? I can't imagine that working." I could tell the words pained her to say, and a part of me believed that she didn't mean it. Call it a gut feeling, but I knew Caelyn sometimes better than she knew herself. She was making up excuses.

Hell, she even said it confused her and that this wasn't easy. I only wished William was here so that they could talk or end things. I had a hard time believing he still loved her if he didn't fight to be here for her. This was a hard time for her and her family. I was even surprised Adrian went too. This conference must mean a big deal to Steve if he had to send both his interns. Now, with all things considered, I think Caelyn knew deep down that she didn't love William. But I didn't know the answer to my burning question—did she love me like I loved her?

"Liam?" she said my name, and I could tell it pained her. I was hurting right now too.

"I understand C. It's in the past, and I'll never speak of it again." I put up my walls that I never intended to use with her. I just couldn't help but try to protect myself from getting hurt. How could she not know that I loved her? "What kiss, right?" I chuckled under my breath and tried to get away from her. I tried standing but she grabbed my arm. I looked in her beautiful green eyes and the damage behind them was unmistakable.

As I stared at her, I could tell she wanted and tried to say something. Or several things. But every time she opened her lips, nothing came out. I could see the conflict in her eyes, but she couldn't express how she was feeling. I knew I needed to get away from her because if I stayed any longer I would only get more hurt. She made it clear that she didn't want me. I needed that to sink in. She was with William and not me.

I pulled my arm from her grasp and looked deep into her eyes. "I'll be at my house with Travis until you tell me it's time to leave. That's if you still want to help me show Travis and Bonnie around town." I turned away from her before I saw her cry. I ran back to my house without looking back.

"So, Travis how is football going?" My dad, mom, and Travis sat around the kitchen table when I came downstairs after my shower. I grabbed an apple off the counter and took a bite immediately. No one gave me much attention which I gladly accepted. I wasn't in a chipper mood.

"Real well. We've had our fair share of wins and losses. Season's coming to an end, but the break will be nice," Travis chuckled. "I've had to sit on the bench with an injury from a few weeks ago. I insisted that nothing was wrong, but then Bonnie, Caelyn's roommate, and the paramedics made me go to the hospital. Turns out, I broke a few ribs." He nodded his head remembering the memory of Caelyn's attack. My stomach tightened at the mention of it. It was several weeks ago, but still felt like yesterday.

"Oh yes, I'm sorry to hear that. Liam did mention that." My dad was calm with his answer.

"It was very brave what the two of you did. It makes us happy knowing the two of you were there to help Caelyn," my mother said, looking at me with her concerned eyes. She sighed and began to speak up before the phone's ringing cut her off. We froze at the sound of the phone, all remembering the call we received about the Prices' accident. It was hard to erase such a vivid memory. The phone rang for a second time and we broke from our trance. My mother went to answer it.

"Hello?" Someone on the other line said something to make my mom light up. She responded with a nod of her head and, "I'll let them know hon." She nodded again and happily replied, "I can't wait to see you either. We miss you around here." There was no doubt in my mind that Caelyn was on the other end of that line. My mom loved Caelyn, and she was among the few people who knew how I truly felt about her. "Okay. Okay. Will do. Goodbye hon, see you tomorrow."

The room was silent; we were waiting for my mother to say something. She returned to her seat and took a sip of coffee. She was smiling ear to ear.

"What was that?" my dad asked.

"Caelyn called. Oh, how I miss her Paul." She placed her hands over her heart when she said how much she missed her. Sometimes I felt as if my own mother loved Caelyn more than me.

"Is she coming over?" my dad sounded hopeful. Why did everyone want to see her except me? Usually I was the first to jump at the opportunity to see Caelyn.

"No, no," my mom shook her head softly and closed her eyes. "She told me to tell Liam and Travis, but especially Liam, that 'it's time to leave'. Whatever that means." My mother was confused, but I wasn't. It was time to leave. I smiled in spite of how angry I was with Caelyn and how she was coming back with that line. And it hurt even more that my mom had to tell me about it.

Travis and I grabbed our jackets and put on our shoes. The brisk Maine air was a definite factor in today's adventure. Travis tried to look at me, but I purposefully avoided eye contact. I didn't want to deal with whatever bullshit he was going to throw at me. I opened the front door and found Caelyn and Bonnie at the bottom of Caelyn's driveway, waiting.

On our walk to town, I hung back and let Caelyn do all the talking unless Bonnie or Travis asked me something specific. First, we walked to the lighthouse to show them a piece of our history and the town's history. *Oh, lighthouse, you are not my favorite place right now,* I thought as I looked at it. Next, we walked around the town square and showed them several small businesses like Caelyn's dad's office. From the looks of it, Travis and Bonnie seemed to be eating it up. They loved the town and the stories Caelyn shared along the way. She told them a little more about David through these stories too. She even talked about our sisters, our parents, and then us. The stories provided a nice change and helped me forget what happened this morning. But just as I thought things were returning to normal, my dark cloud came back when she mentioned William. I tried as hard as possible to block out whatever she had to say, but it was too hard. In a way, I was grateful he wouldn't be here this weekend. I didn't think I could see them in a room together without getting upset.

After lunch, the four of us stopped at our favorite ice cream shop. The family-owned shop has homemade flavors and gives a complimentary waffle chip with each order. Once we got inside, I had everyone sit down at a table and told them to trust me. Caelyn laughed while Bonnie and Travis shared a confused look. My comment was directed at the two newcomers because Caelyn already expected this from me. I've been getting ice cream with her almost every week for the past fifteen summers. I knew what she liked, and I had a pretty good idea what the other two would like too.

"Hi, may I have four small bowls with butter pecan in two, birthday cake in one, and chocolate chip in one?" I asked listing the flavors off the top of my head.

"Sure, no problem Liam," the owner's wife, Darla said.

"Thanks Mrs. Q." I smiled a big grin at her. I waited to pay at the counter while she filled the bowls with my requested flavors. She came to the register as soon as she finished, and I handed her a $20. "Keep the change, you work too hard," I winked at her and smiled again. Mrs. Q had been working in this ice cream shop for as long as I could remember. Her husband only worked a few days a week due to some health issues, but she never missed a day. They loved this place and had put so much energy and love into making it succeed. When Mr. Q got extremely sick two summers ago, she refused to sell up. I think she was afraid to let go and I could understand why.

"Why thank you darling. Are you all back for the memorial?" she asked me.

"Yes ma'am. It starts tomorrow, around eleven I believe." I shook my head and waited to grab the ice cream.

"Sounds like the whole town is about to show up tomorrow. David was such a sweet and kind boy. The three of you were inseparable," she said kindly, remembering the days when Caelyn, David, and I would come get ice cream on a hot summer's day. "We miss him dearly, you know? I'm sure you do too, as well as Caelyn. You're all in our prayers honey."

"Thank you so much. We really appreciate it." That was all I could say without getting choked up. She smiled again, and I grabbed the ice cream from the counter top.

I turned around and saw Caelyn beaming at me. Her eyes lit up when I returned the smile. I focused on her face and got lost in her eyes. It was then that I realized I had been acting incredibly petty all day long. She never meant to hurt me, but instead was being honest. I understood. I also understood that there was a bigger issue, David's memorial. It was selfish to act the way I was when we were home to celebrate and remember David.

"Alrighty, I hope I picked the correct flavors," I anxiously put down the respective ice creams in front of my friends. Everyone took a bite, and I waited to hear how I had done. Travis took one bite and rolled his eyes in amazement. Bonnie took several bites and then mouthed a wow to the table. Caelyn just smiled down at her cup, enjoying her butter pecan which was her favorite flavor. I had done well.

Eleven

Caelyn

It was the day of David's memorial and the four-year anniversary of his death. It had been four years since I touched the ocean water, four years since I heard his voice, and four years since I was in the hospital myself. It felt like yesterday that we lost my brother, twin, and best friend.

I woke up this morning and immediately showered to wake myself up. After my shower, Bonnie offered to get us a cup of coffee downstairs so we could drink it while getting ready. I accepted the offer, ready for that first sip of coffee. We were up until two this morning talking about my brother, and I was extremely grateful I had her here with me. She had been extremely supportive and a great listener when I told her stories and details surrounding his death. I also shared with her the latest drama with Liam and me. I was unsure of what to do and she openly said that she loved Liam as a friend, but thought we would make a great couple. This did not help my confusion since I was the one in a relationship with William, not Liam.

I willingly left out the fact that my relationship wasn't great right now. Although, I knew Bonnie knew it wasn't great. She had been there for me these past few weeks when William wouldn't call and check in on me, or when he had and the screaming matches ensued. She knew how I felt and we had talked about it once before, but since William wasn't here this weekend, we couldn't talk things over in person. I was confused and hurt by William's actions and strongly believed that this was a perfect excuse for him not to see me. I knew what it felt like to be prioritized and this wasn't anywhere near.

I took a sip of my coffee just as Bonnie got in the shower. I set down the red mug and stared at the clothes laid on my bed. I took a deep breath and threw on the dress. My mom and I agreed to avoid black, thinking we would avoid being a depressing figure at the memorial service. I had chosen a beautiful embroidered shift dress. It was deep red with cinched sleeves that almost touched my knees. Up one sleeve, from the cuff, and continuing down the side of the dress ran some beautiful embroidery. The flowers and vine work were amazing and intricate. I couldn't believe my mom had found something so beautiful here in the Cape. It fit perfectly, and I paired it with black-heeled booties. For jewelry, I chose a simple necklace with a diamond pendant, diamond earrings, and a ruby ring I had gotten for my birthday last year.

As Bonnie showered, I decided to let my hair dry up in a towel as I did my makeup. I didn't want to overdo it since I knew my crying would ruin anything I tried to do. I put a little blush on my cheeks and applied a natural base to my lids. Then, I applied a little mascara to finish off the look. I looked at the girl staring back at me through the mirror, and mentally reminded her to stay strong. Although today would be rough, it was about David and that was all that mattered. Finally, after my hair dried enough, I ran a little Moroccan Oil through the ends so I could let it go natural.

Bonnie had chosen a beautiful, light grey dress that hugged her petite figure. Her shoulder-length brown hair had been tied into a ballerina bun on the top of her head, which amazed me. Her makeup was a little darker than my own and she complemented her lips with a dark burgundy shade. She then tied in the whole outfit with the tallest pair of heels I had ever seen. And with that, we were ready to leave. We descended the stairs to find my parents by the front door.

"Are we late?" I asked concerned.

"Right on time." My father placed a kiss on my cheek, and we were out of the door. We walked to the car, and I noticed that my parents had matched their color scheme along with my own. My father wore black pants, black dress shoes, and a red shirt. His tie matched the flowers on my dress perfectly. He then wore his black sports coat to tie together the look. My mother also wore primarily red. However, her dress was floor length and a black cardigan covered her shoulders. I had to agree that the Price family cleaned up nicely.

The day was beautiful, but a little chilly for my liking. I was so happy that I had grabbed my dress coat from the hall closet before we left. The memorial was outside and located near the pier and marina. When I heard the location of the memorial, I couldn't help but smile. They had picked one of my brother's favorite places in town. We arrived in the center of town and parked along the street so we could walk the rest of the way.

People had already started to convene around the tent and chairs that were set up by the marina. I recognized many faces that belonged to business owners around town, most likely the ones who had donated money to make this happen. I was also comforted by seeing my grandparents, the Carter family, and Travis. I wished that Adrian could have been with us, but I knew she was helping my father with work so he could be here. As we approached, we shook hands with the donors in appreciation for what they had done. It was absolutely amazing, and we couldn't thank them enough.

The first of the Carters to approach me was Evelyn. She gave me a warm hug and complimented my dress. I thanked her for coming and gave her an extra hug. Next up was Lisa and Paul. They smiled and held on to me extra tight. I found myself feeling comforted in their grip. These two individuals were like my second parents, and I loved them like my own.

"Thank you for coming," I grinned at the two of them. A single tear escaped my eye, and I let it fall.

"Anything for David, sweetheart. He was like another son to us," Lisa said grabbing my hands. They felt warm and soft, something I gladly welcomed in this chilly air. Paul and she smiled one last time and went to greet my parents.

Finally, Liam came into view once his parents walked away. He patiently stood off to the side with Travis and Bonnie. Liam smiled his contagious grin, and I took a moment to fully see and appreciate him. He wore dark grey dress pants with black shoes and a matching jacket over a sage green button down. His shirt was unbuttoned a few buttons at the top which allowed for his tan skin to peek out. His dark brown hair was not as unkempt as usual, but still had that slightly messy look about it. His chocolate brown eyes looked down the length of my body more than once, and I could feel my cheeks growing rosier with every step I took towards him.

"Every time I see you, you take my breath away C." Liam slowly wrapped his arms around my waist. This hug felt different than our other hugs. He pulled me tight against him which allowed for my arms to wrap around him. I cupped one hand at the back of his neck and took a deep breath. I smelled the Maine air and Liam's aftershave. I was comforted by the smell because I was all too familiar with both.

"You're not looking too bad yourself." I smiled and we parted, slowly. I looked over at Travis and Bonnie who seemed to be giving us a weird look. I tried to distract them and change the topic. "Travis, you look very handsome yourself. Bonnie, you already look beautiful so I don't need to remind you." I laughed and the group followed with their own chuckles. I loved my little group. Just then, I thought David would have loved them too.

Everyone had started to make their way to their seats, and we followed suit. In the front row, my grandparents sat on the far right-hand side, my parents and I sat in the middle, and the Carters sat to our left. This meant that Liam and I could sit next to one another. I looked around and saw that Travis and Bonnie sat directly behind us. I smiled at them and they both returned a genuine smile. I placed my hands in my lap when I turned around and watched as a man, in a nicely pressed suit, made his way to the front podium. It was starting and my tears were soon to follow.

"Good morning everyone. I'd like to thank all of you, especially our donors and the Price family for being here today to memorialize a boy this whole community knew and loved, David Price. David was special to so many people, for countless reasons. His passing came unexpectedly four years ago when he and his mother, father, and twin sister were involved in a terrible car accident." The sniffles in the crowd had already begun and my own tears rolled down my cheeks. My father wrapped his arm around my mother as she dabbed at her eyes with a Kleenex. "Immediately, the four of them were taken to the hospital. Steve and Beth experienced minimal injuries while David and Caelyn were left fighting for their lives. Doctors worked tirelessly for hours, but sadly David was pronounced dead that evening in the hospital." The man stopped to let the words sink in. I tried to compose myself as I looked over to Liam. To my surprise, I saw Liam's own tears. Without thinking, I reached my hand over and entwined our fingers. He squeezed my hand, and I squeezed back. We would get through this.

A few other men stood up to say a few words about my brother and the sentiment was beautiful. Their kind words made me smile and cry as if it was his funeral all over again. Finally, the same man from the beginning returned to the front and began to speak again. "David is survived by his parents, Steve and Beth Price, loving sisters Adrian and Caelyn, grandparents, and loving friends, especially Liam Carter. Myself, along with my fellow donors, would like to present this memorial for David Michael Price. This is in remembrance of a wonderful young man, son, brother, and friend." Then, a sheet covering one side of the tent was pulled down to reveal a beautiful landscape. An iron bench sat directly in front of the water with a place to store fishing poles. The rocks and mulch were laid perfectly around the bench to make a small park. The sight was breathtaking, and I knew David would have loved it.

My mother and father stood up from their seats as I remained sitting. The two of them made their way to the podium, hand in hand. My mother's face was blotchy from crying and my father's eyes were rimmed with red.

"Words cannot begin to describe how thankful our family is for this generous memorial for our son, David. With that, words cannot even begin to describe the feeling of losing a child so young. But with family, friends, and our community, we have been surrounded with love and support. It has been astounding knowing we have so many supporters. My wife, two daughters, and I would love to thank you for all you have done. This is truly amazing." My dad choked as he said those last words. He looked around at the landscaping and tears filled his eyes. "David would have loved this," my mom said, wrapping her arms around his arm. She tried to soothe him as much as possible. Without another word, the two of them returned to their seats. The sobs coming from the audience were undeniable. The man in the suit returned to the podium to welcome the next speaker.

"I'd now like to welcome Liam Carter, a friend of the Price family, to the podium."

Liam let go of my hand, and I stared in astonishment as he made his way to the front of the crowd. I had no idea that he was going to be speaking, and by the looks of it, everyone else was surprised too. He stood there, took several deep breaths, and met my eyes before speaking. I tried to smile, but my grief was almost all-consuming.

"David Michael Price was my best friend. Correction, one of my best friends. My other best friend is his twin sister, Caelyn. Ever since I can remember, David and Caelyn were always there for me. My parents always told me that the three of us were inseparable, and let me tell you we were." He smiled his genuine smile and looked at the audience. Then, his face turned somber as he continued, "I was offered the opportunity to speak at David's funeral four years ago, but I declined the offer. Some of you may think that's terrible and incredibly vain of me. But let me explain. How was I going to speak about him when I was unable to comprehend what had even happened?" he asked rhetorically. "I remember the day as if it was yesterday and the memory always sends a chill through my whole body. We had received a phone call right as we were supposed to meet the Prices for dinner. I came into the kitchen to see my mother on the tile floor in tears. Without an explanation, my sister and I piled into our family car to drive to an unknown location. We drove straight to the hospital and to my surprise, David, who I had been speaking to just minutes before, had died in a car crash. At sixteen years old, your brain cannot begin to interpret news like that unless you see the proof. And let me tell you, I saw the proof two weeks later when we were burying his body." He paused and took a deep breath. I used my hand to cover my sobs. The memory was too vivid. "Through it all, I had many people supporting me so that I could support others affected with the death of David. Caelyn, David's sister, has been my rock and shoulder to lean on. However, I'll be honest, I was so concerned and blinded with her well-being that I tried to hide and deny my own grief. She was my rock in that uncertain time and continues to steady me in this uncertain world." He looked straight into my eyes as he said that last part. My mom reached for my hand as the tears streamed down my face.

"Losing David has been one of the hardest things I have ever gone through, if not the absolute hardest. This memorial not only means a lot to the Price family, but also to me. So, when I had this idea to remember David, I knew I needed some help. I wanted David to be remembered as the man he was and would have become." Did he just say it was his idea? "Speaking as a close friend, I know he would have spent every moment out there fishing or even looking out at the marina. So, thank you very much to those who helped me execute this beautiful memorial. I am so grateful." Liam nodded his head in gratitude as the audience clapped. He returned to his seat and wrapped his arm around my back. I pulled away from my mom and leaned into Liam's touch.

"Thank you," I choked out. He pulled me closer to him and kissed my temple. My eyes momentarily closed and a sense of calmness overcame me. A pair of hands lightly touched my shoulders, and I turned around to smile at Travis and Bonnie. I had the most supportive friends. I could not thank them enough for coming to this.

The man in the suit returned to the podium. He gave his remarks and invited everyone to stay and look at the landscape in more detail. The next few hours became a blur as many people approached my family and Liam, all of them sharing their fondest memories of my brother and offering us any comfort they could. We stood and talked to the donors for about half an hour and thanked them for all they had done. We thanked Liam for coming up with the idea and starting the process. No one had any clue he was behind it, even his own parents. This was so much more than we could have ever imagined. Towards the end of the afternoon, Liam, Evelyn, Travis, Bonnie and I visited David's grave because it was tradition. I took fresh flowers and we said a few parting words. Just as we were saying goodbye, the wind picked up a few leaves that caressed the group, and I couldn't help but think it was David saying goodbye. I felt comfort in seeing my brother's presence today, and I was grateful to be surrounded by people who shared in remembering him.

"So, tell me one of your favorite memories of David, Liam," Bonnie said as the four of us sat in my living room that night. We had changed out of our dressier clothes into something more comfortable. I had brought Liam's sweatshirt and sweatpants back with me for the weekend, and I had changed into them. When Liam saw me all he could do was chuckle. Liam, back in the present, was looking up at the ceiling trying to think of a memory.

"Okay, so we were about thirteen and we went on vacation with each other to Colorado. We were going on a ski trip. Our parents had gone out to dinner and the kids had all stayed in the hotel room. Evelyn and Adrian went off to watch some movie while Caelyn, David, and I looked around the hotel. We honestly weren't supposed to leave the room, but we did it anyway. I mean come on? You can't keep me locked up in a room for very long." We all laughed. "Anyways, we roamed the hotel for about an hour and found ourselves at the indoor pool. Caelyn, in her mischievous way, had asked David for his phone to look up something, but I knew better. Why wouldn't she have just used her own? Anyway, he handed over his phone, she took it, and without any hesitation shoved him into the pool. His face was priceless as he emerged for air. Caelyn and I stood laughing our asses off in this room while he swam over to the stairs. He climbed out of the water and walked straight for me. I thought he was just messing around, but he looked furious. He grabbed my arm and pushed me in next. Now it was my own turn to look ridiculous as I surfaced for air. I remember seeing Caelyn hurled over on her knees because she was laughing so much, and David just stood there with this smartass smirk. Which might I add, he had perfected. Am I wrong?" Liam asked me.

"No, you're very right," I laughed, remembering.

"So yeah, that has to be one of my favorite memories because he never really got back at Caelyn for anything. He always went for me because I laughed and taunted him." I started to laugh thinking of more instances when he targeted Liam instead of me. "She was his favorite, and I was always envious." I elbowed him in his side, and he fell over onto the carpet. "Ouch. Thanks a lot."

"I was not his favorite, take that back," I laughed and pushed him over as he tried to sit back up.

"Wait, so you and David weren't very close?" Travis asked confused.

"Oh, no we were very close," I responded. Liam sat back up and I made a motion to push him again and he flinched. I smiled and then turned my attention back to Travis and Bonnie. Bonnie had her own smirk on her face, obviously thinking of something we would talk about later. "David and I had a different relationship than Liam and he had. And we should have. I was his twin sister, but Liam was his best guy friend. You know?"

"I hadn't realized how close the three of you actually were. I had heard everyone talk about it today, but your stories really sell it." Bonnie was starting to tear up.

"What's wrong Bonnie?" I asked.

"Nothing. I just feel terrible for you two. Not only did you lose a brother, but you lost a best friend. I don't know how you ever healed from losing him." Travis reached over and rubbed her back. That action, though small, was something she and I definitely needed to discuss later.

"It takes time, honestly," I said.

"And it helps when you have someone to help you through it," Liam added.

"Exactly!" I exclaimed. "I can't imagine going through what I did, if Liam wasn't there." I looked at him thoughtfully before saying my next words. "Liam saved me. He pulled me out of despair and showed me the light. I owe my life to Liam." The room grew silent and for a moment, it was as if Liam and I were the only two in the room.

For the next few hours the four of us shared stories from our childhoods before crashing in the living room. Before falling into a deep sleep, Liam covered me with a blanket and kissed my forehead.

Twelve

Liam

I awoke with a start, breathing heavily. I figured I had a nightmare, but my mind was clouded with the faint dull of a headache. I tried to focus on my surroundings and saw Travis passed out on the floor, Bonnie in the adjacent recliner, and Caelyn asleep on the opposite end of the couch. I didn't smell the fresh coffee that Caelyn's mom usually has brewing, so I figured it was sometime between six and six forty-five. To my surprise, the clock below the TV read seven a.m. I pushed myself off the couch and walked into the kitchen to start a pot of black coffee for everyone. While that was brewing, my mind raced with thoughts about Caelyn.

Yesterday's service and events were perfectly dedicated to David. I knew just how much it meant to Caelyn, her family, and my family. This one small step allowed all of us some more closure. Thinking back to the memorial service, I remembered when Caelyn reached for my hand in comfort. I remembered her sobs as she listened to the many speeches and kind remarks from the community. I perfectly remembered her face when she found out I helped organize the memorial. Her eyes widened in shock and her features softened. For a moment, she didn't sob. Instead, two tears rolled down her rosy cheeks, and I knew they were happy tears rather than sad. As soon as I finished my speech, the one that took me weeks to write and perfect, she took hold of my arm and thanked me. The gesture was intimate and warm which made my heart flutter.

Now considering what happened yesterday and the day before, I felt stumped. No matter how good yesterday felt or the way she looked at me, I couldn't erase those words from my head, *we shouldn't have kissed.* I knew we shouldn't have, that wasn't the issue. It was the pain I saw in her eyes when she said those four words. Some small part of me knew she loved it, but another part of me felt guilt and regret. I figuratively kicked myself for putting her in an uncomfortable position with William. I never meant to wedge myself between them, even if I wished an end to their awful relationship.

Back in the present, I realized I forgot to hit brew on the coffee machine. I hit the silver button, reached for a water glass in the cabinet, and filled the cup to the brim. I downed the glass in a matter of seconds. Just as I set the glass down, I heard a car door shut outside. Being the curious person I am, I went to the front door to check it out. I peered out the small windows to the side of the door frame and saw William and Adrian get out of a car. *Great,* I thought to myself, *what a terrific start to my morning.*

William grabbed Adrian's suitcase from the trunk of the car and dropped it by her feet. He leaned in for a hug, which looked normal. They worked together and had spent a lot of time with one another as of late. Also, he had been dating Caelyn for a little over a year now, so I'm sure they had grown closer throughout their relationship. But then, the hug turned into something else. As they both pulled slightly away from the other, William leaned in to kiss Adrian. I averted my gaze and looked down at the rug under my feet. My mind was spinning. Had I seen that correctly? I quickly looked from the rug and saw that their embrace had turned into something more heated. Again, I looked away and stormed off to the living room. Caelyn had to see this right now.

When I rounded the corner, I saw Caelyn sound asleep on the couch. I panicked and chose not to wake her. I remained frozen in the doorway until I heard the front door close.

"Hey Liam," Adrian's voice bellowed through the foyer, almost waking up the whole house. I immediately tried to quiet her down. "Is everyone still sleeping?"

"We had a long night," I said curtly. I hurried past her impulsively. I had a feeling I might regret what I was about to do. "I'll be right back. If Caelyn wakes up, tell her I'll be back in a second." I ran out the front door just as William backed out of the driveway. Still running, I came to his window and knocked on the glass. Slowly he rolled down the window.

"What is it, Liam?" he asked as he rolled his eyes.

"You're not going to come in and say hi to your girlfriend?" I snarled back at him.

"Well I'm sure the two of you don't miss me."

"What's that supposed to mean?"

"Don't start with me, Liam. It's too early for me to deal with your shit," he said, backing out some more. I reached through the window and grabbed his shirt, and he immediately slammed on the brake.

"My shit? How about you explain to me what I just saw about a minute ago?" I raised an eyebrow at him. He stared at me like a deer caught in headlights. "Hmm?" I cocked my head to the side. I caught him.

"If you dare say anything, I will ruin you." He lowered his voice and his eyes bore deep into my soul. I wasn't going to back down. "You'll regret saying anything once I'm done with you. You think

I couldn't defend myself and make you look bad in the process? Maybe tell Caelyn it was you kissing Adrian, and I caught you before coming in to surprise her this morning. However, before I even made it in the door, I was shocked to see the two of you making out. Then, I knew the news would wreck her so I needed time to calm down before sharing that her best friend was kissing her sister." He looked me dead in the eyes and continued, "I'm studying to become a lawyer, I can twist anything so long as it benefits me, Liam."

"I'd like to see you try. Who do you think she'll believe? A cheating, cowardly boyfriend or her life-long best friend who saved her life?"

"Don't test me, Carter. I'm sure you've been messing around with Caelyn, and she's too afraid to tell me."

"Don't test you? William, you're cheating on her with her sister. No wonder she's confused who to pick! You're a master manipulator! Why don't you just break up with her?" I asked incredulously. "You know, don't answer that. You know she's twice the woman you'll ever deserve. You're a snake of a man if you decide to drag her into this mess."

"What do you know?" he said threateningly.

"I'm pretty sure I just saw you feeling up Adrian in their front drive. There's no other explanation for what I saw." I patted my hand on his car door after he didn't have an answer for me. "You have a good day now, William. I'll be sure to tell Caelyn that you stopped by while she was sleeping." I chuckled and walked back up to the front door. What was I going to do now? Should I wait for Adrian or William to come clean or was it my responsibility to tell Caelyn? I had no idea what was right.

After William left, I returned to the kitchen for the coffee I made, though I really felt like I needed something much stronger after what I just saw. I downed a cup and went to wake up Travis. I wanted to go shower and get out of this house before I saw Adrian again. Or even worse, spoke to Caelyn. He stirred at first, and I shook him harder to get him moving.

"Get up Travis," I harshly whispered.

"Alright, where's the fire?" he asked groggily. *If only he knew*, I thought.

"I just wanna go shower. Can you please hurry and be quiet?"

We successfully made it back to my house without waking anyone. As I laid on my bed after my shower, I contemplated what to do. On the one hand, I thought Caelyn needed to know right away. On the other, I had many reasons not to tell her too. First, now was a rough time with the anniversary of David's death. Second, she had just gotten over the feeling of someone almost taking advantage of her. Third, she was already confused about her relationship, and adding this issue in would only lead her to believe I was making something up for personal gain. She needed to hear this from William and Adrian. I wanted to give them a chance to speak up and do the right thing before I got involved. In that moment, I thought that was the best plan.

Travis came out of the bathroom, not paying any attention to my inner turmoil. I really wished he wasn't so blind to things. Instead he started up another conversation.

"So, I don't think I've ever truly expressed how sorry I am." His back was to me as he packed his toiletries.

"What do you mean, man?" I asked totally confused.

"You know, with losing David. This weekend totally put everything into perspective to me. I am so sorry, Liam. Really I am." He looked over his shoulder, and I could tell by his facial expression that he truly meant it.

"Don't worry about it. It was a long time ago," I said, trying to brush it off.

"No, Liam," he shook his head. "I can't imagine losing a friend so young. I definitely can't imagine what you, Caelyn, and both of your families went through. Hell, are still going through." He looked down to my carpeted floor. "I'm also sorry for what I brought up the other night. It was uncalled for and I'm sorry." I nodded in response. He took a deep breath, "I know we haven't known each other that long, but I don't know what I'd do without you. No, I'm not confessing my love for you," he chuckled trying to backtrack, "I just mean that you're my best friend, and I can't imagine losing you like you lost David. That's all I'm saying." He began to ramble and cringed at his own words. I walked over from the bed and clapped my hand on his back.

"Travis, thank you." He nodded his head back to me. And just like that, our moment was over. Travis and I didn't normally get into deep conversations very often, but when we did I was sure that he was capable of real, deep feelings. "Not that we were on this subject, but what's going on with you and Bonnie?"

I've never seen someone so distressed in my life when he heard those words. "Wait, is it obvious?" Obvious? What was he talking about? I just asked what was going on? He must have read the confusion on my face, so he continued to talk. "Is it obvious that I like her?"

"I mean, I've never seen you comfort a girl in public before. Like when I was giving my speech I saw that you were rubbing her back as she cried, and then afterwards you kept touching her back and asking if she was okay." The pieces started to come together a bit more. Of course he liked her and maybe even felt stronger than he thought he did. "If I'm not mistaken, I'd probably think that you might even love her." I started walking to the doorway. I loved messing with him.

"Woah there. Says the boy who loves his best friend, but doesn't have the guts to tell her. You can't talk," he scoffed and laughed at me. I was already out in the hall and chose to ignore that last comment.

"You told Travis that you love Caelyn?" My mom and dad emerged from their room. What the hell?

"Mom!"

"Liam, we already knew it, we're just glad you expressed it," my dad smirked. "It's old news Travis, but he's never said it himself. At least, out loud." They shared a look. Travis must have followed me into the hallway.

"I would've thought you told your parents." Travis laughed. What was going on here? How did my parents hear our conversation?

"Mom, Dad, Travis, stop. I do not love Caelyn," I said exasperated.

"Sure hon, your secret is safe with us," my mom said retreating into her room. My dad followed behind her after he let out a chuckle. I was left in the hallway staring between my retreating parents and Travis. He smiled ear to ear and went back into my room.

"Good talk buddy," I laughed and went to brush my teeth. "We're leaving when I'm done!" I shouted through the walls and wasn't sure if he heard me. Oh well. That was interesting. Not only did that conversation set my nerves on high, but butterflies filled my stomach at the thought of loving Caelyn. Did I truly love her? I was a mess of emotions and questions myself. Did I even know what that meant?

"Please, oh please let me know when you get to campus," my mom begged as I gave her a big hug. She was on the verge of tears, like always.

"Yes Mom," I said laughing at her. "I know how much you worry." We parted and I could see the relief on her face. Since our interesting conversation this morning, no one had brought it up again. I was beginning to wonder if it even happened.

Next, I went to give my dad a big hug and just as we were parting he said, "Proud of you son." I smiled at the compliment. That was a little rare around here. "Looking forward to having you home again at Thanksgiving. Maybe you can come and help out with the business."

"Of course."

Just then the Prices and Bonnie were walking across the street and up the drive. They started their goodbyes, and Steve and Beth came over to Travis and me. They had enjoyed having Bonnie and Travis here this weekend. It was refreshing for our parents to see some new faces who we called friends. Steve came over to me after shaking Travis's hand.

"Liam, always a pleasure," he said, firmly shaking my hand. He pulled on my arm to have me lean forward, so I did. "Also, thank you for taking such good care of our little girl. She insists she's not so little, but you know she's our baby. I feel so much better sending her back to school because she has you there. It's not like I can say the same about that boyfriend of hers, but that's a whole other conversation," he laughed and we both pulled back to an upright, standing position.

"Anything for Caelyn, Steve. You know I wouldn't let anything happen to her." He shook his head and made way so his wife could give me a hug.

She held on tightly for a few extra seconds so that she could tell me something. My eyes got wide and a sense of happiness overcame me. She pulled away, and I smiled at her. I didn't have an answer for her right then, but we seemed to connect through our glances. Steve and Beth both smiled and wished me luck with everything. Gosh, I really did love them like they were my own family.

"Alright, you all better get on the road. Please drive safely and we'll see the two of you at Thanksgiving," Steve said, directing the last part to Caelyn and me.

We said our final goodbyes and climbed into the truck. The girls took the back seat while Travis and I rode up front. Almost as soon as we left our street, Caelyn was passed out in the back. Bonnie looked out the window at the scenery as we exited Cape Elizabeth, and Travis fidgeted with the radio to keep himself busy. All I could do was drive the two hours back to campus, periodically checking the rearview mirror to see Caelyn's sleeping figure.

Thirteen

Caelyn

Thanksgiving Break was fast approaching, and I couldn't wait for another chance to see my family. Being home for David's memorial made me realize how much I missed my people and Cape Elizabeth. At this point, I no longer missed William and it was a weird revelation. But no one knew, except for Bonnie. I learned that, the morning after the memorial, William and Adrian arrived back and to my surprise, William dropped off Adrian without saying hi. At first I was hurt, but then the hurt turned into anger. Something had to be going on and now he was playing me. I tried calling but my calls were sent straight to voicemail.

Adrian assured me that he was tired, he'd call soon, and not to worry. I reluctantly listened to her excuses and tried to block it out of my head. After a quick hug, we sat down to have coffee together. She told me about her weekend as I explained the memorial. The conference was a huge deal which allowed her to meet new firms and professionals. She lit up when we talked about law, and the calm conversation was a refreshing change for our relationship. I was used to snarky and passive aggressive comments these past few years. Even though some thought we should be mad, we mostly just missed her yesterday and she apologized profusely for missing out on tradition. I understood where she was coming from and let her absence go.

Since that morning, William had been extremely short over text and barely bothered to answer my calls. After talking with Bonnie and sharing the things I once hid from her, I decided that enough was enough. I planned to have a conversation with him when I got home for break because I couldn't do this anymore. Although Bonnie tried to convince me to call and end things, I thought I owed him more than a call or text message. I wanted to tell him how unfair he had been treating me so I could see his reaction in person. I was about ninety-five percent sure that I wanted to end things over the break, but until I got home, I wouldn't allude to a breakup. I didn't want him to have the upper hand and end things himself. I wanted to be the one who initiated it and stood my ground.

In the weeks since the attack and memorial, I had been trying to work on myself. I wanted to use what happened to me the night of the ball, and grow from it. I didn't want to be scared and hide for the rest of my life. Hell, that's what I was doing for the weeks after the attack. All it took was staring at myself in the mirror before the memorial. I looked broken, unsure, scarred, and small. This wasn't the life I wanted, and it wasn't the life I promised David. Then, considering my thoughts and feelings about William, I knew it was time to make a change. I needed to focus on myself and remove the negativity once and for all.

Besides the drama with William and focusing on my personal growth, I had been extremely busy with classes, swim practice, and meets. My midterms came back a lot better than what I had been expecting, and I was proud of myself for pushing through. I didn't want to receive special treatment after the incident, but my doctor and BU emphasized I needed time to heal. I accepted the assistance then and combined with the time home for the memorial, I came back energized and ready to go.

Around five weeks after the attack, I no longer had the terrible nightmares. I returned to my dorm room to sleep in my own bed. I had Bonnie as my support, and I was relieved to be making progress. I was thrilled at first to be back to my normal life, but as the days and nights went on, I really started to miss Liam. Like I really, really missed seeing him all the time. I still saw him in class, swim practice, and the weekends, but something felt different.

After we got back from the Cape, he distanced himself from me for about a week. He claimed that going home for the memorial had taken a lot out of him, so I respected his request for space. Then, one morning he asked if I wanted to go for a run, and the butterflies I felt were undeniable. We met up outside of my dorm and ran several miles. Once we were heading back to my dorm for breakfast, he stopped and thanked me. It was a simple thank you, and I knew our rhythm had returned. In the swim realm, we continued to kick ass during our meets. Wilson and Barnes couldn't keep up, and Coach was thoroughly impressed. Liam was getting better and better every day, and I loved watching him grow. It was an awesome feeling when I could cheer him on in the pool and vice versa. We were each other's support system now as we had been for the past four years.

It was the Friday before Thanksgiving Break and Coach decided to take just the boys to a swim meet out of town. They were travelling to Virginia for the weekend to compete against a few men's teams. I had planned on saying goodbye to Liam before he left, but got held up with one of my professors during their office hours. Instead of seeing me, he sent a text saying he'd see me on Sunday. Let's not forget that he threw in a "you need to behave." Ha, behave. Bonnie and I had been planning on going to a party, upon Travis's request, that night at a fraternity house. I knew Liam wasn't very happy because he wasn't going to be home if I needed him, but I needed to get out and have some fun. It had been so long since I let loose. I spent so much time playing catch up in class and in the pool, that I hadn't had much fun these past few weeks.

Bonnie and I spent the early evening trying on clothes and getting ready before Travis picked us up. I had sent a text to William that I was going out with friends tonight and if he wanted to talk he needed to call me tomorrow. I got back a text that said, *We will talk when you come home.* What the hell did that mean? I was fuming and honestly a little scared he would end things before I had the chance. So, I immediately got my phone and texted Liam.

Sent at 7:04 p.m.: *I miss you come back. I'm totally going to be third wheeling tonight.*

Received at 7:06 p.m.: *Miss you too C.*

Sent at 7:15 p.m.: *What no comment about the third wheeling?*

Received at 7:21 p.m.: *I chose to ignore it ;) Just focus on having fun and it'll be okay. Travis won't dare try anything.*

Sent at 7:45 p.m.: *It'd be more fun if you were with us. Swim hard for me tomorrow!*

Received at 8:00 p.m.: *I'll be swimming for you! Text me when you get back in tonight, okay?*

Sent at 8:08 p.m.: *:) I will!*

"Girl I know you're not texting William if you are grinning that big," Bonnie said as she applied her last coat of mascara.

"Oh, shut up," I said, putting on lip stick. I had chosen a mauve matte color to match my jean, mid-thigh length skirt and white cropped top. I had picked out a pair of Converse to complement the outfit too. My hair was down in loose curls to cover my shoulders from the evening chill. "How do I look?" I asked facing Bonnie.

"If only Liam were here." Bonnie tsked and tied her shoe laces. She had chosen a black, tight two-piece outfit and wore bright red lipstick. Her hair was pulled into a shocking ballerina bun again. She looked beautiful, and I knew Travis would think so too.

"Well Travis is here, and I have a feeling he won't be able to take his eyes off you," I said matter-of-factly as we shut our door. She stopped in her tracks, and I had to turn around to face her.

"Is it that obvious?" she asked, insecure all of sudden. "I mean, what does it matter? He would never go for someone like me." She looked down at the floor.

"I don't know Bonnie. I think you'd be surprised."

"If it happens, it happens. Sure, I would love to be with him, but it's not just up to me."

"Well if that's how you feel, you shouldn't hold anything back. Especially tonight, okay?" I told her. She smiled and nodded her head. And with that settled, we walked downstairs to meet Travis.

Just as I suspected, Travis's jaw dropped as he saw Bonnie come out of the door.

"You ladies look amazing, as always," he stammered. He stared at Bonnie which made me smile. I said a quick prayer that everything went well tonight.

It was about midnight, and I was a few too many tequila shots in. Bonnie was my party buddy for the evening, and Travis agreed to be our designated driver and caregiver if one of us got out of hand. Anyway, the music in the fraternity house was loud enough that the walls shook with every beat. The rooms of the house were packed on the first two floors, and I'm sure a lot of the bedrooms were in use too. Bonnie and I stayed on the main level close to the makeshift dance floor while Travis got us drinks.

Plenty of guys had tried to make a move on us, but Travis was never too far away so he could scare them off. I was a little drunk, but not drunk enough to do something with another guy. If Liam were here, I might have done or said something stupid to him, and I'm sure I wouldn't remember it come morning. An hour went by and Bonnie and I were covered in sweat from dancing. At this point I had done another handful of shots, trying hard to erase the thought of what an awful boyfriend I had. I was mad at myself for not seeing it until recently too. The alcohol numbed my emotions and allowed me to have a night free from deep thoughts about William. I regretted staying in this relationship for so long.

Around two in the morning, Travis pulled at my elbow to get me off a table. I had, at some time during the last hour, taken off my crop top which left me in my white bralette. It wasn't completely slutty, but definitely not my proudest moment. Bonnie handed me my shirt and the three of us made our way to the front door.

"But I'm not ready to leave Travis," I whined, trying to walk back into the party.

"Nope, time to go home," he said as we walked into the cold night. The air was a shock to my body, and I almost immediately sobered up. The back of my neck was wet from sweat and the rest of my body had a coating of it as well. I was having a hard time walking straight and decided that it was a good thing we were leaving. We made it to Travis's truck and he helped each of us into the car. Bonnie was more sober than I was, and I saw that she couldn't take her eyes off Travis as he closed her door and climbed into his side. "I'm taking you back to my apartment in case one, or both, of you gets sick. No arguing." He was being bossy but that could have only been what my drunk brain thought at two in the morning.

We parked in front of the apartment complex, piled out of the truck, and walked up the stairs to their apartment. Travis unlocked the door just in time for Bonnie to run to the bathroom. I had a feeling she was getting sick.

"Doyou wantme to helpher?" I slurred. I pointed over towards the direction of his bathroom but my arm fell to my side because it was beyond heavy.

"No, I'll take care of her. You can sleep in Liam's room," he said.

"You takegood careofher mister. And don'tyou dare takeadvantage ofher." I stared into his eyes and his hands flew up defensively.

"I would never." He smiled in her direction. "Get to bed Caelyn."

After I rinsed off in Liam's shower, I changed into a sweatshirt of his. It was almost like a full-on dress. I grabbed my phone off the counter of the bathroom, about to call Liam, when I stopped, frozen in my tracks.

"Surprise." Liam smiled from where he sat on the bed. A big grin overcame me and I rushed into his arms. He fell back onto the mattress, his back flush on the sheets. I pulled away briefly and had a strong sense of déjà vu. His hands pushed back the stray hairs that had fallen forward.

"What are you doing?" My words were still a little slurred, but I tried hard to fight it off.

"Virginia has bad weather coming this weekend so they just cancelled it to be safe. There were several teams driving and flying out of state. I convinced Coach to come back tonight so that we didn't get stuck there. We weren't even halfway there, so we made a smart decision."

"Well I missed you," I snuggled my face into the crook of his neck and shoulder. His arms wrapped tighter around me. It was such a good feeling. Every care in the world erased from my mind.

"I'm going to shower quickly and then I'm going to bed. Travis already told me what was going on so go ahead and make yourself comfortable." He got up and disappeared into the bathroom, but left the door cracked. I was still feeling the effects of alcohol in my system, and I dared a peek into the bathroom. He'd already jumped in the shower, in though.

Next I walked over to the side that Liam doesn't sleep on and pulled back the covers. I crawled in and snuggled up underneath. They smelled just like him. I heard the water turn off, and Liam came out a few seconds later in a towel. We made eye contact and instead of looking away, I continued to stare at him. He broke it off when he grabbed a pair of boxers from his dresser. He slid them on without revealing anything.

He walked over to his side of the bed and pulled back the covers. He slid in and turned to face me. My breathing grew faster and faster, and I was having a hard time thinking. Stupid alcohol. I always felt a little more confident with it in my system, which at that moment could be a good or a bad thing.

"Why are you so far away?" I asked quietly. He immediately scooted closer to me. "Much better." I smiled at him and could smell the fresh mouthwash scent.

"Did you have fun tonight?" he asked, closing his eyes as his head rested on the edge of his pillow.

"Yes, I feel like I acted a little stupid though. I had too many shots," I admitted guiltily. "But I wish you could have been there. Travis isn't so 'caring' when it comes to alcohol. He's the first person to push a shot your way and persuade you to have another. Even when you insist you've had enough." I laughed. This moment was perfect. Liam was home instead of being several states away. I was completely happy. *Wait, did I just say he was home?*

"Travis told me."

"Oh gosh," I brought my hands up to cover my face. "I'm so embarrassed. I have no idea how that happened," I said referring to my top coming off while I was dancing. I peeked through my hands and saw his eyes were still closed, but he was smiling anyway. "I'm sure if you were there it never would have happened."

He thought for a minute and grew very serious. "I'm sure it would have happened, but it would have been my idea." My mouth must have fallen open because he started to laugh. He didn't defend his comment, and I was speechless. I stammered for some words, but ended looking more like a fool.

He scooted a little closer to me and put his arm over my side. My breath caught, and I heard him take a deep breath. His hand ran up and down my back. The movement was soft and sweet. I moved a little closer myself and his pressure on my back grew. I could feel every hair on my body stand up as he continued to rub my back. Feeling brave, I inched my face closer to his so that our noses almost touched. It was his turn to catch his breath.

I could feel his hot breath on my skin, and I could almost hear his heart beat. This was where I wanted to be. This was who I wanted to be with. I truly felt that William was no longer the man for me, but that didn't change the fact that we were still in a relationship. Still, I didn't back down while I was with Liam. It was in this moment, and I'm not sure if it was because of the alcohol or not, that I wanted to kiss him. I wanted to feel his lips on mine. I wanted to feel his arms wrap tighter around my body. I moved my face a little more and we were centimeters away from kissing. I could almost taste his lips when he stopped me.

"C," he whispered, not moving.

"Hm?" My eyes were closed, and I was breathing in his scent. He smelled freshly of shampoo and mouthwash and it was almost intoxicating. Why wouldn't he just let me kiss him?

"As much as I want this, I think you're still drunk," he whispered slowly. "I don't want you to do something you'll regret later." He inched away and opened his eyes. He took his hand back and lifted my chin so he could look at me. He stared deeply into my eyes, and I looked up at him in a trance.

"What?" I asked him. I had a feeling he was thinking about something.

"You're just so beautiful Caelyn. So incredibly beautiful that it hurts," he said, closing his eyes for a second. "You make my days brighter, C. When I'm with you, I feel so special and loved. And when I don't see you, I feel like I'm missing a part of me. You make me so happy, and I hate that I can't hold you like this in public." His eyebrows furrowed in frustration. "I don't want to hide these feelings anymore." I was surprised that he was being so open and honest with me right now. With every word he was saying, the butterflies intensified in my stomach. Tears began to well up in my eyes. "C, I need to tell you something," he paused and bit his lip.

Just then, I felt like I was going to get sick. I jumped out of bed so quickly and ran to the bathroom, stumbling over the bathroom rug in the process. I clung to the sides of the toilet and emptied all contents in my stomach. I knew the retching was anything but attractive, but Liam was out of bed and by my side in seconds. He was there holding back my hair as I continued to puke for a good thirty minutes.

Once he figured that I could keep some water down, he filled a plastic cup to the brim and made me drink something along with some aspirin. I gladly accepted the cup and medicine, and laid down on the cool tile. Liam wet a wash cloth and dabbed it along my forehead and neck.

"I'm never drinking again," I complained. Liam just laughed and walked into the other room. A few minutes later, as I began to doze off on the tile, he returned and carried me to bed. After he was sure I was tucked in, he laid down on his side. "Hey, what were you trying to tell me earlier?" I said through a yawn.

"Don't worry, we'll talk about it later. Just get some rest C," he yawned too.

I'm not sure when we both fell asleep, but I awoke wrapped in his arms early the next morning. Without waking him, I climbed out of bed, left a note, and went back to my dorm. When I walked in, Bonnie was nowhere in sight so I figured she stayed with Travis. The last thing I wanted to do was pry, but I couldn't wait to hear what happened. I shot her a text asking her to let me know when she got back to the room. I then added I went to practice so my absence didn't worry her. I changed into my suit, put sweats over the top, and went to the pool.

There wasn't a formal practice today since Coach and the boys were supposed to be in Virginia for a meet. I decided since I missed too many practices that I needed to put in the extra training. When I walked into the building and saw the pool, I realized I had it all to myself. I decided to dive in and start with a few warm up laps. When I felt warmed up, I started to run through our relay. I glanced at the clock when I began and saw it when I had finished. My time hadn't changed, but I wanted to push myself to get better. Ever since the assault I felt that I had fallen behind everyone, just because I hadn't been to a few practices. With the all-clear sign from my doctor, I began to swim more intensively. However, I still wasn't quite back up to speed. Some would beg to differ, but I needed to feel happy with my techniques and times.

An hour went by, then another, and I still hadn't noticed anyone come in. As I was cooling down with the back stroke, I heard the door open and close. Not long after that I touched the side and took off my goggles. I peered around the pool and saw I had company.

"I didn't realize you were putting in the extra practices," Tony Wilson's voice echoed in the room. I rolled my eyes and pulled myself out of the pool.

"I could say the same to you Wilson," I commented. I grabbed my towel and began to dry off. Since meeting Tony, I had gotten a bad vibe from him. He was all talk, and I honestly didn't care for his attitude. Let's just say, he'd been on my bad side ever since that first encounter.

"Well it must be refreshing to actually get out without feeling like someone's going to rape you."

"Excuse me?" I stopped drying off and stared at him in disbelief. Did I just hear him correctly? What the hell did he know, anyway?

"Everyone is talking about what happened to you back in September. I can't tell from your swimsuits if you're showing yet, but you can't always tell when someone's pregnant. Right?" He turned to face me now.

"What the hell are you talking about?" I raised my voice. Tony had some nerve talking to me like this.

"The word on the street says that Carter couldn't get to you in time and that drunk got you pregnant. I'm sorry to hear it. You know, because we all know how much Liam cares for you," he said, starting to come closer to me. I kept my eyes on him with every step he took. My blood had begun to boil, and I knew I'd punch him if he got too close. "Word on the street also says you didn't even put up a fight. I'm guessing you're pretty easy then, hm?" He was right in front of me now. I could see the smug smile on his lips. "Can I have a turn?" My eyes bugged, and I was seething with anger and disgust.

"Shut the hell up Tony!" I screamed at him. I could feel the tears burning my eyes. I couldn't show this weakness in front of him. I just couldn't, not when I had come so far.

"No defending? Wow, you are much easier than I thought; in every sense." He laughed and that's when I lost composure. I wound up my fist and threw the biggest punch to the side of Tony's face. He felt the connection of my fist on his cheek, and his hands flew up to hold the already red mark, as he stumbled to the ground.

"Don't you dare talk about me like that. You have no right to be going around and spreading rumors," I talked down to him. "It just shows the type of man you are. You are a prick. An asshole. A snake of a man. I don't know how you can even look at yourself every day," I scoffed. He looked up at me in pain, still holding his cheek. I wanted to put him down like how he put me down. "You disgust me and I never want to hear my name come out of that repulsive mouth of yours."

I turned around without another word from Tony. I grabbed my bag on the floor and walked hurriedly out the front doors. The wind chill was brutal against my swimsuit, but I pushed on to my dorm. I made it to the doors and ran up the stairs and into my room. After hastily grabbing my shower stuff, I slammed the door and went to the bathroom. I peeled off my suit and got into the shower. Then, and only then, did I allow the tears to come.

I stood in the hot water, letting the droplets trickle down my body as the tears became all-consuming. I had no clue that there were rumors going around about me. And not just simple, stupid rumors either. They were cruel and offensive. The feeling of my assailant's hands on my body returned, and I was left feeling filthy. I scrubbed my skin until it felt raw and washed my hair twice. No matter what I did, the feeling didn't go away. I grabbed my torso remembering the feeling of the blows. The pain of that moment returned, and I couldn't stop the tears from flowing.

I continued to stand in the water until my hands looked like prunes. I shut off the water and dried off. I walked to my room and chose a pair of sweatpants and a baggy t-shirt. I sulked off to my bed and pulled the covers back, crawling in. Thanks to Tony I was back to feeling like a piece of shit again.

I woke up a few hours later to Bonnie and the boys walking into our common room. I turned away to face the wall so they couldn't see how puffy my face was. I didn't want to face them because I was afraid and embarrassed. What if they had heard these same rumors? Why didn't they tell me about it? The three of them laughed as they walked in the bedroom.

"Caelyn? Are you here? Why aren't you answering your phone?" Bonnie yelled. I looked at my phone and the time read seven-twenty p.m. I saw three missed calls from Bonnie and two missed calls from Liam. I guess my little rest turned into a slumber. I'd been asleep for nine hours.

"I'm in here," I said weakly. Bonnie and the boys walked in just then.

"Why are you in bed? It's seven-something Caelyn! Come on, let's go get some dinner," Bonnie begged.

"I'm okay. I'm not feeling very well." It wasn't a total lie. I wasn't feeling well. Correction, I was feeling sad and worthless.

"How about we go get food and bring it back here? Have a movie night?" Bonnie knew how to get to me, but I still wasn't feeling up to the company. I just didn't feel like being around anyone. Well, anyone besides Liam.

"I don't want to ruin your plans. Really, please go have fun," I insisted. My back was still to them as I faced the wall, knowing how swollen my face would be from all the crying.

"Boys, how about you go pick up some food and we'll watch the movie when you get back?" she suggested. I didn't think the boys fought her because the dorm door opened and closed within the next few seconds. I took a deep breath once I heard them leave. I turned over to face Bonnie because I needed to talk to someone. If it wasn't Liam, then it could be Bonnie. "Oh honey, what's wrong?" she said with genuine concern. She sat down on the side of my bed and grabbed my hand. The tears started to prickle.

"I went for a swim this morning and after I was done, I ran into Tony Wilson at the pool," I started to tell her. The tears were inevitable, but I continued to tell Bonnie every detail. Including the fact that I punched Tony in the face afterwards. Bonnie listened intently and reacted just as I thought she would. She freaked out and wanted to go kick Wilson's ass. I told her I already hit him so it wasn't that big of a deal anymore. She begged to differ and that's what I loved about her. I knew Bonnie would always have my back and take my side.

She continued to sit with me until the boys got back with dinner. During that time, I also asked her what had happened last night and/or this morning between her and Travis. I couldn't wait for her to bring it up, I was too impatient. She explained that when she had gotten sick he pulled her hair back out of her face and comforted her until she was ready to get up. He insisted that she take the bed while he took the floor, which I thought was sweet. She said that after they both laid down, they started talking about anything and everything—family, past relationships, favorite foods and animals, and even their future plans. She said it was nice to finally have a real, deep conversation with him. Then, she explained that they fell asleep around six a.m. and woke up about an hour ago starving.

I had a hard time imagining Travis in that story, but knew he had a softer side I hadn't seen yet. He was a great guy, and I had picked up on his feelings towards her not that long ago. I was glad something was finally happening between the two of them. When she was done telling me about her night, I asked what time Liam got up. She wasn't sure, but said it couldn't have been much before them. I wasn't surprised because I had kept him up late. I'm glad I got out of there so he could sleep. I just wish I hadn't run in to Tony when I left.

Finally, the four of us ate dinner after I pulled my butt out of bed. Liam immediately noticed something was wrong with me and gave me a huge hug. I melted in his arms and welcomed the comfort of him. After dinner, we popped in an action movie called *London Has Fallen* with Gerard Butler. It was actually really good and kept my brain occupied for a while. I was exhausted after the movie ended and insisted I should go to bed. Bonnie looked at me sad because she knew how upset I was. Travis asked if anyone wanted ice cream and Bonnie jumped at the opportunity to have some alone-time with him. Liam declined the offer, even though he loves ice cream.

The two of them left, and I went to lay down in bed. Not long after I laid down, Liam came and sat on the edge of the bed. He leaned over and lay face down on the comforter. After a good five minutes like that, he finally spoke to me.

"You want to talk about it?" he said, testing the waters. I knew he felt uneasy, but he asked anyway.

"Not really," I admitted turning onto my side. He watched me intently. "Will you just lay with me for a little? At least until I fall asleep?" I asked sleepily. He didn't answer verbally but came beside me. He laid down on his side too, facing me.

"You will tell me, right?" he asked, but didn't leave time for me to answer. "Because I'm worried, Caelyn. Did something bad happen? Did someone touch you?" His voice broke, and he broke me. I crumbled into him and cried into his chest. He wrapped his arms around me and rubbed my back.

After I felt the tears slow down, I took a chance at something. My head was tucked in between his neck and shoulder like earlier this morning. Instead of pulling away, I stayed close to him and put my lips right where his neck and shoulder met. I kept my lips there for a while before kissing up his neck. Each kiss was soft and the further I went up, the more I could feel his heart beat faster and faster. I got to his jaw line, and I felt his breath catch when my lips made contact with his skin. I brought my hand up to his neck so that I could pull him closer to me. His hand grabbed mine, and he just held it for a second. After a while, he took my hand and kissed the palm. I wanted him to do something else, but he didn't. Instead, he rubbed my back. The motion made me calm down and lulled me to sleep. I didn't even hear Bonnie and Travis get back. I most definitely didn't feel Liam leave that night either.

On Sunday I packed my bag for the break, picking enough clothes, jewelry, and toiletries for a week. Liam and I discussed leaving Wednesday since Monday and Tuesday consisted of exams and deadlines. I'd worked my butt off this past week to prep for those assignments because I was trying to apply for another scholarship. Between studying and training in the pool, I ended up telling Liam about my encounter with Tony on Sunday night. Of course he was livid. However, when Monday and Tuesday's practices rolled around, Tony didn't show up. My guess was he already left for Thanksgiving break. Whatever the case, I was glad that he wasn't there.

I pushed myself at practices to improve my times and worked harder to beat Lacie, who had bettered her times. She wasn't totally up to my skill level, but she had improved tremendously. Throughout the past few practices I picked up on Lacie glancing at Liam as he got in and out of the pool. Liam, just like every other guy, claimed he hadn't noticed. I tried to let it go, but was intrigued to say the least. Then, on Tuesday night, we had our final practice before the break. It was laid-back and the team seemed to be letting off the week's steam. I found myself hanging out with a group of girls, listening to their drama.

"Did you hear about Lacie?" asked Grace Tills. She was a sophomore who swam a fantastic breast stroke. She was also one of the few girls who brought the gossip to practice.

"Poor thing, she never had a chance. I mean everyone wishes they had some of that ass," Brooklyn Sutton, another sophomore who swam primarily freestyle, commented back. I was so confused. A few of the other girls nodded their heads. Was I the only one not aware of what they were talking about?

"What are we talking about?" I asked with a shy smile, embarrassed to be in the dark.

"Lacie and Liam started hooking up last year and then they tried it up again when school started, but he stopped it. Must've had a reason why he stopped. Last I knew, they were having a lot of fun together." The group of girls laughed, and I tried to fake a smile. My heart pulled in my chest, and I felt queasy. Lacie and Liam? "I've heard that she's been devastated, but he won't try it again. She told us that he wanted a relationship with someone else."

The group continued to talk about Liam and Lacie's past hook ups, or at least the rumors they heard. I had now begun to understand why Lacie gave Liam those puppy dog looks almost every practice. I was appalled at the image of the two of them together; it made me feel sick to my stomach. But why? I was tired of always feeling like this when someone mentioned Liam and some other girl. Meanwhile, the boys were finishing up their drills and the girls lined up to jump into the pool. I stood on the concrete, above the pool, in Liam's lane. I could make out his back muscles contracting as he finished with the free. I found myself not being able to break eye contact with his body. Was I just like those other girls? Did I think that Liam only had eyes for me and no one else? Obviously, several other girls felt the same way. Well at least one, and she'd been left heartbroken.

Trying to block out the shocking information, I focused on the water in front of me. Just me and the pool, me and the pool. It seemed as if all the noise left the room as Liam's hand touched the edge. I jumped in and swam like a beast. I had never completed a set of drills like that before. I was angry, but I didn't want this news to hinder my ability to swim. The chlorine seeped into my skin and quelled my anger. Then, my mind ran through another set of emotions. I was annoyed and jealous that Liam would pick Lacie, of all people, to fool around with. Also, why hadn't he told me?

When Coach blew the whistle to signal the end of practice, I saw the clock read nine p.m. I took my time getting to the showers as others hustled to go study. Choosing to leave my wet hair down, I exited the locker room to find Liam waiting for me on the bench by the front doors. I averted his gaze as he stood up, and we walked silently to my dorm. The silence only made me grow more and more upset, and I wasn't sure why.

About ten minutes later we reached the front of my dorm, and I told him I'd see him later tomorrow. Tomorrow, being the day before Thanksgiving, was going to be busy as soon as I stepped foot in my front door. I definitely needed the rest. Before hearing his response, I retreated through the doors and up the stairs. *Why do you close yourself off like that?* I questioned myself and my poor attitude for the rest of the night.

When I awoke the next morning, my body felt sore from yesterday's practice. I hurried to shower and got ready before making my way to the coffee shop. Just as I tied my tennis shoes, Bonnie asked to join.

"So, how is this weekend going to work?" she asked me as we walked out the building.

"Well, you already know William said we'd talk when I got home," I said rolling my eyes. "I want to be the one to end things though, and I'm afraid he'll beat me to the punch. But I definitely don't want Liam to find out before I do anything, you know?" I was thinking out loud. My mind raced with what I needed to do. Why was I feeling so uncertain about my decision?

"I understand I guess," she nodded along and thought to herself for a moment. "Wouldn't it help to just be honest with Liam? I think you feel so uncertain because you don't know what this will mean for you two," she said reading my mind.

"You're right." I felt unsure and questioned everything. If Liam chose to do things with Lacie, did he even have feelings for me? Why would he choose me at the end of the day?

"Nothing will feel like the right thing Caelyn," she said. "The only right thing is to break up with this no-good, slimy boyfriend!"

"You're right, as always," I chuckled at my best friend. We walked into the coffee shop and placed our orders. My mind was spinning with what-if scenarios, and I started to feel dizzy. I think Bonnie saw my inner turmoil and she broke me out of my spell.

"I think Travis is coming to visit me over Thanksgiving break," she blurted out. For a moment, I thought I heard her incorrectly.

"What!" I exclaimed.

"Don't make a big deal out of it, please. We were just talking about our plans and I sort of invited him. I don't know why it came out of my mouth, but it did," she rambled. "Do you think I made the wrong decision?"

"Hell no! Bonnie this is great news, of course it is!" I looked at her excitedly and her cheeks blushed. It was refreshing to see her like this.

"I hope so," she said quietly.

"I am so happy for you Bonnie," I grabbed her hand across the table and gave it a little squeeze.

"Who knows, maybe we will both have some exciting news to share after break," she said, alluding to the unknown with a wink.

"Bonnie!" I swatted her hand and we laughed right there in the shop. Several bystanders stared at our loud outburst, but I didn't care. I soaked in this moment with my roommate and best friend, and reflected on how lucky I was to have found someone so special and kind.

Around three p.m., my phone buzzed with a text from Liam. I ran over to Bonnie, who sat on our couch, and gave her a huge hug. I wished her a good Thanksgiving break, shared a meaningful glance, and was on my way. Meanwhile, Liam was downstairs waiting in his truck as I walked outside. As soon as he saw me he was out of the truck to help me put my bag in the back. I tried to smile at him, but I knew it didn't reach my eyes. I had done a lot of thinking these past couple of days, and I couldn't be more prepared for this break. I just wanted to go home, break up with William, see my family, sleep in my bed, and eat a shit ton of food tomorrow. Oh, and don't forget about the swim contest.

Remember the swim contest that happens the night before Thanksgiving? I'd dreamed of participating since I heard Liam talk about it last year. I wanted to show everyone what I was capable of, but I was still nervous. I hadn't been in the ocean for four years. It had been four years since my check out dive, the crash, and the day my life turned upside down. With those nerves and those of my parents and Liam, I was scared I would be talked out of my decision. I promised myself I would do this. Why else would I have spent so much time in the pool these past few weeks? I was training to become stronger and faster, both mentally and physically. This wasn't just for me, it was for David and Liam. I had so much to prove.

My phone dinged, bringing me back to the present with a text from William. I slid the phone open and read his text, *Want to hang tonight? I feel like we should talk.* I rolled my eyes and typed a response after checking the GPS, *I get home in an hour and I think my parents have plans tonight.* His response was quick, *I'll come over then.*

"Everything alright?" Liam asked looking over at my phone in my hands. He kept checking my hands, my face, then the road. He did this until I answered. I put on my best lying voice and said what I wanted him to know. I guess in that split-second I chose to keep my decision from him, against Bonnie's recommendation.

"William texted me and we're going to hang out tonight." I glanced at Liam and his jaw tightened. I wanted to drive the lie home so I added, "Finally, right? I missed him so much." I knew as soon as I said those words, Liam would be devastated. I hated lying to Liam because he didn't deserve my dishonesty. With one more look at him, I knew I'd upset him to the core. I could read his body language like my own, and I knew he was trying to hold it together.

Of course, I didn't miss William at all. Actually, I was quite done with him and couldn't wait to be done with the relationship. However, some small part of me, and I mean small, had this idea that seeing him would scare me out of doing the right thing. I was afraid he would manipulate me into thinking I was in the wrong and that he did nothing to jeopardize our relationship. *Stay strong Caelyn, you know he did this to you,* I had to remind myself. I think my response was more about convincing Liam that nothing was wrong.

"Oh good," he said slowly. I saw his knuckles turn white on the steering wheel. He quickly unclenched them and cleared his throat. "Have fun C. I guess I'll see you tomorrow morning then? For Thanksgiving?" He tried to switch the topic of conversation.

"Yep. I just invited William to come too," I smiled tight lipped, and Liam's face was expressionless. I felt guilty for rubbing that in, but knew the only reason why I asked was to keep up this façade. Just then, I got a text back from William, *Adrian already invited me, but I'm there. Will you be dressing like a pilgrim or an Indian? ;)* I had to hold back the vomit rising in my throat. What had I just done? Also, why did Adrian invite my boyfriend to Thanksgiving?

Fourteen

Liam

The clock read 7:43 p.m. on the bedside table as I laid on my bed. I had just over two hours to be at the beach for the annual swim contest. I was anxious, yet very excited, to see some of my old class-mates who would also be racing. My parents were still downstairs in the family room with the Prices, and I wasn't sure what time they would be leaving. This competition was no secret to the adults here in Cape Elizabeth, but that didn't mean they approved. I was afraid my parents would stop me as soon as my feet hit the hardwood at the foot of the stairs. I laid on my back, staring at my ceiling, con-templating if it was worth going or if I should just stay home.

Thanksgiving break always began with this huge swim contest at one of the secluded beaches here in town. All college kids from the Cape were invited to partake in the competition, however not everyone did it, afraid of the frigid water temperature. The rules were simple:

1. no wetsuit or additional clothing besides your swimsuit,

2. one person would sit in a lifeguard stand on the beach (to oversee the races),

3. each grade would have their own heat to determine winners for the final race,

4. the final race comprised of all winners—one freshman, sophomore, junior, and senior,

5. and failure to complete the race meant disqualification.

At the start of each race, the official would call into a megaphone to have the swimmers line up along the water's edge. They would then count down from five. After counting down, they would blow their whistle. Then the race was off and it was every person for themselves.

I thought back to last year, afraid of getting hurt again or even failing and becoming a laughing stock among my old classmates. I knew my chances of getting hurt were slim because that didn't happen often. My injury last year was a fluke. I was confident I would be one of the better swimmers competing this year. Ultimately, I realized that if I backed out now, I'd still become a laughing stock so I got up to get ready. If David were here, he would've called me the biggest chicken-shit, and I would've agreed with him.

Thinking about him made me recall a fond memory. It was the beginning of my sophomore year and David and Caelyn's freshman year, two months before his death. The three of us stood in front of the lighthouse in the middle of a run. Caelyn walked over to look at the water's edge while David and I grabbed our knees to steady our breathing. We had just started running regularly, and I was not in the best shape.

"How is she not dying?" I asked between labored breaths.

"She's been waking up every morning to run this exact route for weeks now," David replied matter-of-factly. How did I not know this? I looked over at Caelyn who still stood with her back towards the two of us. "She's trying to get in shape apparently. She says she likes it," he started to stand up, "and I believe her. I know she's trying to improve her breathing so she doesn't suck up all the air in her dive tank. You know?" I nodded my head. They had been telling me the challenges of breathing on a tank rather than breathing normally. "She's also taken an interest in maybe joining track in the spring. Keith Gil has been trying to persuade her. If you ask me, his persuasion is a little friendlier than normal. She's told me not to worry because she's not doing this for him." He rolled his eyes, looking over at his sister, "I don't know man. She's trying to find out what she likes and dislikes I guess." He looked at me with a straight face, but returned his look to C.

I stayed silent for a while as David and I stared over at Caelyn. I was learning quite a few new facts about her.

"You don't think we're losing her, right?" I asked somberly.

"No, she loves us. She knows this is our little pack Liam." Just then Caelyn turned around and smiled at the two of us. She made her way over to the bench. "C's just being a girl."

"I'm sorry, I'm being a what?" Caelyn looked shocked at David's comment.

"A girl, sis, a girl. That is what you are, correct?" David said, being a smart ass. She glared at him for several seconds.

"I'm sorry but this girl can't hear over how pathetic you two are. I literally heard that whole conversation David. You might want to learn how to speak quieter bub," she smiled and sat in the middle of the bench. We followed suit and sat on either side of her. "Besides, this girl is a much better runner than the both of you combined." She punched our arms playfully.

"I'm hurt C, you know I can't run very well," I complained.

"Tough luck Liam," she said, flashing a huge grin at me. I so badly wanted to make her stop the taunting.

"Okay Liam, how about this," David began, "you and I will now be joining Caelyn on these morning runs. That means at least three days a week." Caelyn shot him a bemused look. "Let's not go too crazy, am I right?" He smiled and laughed at himself. Little did he know I was planning on joining her on every run. I was afraid that if I didn't, I'd miss out on being around Caelyn so much, ever since she'd started hanging out with more girls her age and flaking on plans with us. What would happen if this Keith guy became her boyfriend? I immediately shoved the thought out of my mind, knowing that wouldn't happen. However, I did know one thing. I wanted to keep her to myself. Well, to myself and David.

"Do you think we will ever do those swim contests once we graduate?" Caelyn asked randomly. She was looking out past the lighthouse to the water. David and I exchanged a look before we answered.

"What makes you ask that?" I questioned.

"I heard one of the upperclassmen talk about it the other day. It kind of makes me nervous, but I was just wondering what you guys thought," she said but then added, "I mean if you guys do it, so will I."

"I mean it's like a rite of passage you know?" David said shrugging.

No one else said anything for a while. Each of us were thinking about the horror stories we had heard; Evelyn had told me, and Adrian refused to talk about it in front of her mom and dad. David put his arm around Caelyn, and she rested her head on his shoulder. Then she placed her hand on my leg and said, "I'm not going to leave you two anytime soon; I hope you know that."

Without another word, she stood up and started to run home.

I crept quietly down the stairs, but as soon as my feet hit the hardwood I was called into the kitchen. I knew it. I slowly walked into the other room to find my parents, Evelyn, and the Prices standing around the kitchen counter. I waited for the harassment.

"Do you want me to drive you?" Evelyn asked randomly. I blinked several times to make sure I understood her correctly. What?

"No, I think I'll be okay Ev," I said slowly. I looked around at the other faces, and everyone seemed to share the same somber look. I slowly started to turn around before I heard Beth speak up.

"Liam, I think Caelyn is going."

"What do you mean Caelyn is going? Going where?" I asked warily. I began to worry and my blood pressure spiked. Did she mean she was going to the swim contest? Steve seemed to answer my question.

"Liam, she hasn't been in the ocean since the day of the crash," he said, sounding worried.

"Why would she choose to go in the water now?" I asked incredulously. I ran a hand through my hair, no doubt messing it up more.

"I don't know, maybe she's trying to prove something," Steve said.

"Okay," I said slowly. "What makes you think she's going tonight?" I didn't quite understand them. If she hadn't gone in since, then what would make her do it now? And why was I the last one to find out?

"Liam, I know my daughter, and I know you know her too. This was something David always wanted to do."

I understood and nothing was left to say. She wanted to do this for David. It was plain and simple. Yet, I didn't like the fact that she was going and didn't tell me. What was going on earlier? We literally had two hours in the car and she said nothing. Nothing except the fact she was going to be spending the evening with William.

"Why didn't William try and talk her out of it? I thought they were together tonight." She told me they were hanging out, and

I was devastated. William was back in the picture, and I was out. Well, it wasn't like I was ever "in" the picture, but I still liked spending one-on-one time with Caelyn. I wanted that to be a regular thing, but now William had weaseled his way back into Caelyn's heart.

"He cancelled last minute. Liam, you know he wouldn't have even cared," Beth chimed in. "He doesn't care like you Liam. He wouldn't have thought twice if she said she was going. Hell, he might've offered to drive her."

I looked at Evelyn, who stood there waiting for my response. Thinking over her offer once more, I decided I didn't want to drive because I knew Caelyn would have driven her own car. I planned to get there and drive the both of us home. For the duration of the car ride, Evelyn and I sat in silence. I was too worried to talk to her. I didn't want Caelyn to do anything stupid. This whole contest was stupid enough and she didn't need to be a part of it. After the five-minute drive, we pulled into the parking lot and Evelyn reached over to grab my arm.

"Liam," that's all she said. I knew what she meant; she didn't have to say anything else. My sister and I had a connection all right, but it wasn't like your typical sibling relationship. When she said my name, she had a certain tone and look on her face. I knew what she wanted to say. I smiled at her and placed my hand over hers. Seconds later I was jumping out of the car to find Caelyn.

I sprinted down the beach to find it crowded with college students. When people recognized me, I heard whoops and hollers. Several guys stopped me to shake my hand and asked how our season was going. I'm sure I came off as distracted, since I broke away and gave them the best excuse I could think of in the moment. My eyes squinted in the dim light looking for any sign of her. Then, I found her. She was unmistakable. I sighed in relief and approached her. The closer I got, I noticed she was wearing her red, one-piece swimsuit. She smiled at the sight of me, clearly off guard. Then she saw my face and how unhappy I looked. The smile faded and she clung to her sides.

"Liam, don't," she warned me.

"Don't what?" I said a little too loudly. A few people looked over at us. She let go of her sides and reached up to cover my mouth. The gesture was pretty intimate considering we were just friends. I didn't think she realized what she did until I flicked my eyes down to her hand on my mouth. She dropped it as quickly as she covered it.

"Don't cause a scene," she seethed through gritted teeth. She smiled and looked around to those staring.

"This is not causing a scene, but I can if you want me to," I warned, not letting my eyes drop from hers. She had an uneasy look about her.

"Please stop, you can't change my mind. I'm doing this," she told me and walked over to the water. The rest of the freshmen were lining up too.

"But you haven't gotten in since that day C," I begged her.

"So?" she snarled back.

"What do you mean 'so'? What if you have a panic attack? What if you freeze? What if you get hurt?" I rambled, trying to reason with her. I didn't like the idea of her getting into that water.

"Liam, don't worry about me. I'll be fine." She looked out at the water and then looked me directly in the eyes. "I have to do this."

"Why? What could you possibly need to prove?" I asked exasperated. Her eyes bore into mine. I could see her internal struggle, but there was strength within the apprehension.

"I have to do it for David." The words stung more than the cold water at my feet. I stared into her sea green eyes as they welled up with tears. The official told the swimmers to take their mark and Caelyn turned to face the water. I didn't want to watch her, so I turned away from the shore and looked back among the people conversing. The whistle blew and everyone erupted into cheers. My eyes stung with tears of my own as my head spun. Cheers for Caelyn grounded me, and I dared a look at the water. The waves were mostly calm and the moon shone bright overhead. The whole scene looked a little too ominous.

I couldn't help but join the cheers for Caelyn as I believed she took the lead. As I screamed her name I saw my own breath cloud in front of me. It was hard to make out who was who, but no one was quite as good as she was. Some swimmers had started their journey back to shore, and I saw a red swimsuit take the lead in the dark water. I let out a breath I didn't know I had been holding and waited for her to reach the shore. The frigid air bit at my skin and my worry for her safety increased.

Finally, after what seemed like eons, Caelyn emerged from the water, her face blueish. She shook uncontrollably and rid her face of the salt water. The official screamed, "Price advances to the finals!" and the whole crowd cheered. I ran over to her and hugged her tight. She hugged me back immediately but continued to tremble in my grasp. Our previous conversation had been dropped. I didn't worry about why I was upset. I just needed to hold her in my arms. Nothing happened and she was safe. My whole body warmed as I touched her.

"Oh. My. Gosh. No one tells you how cold it is Liam," she spoke through her shivers. I heard her teeth chatter over my laughter. With that, I gripped her tighter and ran my hands along her arms to warm her up. I let go for a second to look at her better, and her face was still blue. "I'm fine. I'm fine. I just need a towel and my sweatshirt."

Without another word, I took off my own and helped her put it on. I then handed her my own towel and continued to rub my hands along her arms to warm her up. She smiled up at me with a chattering jaw.

"Don't do that to me again, C." I took both hands and placed them on either side of her face and pulled her to me. I kissed her forehead and kept my lips on her skin longer than I should've, but I couldn't help it. She sighed into me and wrapped her hands, still holding the towel, around my waist. I wanted to stay like this forever, but the official called out my grade. I looked down at her and regretted letting her go. I didn't want to leave.

"Go win for me," she said with a full grin. The uneasy feeling in my gut spiked thinking about her racing again.

My grade was much bigger than the freshmen and there was a little more competition ahead of me. But she told me to go win, so that's what I was going to do. There was no way she would swim again without me by her side. The whistle blew into the cold air, and I broke into a sprint. When the water was about waist high I broke into a freestyle to swim to the buoy. The water was absolutely freezing and felt like shards of glass against my skin. I gasped for air and felt the cold air enter my lungs.

I got close to the buoy which meant I was halfway done. I disregarded the other contestants because I had to win. There was no other option. I pushed harder towards the buoy and touched it with my left hand before turning around and going back to the beach. This direction was much easier because we weren't fighting against the waves. However, the wind chill was worse on the way back. I pushed harder and harder, kicking my legs as hard as I could. It was like I was competing against Tony Wilson for the first spot on BU's swim team. It had to be mine, just like this spot into the finals had to be too.

The water became shallow enough for me to stand up so I dug my feet into the sand and ran out of the water. My bare chest hit the cold breeze, instantly shocking my system. The shock was almost enough to slow me down, but I couldn't lose my spot in the finals. The water was now about to my knees, and I continued to run until every extremity was out of the water. The water rolled off my body as I stood trying to focus in on the crowd. Before my eyes could fully focus, something slammed into my body. I had to catch myself and them before we toppled over. Caelyn's red suit came into focus as well as her ratty brown hair. Besides, I knew what her touch felt like by now. No one else quite made me feel the electricity and warmth like she did.

"Carter advances to the finals!" I heard through the cheers. My eyes adjusted and Caelyn wrapped the towel around my shoulders.

"C, C," I tried to stop her frantic movements. She looked up and her sea green eyes focused on me. In that moment, she was beyond beautiful. "I'm fine. Sure, that water is a bitch, but I'm fine," I laughed and saw her own expression lighten. I dared to take a risk, "Besides, your hug warmed my whole body just now."

She tucked some hair behind her ear, and I saw the faintest blush rise to her cheeks.

I grabbed the towel from Caelyn and dried off as the next race started. She had regained some of her color, but continued to chatter her teeth. I tried not to touch her because a lot of eyes were on us. It was normal for the finalists to receive a lot of attention as the other finalists were determined. As soon as we won our respective divisions, the crowd's whispering commenced. To be honest, I was a shoo-in but Caelyn must have stumped a few competitors. I tried to block out the comments because I knew people were talking about David.

A female junior and male senior won their events and were set to race Caelyn and I in the final round in a matter of minutes. The crowd was loud with chatter as they predicted the winner of the last race. Caelyn and I stood side by side, barely touching. It helped keep at least one side of me warm.

"If you need to stop, stop and I will stop with you," I told her looking out to the water, avoiding eye contact.

"I'm not stopping and you're not either."

That's all she said before she ripped off my towel and sweatshirt she was using. The official's voice rang through the air, telling us to take our places. The four finalists complied.

The next few minutes went by incredibly slowly. Maybe it was because of the frigid water or that I couldn't see Caelyn, but time seemed to last forever. I felt every single inch of water touch my skin as I glided through it to the buoy. I could feel my muscles cramp up on me on the last leg to the beach and knew I wasn't going to win. *To hell with winning*, I thought. I just wanted to make sure that I was here for Caelyn if she needed me. I thought I was able to make out her red suit next to me as I swam to the buoy, but I had lost track of her on the way back. Terrified that something had happened, I paused and looked for her. My heart felt like it had stopped, but then I saw her on the beach ahead of me.

Caelyn won, which was no surprise. She finished seconds before me and our opponents and was on the beach before I could stand. The crowds surrounded and congratulated her on a successful race. Then, the official handed her an envelope full of money from this year's betting pool. Her smile spread across her face as she thanked everyone. She was living for this moment, and I couldn't have been prouder. David would've been so happy to see her win.

The crowds dwindled, and I was cleared to approach the winner herself. I made my way over to Caelyn who was finishing up talking to some girls I recognized from high school. She said her goodbyes and faced me. She was wearing my sweatshirt and had switched towels. The tension returned from earlier.

Saying nothing, I reached down to grab her bag and walked towards her car. I figured I should drive since it was almost one-thirty a.m. and she must've been exhausted. I unlocked the doors and slid in, turning on the car. Our breaths were hard and clearly visible in the cold cabin of the car. I blasted the heat, but it was taking forever. I looked over at Caelyn and without thinking, grabbed her hands. I brought them between us and breathed hot air onto them. She nervously laughed through her chattering teeth. I slowed down my breathing on our clasped hands and listened for something. Anything. All I could hear were the air vents producing heat.

Caelyn closed the gap and leaned forward, resting her forehead against mine. I stopped blowing on our hands and sucked in a surprised breath. I closed my eyes and relished the moment. Briefly opening my own eyes, I saw that hers were closed and her lips were slightly parted. I leaned in ever so slightly and felt her breath on my lips. She must've sensed how close I was to her and moved towards me. It was slight, but I saw it. I inched forward and she followed suit; it was like a game of cat and mouse. One would move in while the other moved back a little and then vice versa. It was killing me, and I so badly wanted to close the gap, but I couldn't. Some small part of me didn't feel right.

"We need to get home. We have a big day tomorrow," I said slowly. The intensity of the moment left me breathless and we hadn't even done anything. She nodded her head and bit her lip. I put the car in drive and neither of us broke the silence. When I put the car in park, she opened the door, turned towards me as if she wanted to say something, and closed her mouth. She slammed the door and ran up her driveway. Feeling defeated, I left the keys in the cup holder and watched the door shut behind her.

Fifteen

Caelyn

I'd been up tossing and turning for the past hour, the clock reading 4:30 a.m., just two and a half hours since I laid my head down. Although my body was physically exhausted from the competition, I couldn't sleep. I was too busy thinking about what had just happened with Liam. We were close to kissing and yet we didn't. I didn't kiss him even though I wanted to. I knew this meant my feelings for him were one hundred percent confirmed, but that didn't solve the problem I still faced. William and I didn't get the chance to talk yesterday so I didn't break up with him. That meant today was the day. I was going to break up with him when he got here for Thanksgiving dinner.

I knew what I was doing was wrong. The stolen glances and touches were unfair, and I was no better than William right now. Although he was in the wrong for neglecting our relationship, at least he wasn't being dishonest with me. I, on the other hand, was emotionally and physically cheating on him and hated myself for giving in to my feelings for Liam. Part of me was upset with Liam for putting me in this position but knew it was my fault. As sick as I felt about myself and my actions, I finally knew what I needed.

I got out of bed and paced the area of my room, thinking back on these past few months. I remembered the way Liam looked at me at the first party he took me to, how excited he was when we were picked for the relay, how hurt he was when I hurt, and how much he cared for me even if I treated him terribly. Then, I remembered how much I put him through with William. How I hurt him when I repeatedly sided with William in every argument. How had I been so blind? Liam was what I needed and he had been right in front of me this whole time. I laid down on my bed, overwhelmed by my feelings for Liam. I opened my heart to the possibility of everything working out, but stopped short when a thrilling question entered my thoughts: *should I confess my feelings to Liam?* Again, that knot in the pit in my stomach grew and thoughts of the unknown clouded my judgment. Would I ruin our friendship if I voiced my feelings? What would this mean? How would everyone take it? Was I allowed to be feeling this way when I was technically in a relationship?

After running through the list of questions in my head, I knew one thing was certain. I had to break up with William today. Once I did that, I would work through my feelings for Liam and figure out how to tell him. The clock now read 5:15 a.m., and I accepted that I wouldn't be going to sleep anytime soon. I pushed the covers of my queen bed off and sat on the edge. As I ran through my schedule for the day, I contemplated going for a run. I knew it would really help clear my head before the big conversation.

I walked into the hallway and went into the bathroom to get ready. I threw my hair into a pony tail after I brushed my teeth. Before grabbing my running clothes, I heard my phone buzz. It was

5:30 a.m., who could possibly be up? Liam's name lit up on the screen with the message, *Can't sleep... You up?*

A grin spread across my face as I read the words. I responded, *Is that even a question anymore?*

A second later my phone buzzed again, *Wanna go on a run with me?*

My fingers responded before my brain caught up, *Was just about to go myself. Be ready in 5.* What was I doing?

Quickly I threw on leggings, a long sleeve t-shirt, one of David's old sweatshirts, thick socks, tennis shoes, and lastly ear warmers. I checked the temperature on my phone and it only called for a high of 27 degrees today. I shivered at the thought of walking into that cold again. Looks like it'll be another freezing Thanksgiving for Cape Elizabeth, no surprise there. I ran down the stairs quietly and unlocked the front door. I didn't bother leaving a note because I knew I would be back before the rest of the house woke up. I opened the door and the cold Maine air wrapped around my whole body. I immediately felt my muscles grow stiff. I quickly shut the door and jogged to the end of the driveway. I kept my feet moving until I saw Liam's front porch light flicker. Moments later he emerged, bundled up in sweatpants, a sweatshirt, and hat.

"Hey, you." His voice sounded husky and clouds formed in front of his mouth. He pulled his right leg up to stretch and then did the same to the left. It was just hours ago that we were almost kissing. He was avoiding eye contact, but I kept my gaze on him.

"Morning," I squeaked. I bent over and reached for my toes, feeling the stretch up the length of my legs and back. "You ready? I'm freezing," I admitted, my teeth chattering. I wished he would talk more or at least give me a hug. I saw an internal struggle in him when I said I was freezing. Maybe just maybe, he would wrap me up in his arms once again. I craved that touch from him and wondered if he did too. Was he only being nice last night? Did he truly feel the same things I did? Again, more questions clouded my thoughts. Without answering, he started in an easy pace toward town.

The Cape will always hold a special place in my heart for many reasons. One, my best friend in the entire world lived a few feet away from me and two, we lived a few blocks from the center of town. I filled my lungs with the calming smell of salt water and fresh, cold air. It kept me energized as Liam and I continued our run past the lighthouse and back through town. The questions flooded my mind again, and I focused on the pitter patter of our feet as they connected with the cement sidewalks. When I exhausted that option, I focused on our breathing. I could tell his had started to grow a little shallow, and I heard mine do the same.

We made another loop, this time taking a brief stop at the lighthouse. We came to a stop, and I bent over and placed my hands on my knees. Though I didn't normally struggle with my breathing, it was so cold and my body had not recovered from last night's race. I breathed deeply, in and out, until my breathing evened out. Liam's eyes searched the lighthouse, the ocean, and then me. "So, why couldn't you sleep?" he asked first.

"My brain was going a mile a minute. I couldn't stop the chatter, you know? Also, I'm feeling anxious for today," I admitted. It wasn't a lie, but it wasn't the whole truth either. I wasn't sure if I was ready to tell him about my decision with William because I was afraid I would share my feelings for him. I liked what we had going, but didn't want to sabotage it all by saying those three little but meaningful words. I needed to get past today. "I was seriously getting out of bed to go on a run anyway when you texted me."

"Then it's a good thing I couldn't sleep either," he smiled softly. I loved that smile so much that it erased all my nerves. Suddenly, I felt incredibly warm and knew my cheeks were showing their rosy tint. He started to walk over to where I was kneeling, and my heartbeat increased with every step. "I really need to talk to you about something," he started.

"About?" I responded. I hoped he would share his own feelings so I could tell him where I stood. Instead, his words left me dumbfounded.

"William is cheating on you." He blurted out the words, and I could tell he immediately regretted them.

I was taken aback by his statement, but the surprise was hidden on my face because I was still leaning over my knees. I felt something inside me break and my entire body shook as the tears fell from my eyes. Everything started to come full circle once those words were spoken aloud. The days without communication, the flighty attitude he'd had for weeks now, and the constant avoidance since I'd been home. He had been cheating on me. He had been cheating on me. I repeated Liam's words over and over in my head.

I started to shake as the sobs became all-consuming, and Liam caught hold of my waist. He pulled me to him, and I melted into his touch. I grabbed hold of his sweatshirt with my fists and cried into his chest. His left arm tightened his hold along my waist while his right hand rubbed my back. He cooed soothing words into my ear until I regained my composure.

"How do you know for sure?" I choked out in broken English. I didn't wait for him to answer. "I mean, how did I not piece this together? There have been so many signs, and I've been oblivious to them all." My mind was racing with the thoughts that kept me awake just hours ago. My next words flew out of my mouth before I could stop them, "It's a good thing I was already planning on breaking up with him today." I took in a sharp breath of the cold air; the briskness sent a shock through my body. I became frozen in thought. *This is a good thing Caelyn,* I told myself. I knew William wasn't the man for me. He was a coward, a snake, an ass. I deserved so much better, and it was a shame I waited until now to act.

"Wait," Liam stammered. "What do you mean you were planning on breaking up with him?" He kept his hands on my shoulders but kept me at arm's length. I'm not sure if I saw a look of relief or shock. But seeing those dark brown eyes staring so intently into my own, made me stop crying. The pads of his thumbs wiped the stray tears from my cheeks. I took another deep breath, and knew I was going to be okay.

"I've known for a long time that William and I have been over, but something in me held on to the relationship. I'm not sure why, but I did. This news, true or not, just solidified my plan. That's the real reason why I couldn't sleep. You know runs help me clear my head, Liam," I admitted to him. "Also, I've been feeling guilty with what happened between us. I've been unfair to William too."

I was starting to feel a little better now that I knew the truth. By better I mean with my decision, not with the fact that I was being cheated on. That news honestly made me feel terrible, but then I didn't know how I could be upset when I'd done something similar. I thought about who it could have been with or when it could have happened or how many times it happened. My mind was racing with questions, and I was sure I'd never get the whole explanation. I was digging myself into a deep hole the more I thought about the technicalities.

"Hey, don't cry," he pulled me to his chest once more. "He's not worth your tears C. Also, that was my fault, not yours. You have been fair, and I was the one to kiss you. Not the other way around." *That's not totally true,* I thought to myself.

It was awful to even consider what this meant for my relationship with Liam, when I was deeply hurt by William cheating on me. But just when I started to feel guilty about my feelings and actions,

Liam would look at me and all my cares would subside. He was the one that made me happy. He was the one who would never cheat on me; he'd be loyal. He was the one. I pulled away just a bit and before I could even get another word in Liam interrupted me. He looked a little upset.

"But hey, it's almost time we got back."

Oh, my gosh, what time was it? I checked my phone and the time read 6:26 a.m. Oh no, I told mom I would help her with the cooking at nine, and I promised Adrian I would help her clean the downstairs of the house before company got there.

"Crap!"

We ran in silence because we knew we'd make better time getting home. We slowed to a stop in the middle of the street that separated our houses. The street was quiet and a few lights had been turned on since we left. His porch was still lit on and a few lights downstairs were on too. I peered over to my own house and saw almost every light on. Even though I knew that I would be seeing Liam in just a few hours, I didn't want to leave him now.

"Thank you, Liam," I spoke softly as I grabbed his upper arm. "I know that this must've been so incredibly hard for you. Especially because you've been the one telling me that William wasn't right for me. I know that now, and I think deep down I always did. Sometimes it just takes a while to realize that something good is actually standing right in front of you." I let my hand trail down his arm and turned my back to him as I retreated into the house.

As I took the stairs two at a time, I heard my mom yell up the staircase, "Honey is that you? Where have you been?"

"Liam and I went for a run. I'm going to get a quick shower and then Adrian and I will start cleaning. Once I'm done I'll help you in the kitchen, okay?" I yelled from upstairs. My mom's petite figure stood at the bottom of the staircase. She looked beautiful in her green sweater with her hair framing her face.

"Alright Caelyn," she smiled, and I ran to the bathroom. "I'm glad you're home safe."

The cleaning went quickly as Adrian and I split up the work on the main level. I cleaned the family room while she did the study and the bathrooms. I vacuumed the hallway and stairs and then dusted the entry way. My mom had turned on the TV to play music throughout the house as we cleaned for today's guests. This was something I had always loved about Thanksgiving morning. The smell of the oven, the music playing faintly in the background, and my parents moving about the kitchen. Everything was going smoothly except for the fact that Adrian hardly said anything to me all morning. I wondered if she was just tired or maybe she had a bad headache. However, I was accustomed to this attitude since I was a child. I knew not to bother her or pry, and if she wanted to talk she would.

After my chores were done, I entered the kitchen and put on a spare apron. Mom and I fell into a routine as she prepared the cranberry salad and stuffing while I made the mac and cheese and mashed potatoes. Dad ran in and out of the door to the patio as he oversaw the cooking of the turkey. Adrian managed setting up the tables and we were almost ready for our guests.

As mom and I slid some of the dishes into the oven and fridge, the front door started to ring. "I'll go get it," I yelled as I walked to the front door. My grandparents stood on the stoop carrying my grandma's famous sugar cream and pecan pie. I immediately broke into a joyous grin at the sight of them; I had missed them terribly. "Grandma! Grandpa! I'm so happy to see you guys," I said, giving them both tight hugs.

"Caelyn, honey, you are growing to be such a beautiful young lady," my grandpa said hugging me back. The last time I had seen them was during the memorial service. Their cheerful and smiling faces were just what I needed this morning.

Across the street, I could see the Carters' front door opening. I saw Lisa and Paul, followed by Evelyn and Liam, walk down their sidewalk. I kept the front door open for them and greeted them as they stepped onto the walkway.

"Happy Thanksgiving, Carters," I said smiling. Lisa and Paul looked very festive in their matching outfits. Lisa wore a burnt orange sweater dress with tights and high brown boots. Paul wore an orange and cream plaid button down with a cream sweater over top.

"Caelyn, you look very beautiful today," Lisa smiled and gave me a big momma bear hug. "As always." Her features softened as she looked at me. A slight gold tint mixed with her dark brown eyes today, and it made her look much younger.

"Darling, please do not hover," Paul laughed at his wife and stepped up on the stoop to give me a hug as well. We chuckled in unison, and Paul and Lisa began to playfully argue as they continued down the hall towards the kitchen. Evelyn walked a few paces in front of her brother and smiled as she got closer. We exchanged a polite greeting as we hugged, and she disappeared to find my sister.

"You do look beautiful today, C," I could feel the blood rush to my cheeks at the compliment from Liam. I tucked a few stray hairs behind my ear and glanced at the ground. I had decided on wearing my dark green, long sleeve shift dress with a pair of black leggings and ankle boots. I decided to leave my hair down in loose curls because I knew Liam loved that. My makeup was simple, but more than I usually liked to wear.

"You don't look too bad yourself," I looked him over in a way that hopefully didn't show that I was checking him out. Liam had on a pair of dark wash jeans that fit him perfectly. To go with the jeans, he wore a slate gray sweater with a white undershirt and black dress shoes. And to top it all off, his hair was a little messy, just as I liked it.

He gave me a quick hug and when he let go, I had a feeling he was going to say something, but instead, he kissed me on the forehead. He grinned as we both walked through the doorway.

"You okay?" he asked when we walked towards the kitchen and dining room.

"Surprisingly yes, but I'm not sure I'll be able to say that for long. William is also coming to lunch today," I said hesitantly. Liam grabbed my hand briefly, and I felt the energy tingle through my whole palm. He squeezed once but let go before we entered the room. It was his way of showing me he was there for me.

As I visited with the Carters, the doorbell rang and I excused myself to answer it. I opened the door to see the one person I dreaded facing. There, in my doorway, stood my cheating, sleazy boyfriend, William. He smiled and sloppily kissed my cheek, "Dang you look hot." I let him in and closed the door behind him. Mentally, I wiped off his kiss from my cheek. He wore jeans and a button down with the cuffs of his shirt rolled up to expose his fair skin. His hair was short and orderly, but his face had about two or three days' worth of scruff. Seeing him now, I realized that I wasn't physically attracted to him anymore. I'm not sure if that's because of the news I heard or if I was mentally over the relationship.

"Thank you," I said with as little emotion as possible. My skin was crawling, and I found it hard to be around him with the information I knew. "Hey, do you wanna talk before we walk in there?" I asked, trying to get him out of my house.

He looked awkwardly around the foyer and motioned towards the kitchen with his free hand. "Am I late or something? How about we wait till after lunch to talk?"

"No, you're just on time. I just figured you'd want to talk now, since I haven't seen you in a while," I said curtly. He stared back at me, expressionless. Knowing he wasn't going anywhere, I accepted his presence for a few hours. "We're about to say prayer," I said, forcing a smile.

"Great, I brought wine." He took my hand and led me to my kitchen, as if I didn't already know where I was going. Something felt all wrong, but I apparently had to keep up with appearances until after lunch. William and I had some great memories and after all, it was Thanksgiving. I mentally agreed to play nice for the time being. I plastered on the fakest smile I could muster and faced the music.

"Look who made it," I announced and William was greeted by my family and the Carters. I walked with William around the room as he shook my grandpa's hand and hugged my grandma. They welcomed him warmly and asked how he was liking the internship with my father and Adrian.

"It's been amazing so far. I'm very lucky to have this opportunity, and I have this one to thank," he said, grabbing my waist and kissing my cheek. I smiled back and acted like I knew what he was talking about. We had never actually talked about the internship because William claimed I wouldn't be interested. "Adrian and I are working together. She's not as wicked as Caelyn's stories made her out to be. She's a hard worker, and I appreciate having another person around when the work gets to be long and late." I dozed off and saw Liam talking with my mom and dad. We made eye contact across the room, but only briefly. I looked around again and saw Adrian staring at me. Her expression was unreadable.

"Can I have everyone's attention?" My father's voice rang loud in the room. "We are going to say grace and then dig in to this amazing meal." He met my mother's eyes on that last part. "If you would all please join hands," William grabbed my left hand as Liam grabbed my other. They exchanged a brief and tense look, before my dad said prayer. I closed my eyes and bowed my head. "Dear heavenly Father,

I would like to take this time to thank you for all you have provided us this year. We are so very thankful for the company of these great friends, parents, and children. Thank you for allowing us to come together on this beautiful day. Although we are missing one son, we know he is sitting with you at your table today. We would also like to thank you for keeping everyone healthy, and we ask you to keep everyone safe with the coming storms. Bless this food to the nourishment of our bodies. In Your name we pray, Amen."

"Amen," I said along with everyone else in the room.

Guests and family filled their plates and stomachs with all the traditional Thanksgiving fare. This year we added an extra leaf to the dining room table which allowed everyone to fit in the same room. William and Liam sat on either side of me, Adrian and Evelyn sat to the left of William, and the adults filled the other empty chairs. To my surprise, conversation flowed perfectly among the mix of people. Grandpa asked Liam and I about swim while Mom asked Adrian and William about their internship. They both seemed content with the experience, and my dad beamed with the compliments they paid him.

I had never seen Adrian and William interact the way they were at lunch. Pushing aside my thoughts and feelings for William, I was happy Adrian had branched out. It was nice to see her smile and laugh along with the conversation. A few times I saw Adrian touch William's arm and my stomach tightened at the sight. I shrugged off the feeling because it had to be an innocent touch; Adrian was not a flirtatious person. Then, the conversation switched to Evelyn, and she talked about how the move home improved her career opportunities. It was the Carters' turn to beam about the accomplishments of their children. Everything seemed to be going smoothly as the main course came to an end.

By the time the pies were sliced and Cool Whip was scooped, the dessert plates were licked clean. The adults began talking politics, as they always did, and the young adults listened to the friendly banter. It was comedic sitting and listening to my grandparents try and prove my dad wrong. The whole table laughed along with the conversation, and I leaned forward to place my head on my hand, taking in my surroundings. Liam's hand went to rub my back like it was the most normal thing in the world, but I immediately straightened up to see if anyone noticed. William, engaged in an argument about immigration with my father and Paul, saw nothing. Evelyn and Adrian were arguing with my grandma, so their eyes were focused elsewhere. However, my mom and Lisa made eye contact, and Liam and I knew we'd been caught. His hand dropped almost instantly, leaving his cheeks red.

"Okay, okay," my mother and Lisa interrupted. "It's time to start on some dishes, it's five already. Liam and Caelyn, it's your year to help with dishes, and Evelyn and Adrian, you have dining room cleanup."

We excused ourselves from the table, and William asked if he could do anything to help. Without hesitation, my mother waved her hand and said he was a guest. All I could think was, *that lucky bastard.* I heard my grandpa ask if the men wanted to play a round of Euchre while the rest of us cleaned up. I was appalled that William could charm my family and lie so easily. How was he so good at lying and faking?

I walked into the kitchen with a handful of dirty plates, and Liam helped me load them into the dishwasher. After the plates and silverware were loaded, we began hand washing the bigger pots, pans, and trays. I had offered to wash and told Liam to dry so that we'd been done sooner. Midway through the dishes the music from the family room got louder and it was hard to hold back my own dancing and singing. It was now appropriate to play Christmas music until December 25. Liam and I spent the remainder of the time washing and putting away dishes as we danced and screamed the lyrics to our favorite Christmas songs. It had been a long time since I was home and had this much fun. Liam had a big hand in making that possible.

My happiness was interrupted when William walked into the kitchen. Liam and I were mid-laugh, on the ground, with tears streaming down our faces. At some point, Liam had accidentally slipped on the mat in front the kitchen sink. It took a tiny rug to wipe out a stocky man in what seemed like a split second. We both laid on the ground, unable to control our laughter. William cleared his throat, "We're going to play a round of cards, are you guys going to join?" I could hear the snippy tone, but I didn't want to ruin this night just yet. I reached out my hand and William helped me stand up. His hand went to a possessive position at the small of my back as he led me into the family room. "I don't like how you're acting today. It's as if I'm not even here," he whispered into my ear harshly.

"Welcome to the past few months of this relationship," I fired back. William seemed unfazed as he took his spot at the table. He immediately went to ask Adrian to be his partner, so I went to Liam. Two can play at this game, bud.

After several rounds of Kemps, Euchre, Golf, and even a small game of Blackjack, it was already eight p.m. The men had retreated to the family room, drinking beers and watching sports replays. This had been one of the best days I had had in a long time, despite William being here. I loved being with my family and the Carters. It reminded me of old times, and a memory came rushing back.

I remembered, as if it was yesterday, the Christmas before David died. I was sick with the flu, and tried everything to get better. I'd visited the doctor, tried several medications, and had been subjected to bed rest for at least a week. It was tradition that every Christmas

Eve my family and the Carters attended church at three-thirty and came back to eat Christmas Eve dinner at our house. The smell of the delicious food was repulsive to me, and I was up every so often to puke while everyone left for church. Just as I finally dozed off, there was a faint knock at my door.

"Come in," I said hoarsely. My brother stood at the door with a wooden tray and Liam followed, closing the door behind him. I perked up a little at the sight of them, but immediately felt sick. I willed the vomit to stay down this time, and it surprisingly complied. David set a tray of green apple slices, saltine crackers, and a cup of Sprite on my lap. This was my brother, the caring, nurturing type. Liam kept his hands hidden behind his back but smiled a wicked grin, as if he knew something that I didn't.

"What are you hiding?" I asked. In his hands, he held all the Harry Potter movies. I smiled weakly at my two best friends as they put the first movie in the DVD player.

I half expected them to leave once they put it in, but instead, they stayed and took care of me. Every so often Liam and David took turns refilling my glass and wetting a cold rag for my forehead. Neither of them complained or used that moment of weakness against me since. That night, I fell asleep to the soft hum of Christmas music playing downstairs.

As the guys sat in the family room, I tried to focus on the conversation with the ladies in the dining room. I found myself distracted with questions, fears, and uncertainties. Considering the atmosphere, I went to find Liam so I could talk through my thoughts before I acted irrationally. I sat next to Liam's legs on the floor as he sat on the couch. First, I knew it would irritate William and would cause him to a) leave the room, or b) make a comment for me to move. I was hoping for the first option, and I was right on the money. He rolled his eyes, stood up, and went into the kitchen.

"Hey, I need to talk to you," I poked Liam's knee and his eyes focused on me. "I need to talk with you-know-who, right now. He's been the biggest P-R-I-C-K all day, and I can't hold up this façade anymore."

Liam laughed. "Okay. What do you need to talk to me about? It sounds like you've already made up your mind."

"I have, but I wanted to know if you would stand at the doorway of the kitchen when I go in there to confront him. I just want to know someone has my back if he tries anything at all. I know it's Thanksgiving and everyone is here so it might embarrass him. Or, who knows, maybe he'll spin it back on me and cause a bigger scene. But I can't do this relationship anymore, Liam." I leaned my head back in defeat. I closed my eyes tightly, counted to five, and then opened them. Liam looked at me with sincerity in his eyes.

"C, do you even have to ask? I will always be here for you." He brushed some stray hairs away from my forehead. The touch was gentle and subtle, but it sent warmth through my whole body. I took a deep breath and stood up. Liam walked with me to the doorway of the kitchen and briefly stopped right before the frame. He grabbed my hand, "Just say the word, and I'll be right where you need me." He smiled softly and squeezed my hand for comfort. *Here goes nothing.*

I walked through the doorway maintaining a calm composure, wanting to leave things civilly. Instead, I stopped in my tracks about to raise hell with the sight in front of me. I made no sound as I saw Adrian and William in a close embrace. His hands were running up and down her back while hers grasped his shirt as their lips parted to deepen their kiss.

"Liam," I choked, and he was beside me in a flash. The two of them split apart, breathing hard. I stood dumbfounded as my brain played catch up, trying to form whatever words it could. It all made sense: the small, stolen touches today at the table, the easiness of their relationship, their closer bond. My own sister was the girl that William was cheating on me with.

"Caelyn, it's not what you think it is," Adrian said, trying to defuse the situation. Again, I stood speechless. I was replaying the scene repeatedly in my head and growing more and more angry. Yet, it was somewhat humorous too.

I laughed mirthlessly. "What is it Adrian? What the hell is it? Because I'm pretty sure I just saw you two making out. My own boyfriend and sister!"

She moved her lips and nothing came out. I looked at William and he was no better. Liam sifted his weight from one foot to the other, obviously uncomfortable with the situation. *Yeah, me too Liam; you and me both.*

"What the hell is it, Adrian?" I raised my voice a little more. Her eyes uneasily shifted from me to William until he spoke.

"Look Caelyn, I don't think either of us intended for this to hap-pen—"

"I didn't ask you, asshole," I interrupted.

"Caelyn I love him. We're in love," Adrian blurted out. I didn't think anything would shock me more, but here I was, blown away for a second time. *They were in love now?* I stared in complete dis-belief. Then, I heard footsteps approach from behind me, and my mom and Lisa entered the room to join the debacle.

"Love? You love him? We are talking about my boyfriend, William, right?" I grimaced as I said his name. I felt sick.

"Yes, and I love her," William grabbed hold of her hand and ac-tual vomit rose in the back of my throat.

I laughed again at how funny and uncomfortable the situation was. The two of them stood, hand in hand in front of us, defending their actions. Anger flowed through my veins, and I'm sure smoke appeared out of my ears. What sister decides to fall in love with her sister's boyfriend? I had no words for her and that seemed to be the common theme throughout the room. Lisa and my mom were almost as shocked as Liam and I were, and they only heard the last part of this conversation. The more I thought about the situation, the more I saw it as a huge mess. A damn big mess. Before I processed the severity of the situation, another bomb dropped.

"And I'm pregnant."

The vomit came before I could stop it, and I barely made it to the sink in time.

"Pregnant?" my mom yelled. *My thoughts exactly Mom,* I thought between hurls.

The room broke into absolute chaos as Adrian tried to defend her actions to our mother. William stood quietly next to her as my mother tore into her. Next to my mother stood an uncomfortable Lisa whose eyes showed utter shock. I, on the other hand, was still vomiting in the kitchen sink. The vomit was a reaction to the news and resulted from me working myself up all day. I couldn't help but notice a fuming Liam as I tried to clean myself up too.

"William we're done, it's over, I never want to see you again," I said, trying to regain my composure from being slumped over the sink. *Good one Caelyn, hand it to him, there you go,* I said.

"Caelyn, I'm so sorry." He tried to walk over to me but Liam intercepted him. He grabbed ahold of his shoulder and turned him around in one quick motion. His olive-toned fist, once clenched at his side, connected with William's cowardly face. There were multiple shrieks in the room, but none was louder than my own. William came back at Liam and punched him right in the gut.

"Stop, both of you, stop it!" I screamed over their grunts and punches. The two broke apart when I pushed myself in between them. William's face had already begun to bruise and Liam's forehead looked to be wet with sweat.

"You told her, didn't you? You couldn't just wait for one of us to tell her?" William wiped off his forehead with the back of his head. What was he talking about? "You had to be a little bitch and tell on us! How old are you?" he laughed but nothing was funny about this situation. Adrian's head hung low and my mother and Lisa stood confused.

"She deserved to know. You've never been enough for her. You never deserved her. I couldn't just sit back and let you continue on with this," Liam argued.

"Wait, you knew it was Adrian?" I questioned. My mind was going a mile a minute. "For how long?"

Liam didn't answer right away.

"Liam, how long?" my voice rose as my blood boiled.

"A month," he said, putting his head down. His answer rang clear in my ears and I was close to losing all control. He knew about them for a month and didn't tell me. I thought about the time frame and remembered exactly when it happened. My mouth dropped, "But C, I couldn't tell you. It wasn't my place. I hated hurting you, I did. Please understand why I waited," he pleaded with me. "You had been through so much, and I didn't want to add this onto your plate."

I stared back at him and saw the hurt behind his brown eyes. My anger transferred from William and my sister to Liam. How could he do this to me? He saw how much I was struggling with my relationship these past few weeks, and yet he said nothing. My thoughts were interrupted when William spoke up.

"I knew it, all along I've always known." He snickered as he pieced two and two together. "You love her, don't you?" The room was silent besides Liam's breathing.

"What if I do?" Liam asked through clenched teeth. I sucked in a breath.

"I should've seen this coming," William said, shaking his head in disbelief. "Something has happened between the two of you," he laughed. "I'm not blind, Liam. It doesn't matter though. You're just using her; this infatuation will fade. You'll ruin her. How is she any different from the other broken girls you hook up with?"

William's words took Liam aback, leaving him speechless. I stared at Liam waiting for an answer, feeling sick to my stomach. I couldn't believe any of this. Looking from the two of them, to my sister, and then to my mom and Lisa, I was amazed by the fact that no one spoke. I think everyone was in shock, including me. This was all so overwhelming, and I couldn't take it anymore. Tears flooded my eyes, and I ran out of the kitchen. I took the stairs two at a time and slammed my bedroom door shut. I was disappointed and pissed at all three of them right now. How could my sister and William do this to me behind my back? How could Liam not tell me?

I pushed aside my questions, focusing my anger on the situation at hand. I fell to the ground, and the tears fell from my eyes; my body convulsed with each sob.

I heard my door open, but I didn't want anyone up here with me. "Get out!" I screamed not looking up. I sobbed at the thought that my sister was pregnant with my ex-boyfriend's child. Was he really that desperate that he needed to have sex with my sister? What had happened? Where did everything go wrong? I felt sick again.

"C," Liam's soft voice spoke over my sobs. He dropped to the ground to see me eye to eye.

"Liam, I want to be left alone!" I seethed.

"No, I need you to listen to me," Liam demanded. I looked up in surprise at his serious tone.

"And I want to be left alone, Liam."

"I'm in love with you Caelyn. And I have been for a long time. Maybe even years. I'm sorry I didn't tell you," he took a deep breath. I stared at him. "William never deserved you, and I've told you that since you started dating him. I was selfish and never supported you because I've always wanted it to be me instead of him. Maybe I don't deserve you either, but I can't go one more day lying to myself and you about my feelings. I love you." His eyes started to water as he continued his confession. "You're so incredibly strong and I love that about you. When we lost David, I thought you would break, but you fought through. It was extremely difficult but you did it." He grabbed my hands and I tried to pull away. "Caelyn, you're the kindest person I have ever met, and I cherish how sweet you are to everyone in your life. I love that you have a funny and playful side to you, but also know when to be serious. You're amazing from head to toe; I'm not saying perfect because we know no one is. But you are pretty damn close to perfection." I shook my head in disbelief. The lies needed to stop. "Caelyn, it broke my heart to have to tell you about William this morning. Yes, I've known for a month, but you have to understand that I didn't know how to tell you." He started to cry more.

"There it is. You didn't tell me," I choked between sobs of my own. He only shook his head. What the hell was wrong with him? "Liam, you're my best friend, and you didn't tell me. Why the hell not?"

"I was afraid you wouldn't believe me and then William would be able to convince you not to trust me anymore. When in fact you never should have trusted him. I didn't want this to affect you and me." He grimaced at his own words, knowing that he sounded selfish and cowardly. Neither one of them were right in this situation.

"Leave me alone Liam. I don't want you around me anymore," I choked out. I wanted nothing to do with him. I despised his selfish choice because I could've ended a toxic relationship and saved myself a month of heartache.

"Caelyn, you don't mean that," he said, drawing in a shallow breath.

"I most certainly do." I took a deep breath and raised my voice, "Leave. Me. Alone." I pulled my hands away for good and stared coldly into his eyes.

"But I love you," he pleaded, trying to reach for my hands once more. Tears flooded down his cheeks and it broke me seeing him like that. I cried harder as he said those three words to me. I've waited years to hear those exact words from him, but I didn't want to hear them now. I stood up, grabbed my keys from the table by my door, and sprinted down the stairs and out the front door.

Sixteen

Liam

There I was, sitting on Caelyn's bedroom floor, replaying my last conversation with her. I laid my feelings out in the open, poured my heart out, and received nothing in return. Her steps echoed in my ears until she hit the landing. In an instant, I stood up and ran after her. I was not going to lose her because of this.

"Caelyn wait!" I ran down the stairs as quickly as I could and opened the front door. She ran through the pouring rain to her car as thunder shook the house. Lightening lit up the black sky, and I flinched at the sight. "Shit," I closed the door and slipped on my shoes. I looked for my keys but remembered I walked here. "Damnit!" I said in frustration. I ran to the other room and found William and Adrian standing around the kitchen with the adults. Thunder rumbled once more.

"I need your keys," I said to William.

"To hell you do," he smirked at me.

"William, damn it, I need your keys right now. Caelyn just left and she shouldn't be driving like this. One, the storm just started and it's not safe, and two, she's upset. This is everyone's fault. But you're the one that had me keep the secret about you guys, and she knows that now. Just give me your god damn keys, asshole." He stared at me and reached into his pocket. He threw them across the table, and I ran to the door.

"Liam, wait, I'm coming too," Adrian ran after me. I didn't waste time arguing as we ran outside to William's car on the street. It was freezing outside and the rain continued to come down hard.

The engine revved and we drove after Caelyn. I had no idea where she was going, but I knew I needed to get to her. I pulled my phone out and dialed her number by heart. The line rang and rang, but ultimately was sent to voicemail.

"Shit," I ended the call and got to the light in town. I thought for two seconds and then turned on my blinker. I knew where she was going; the lighthouse. I unsuccessfully tried calling her again and the rain continued to pour.

"This is all my fault," Adrian cried in the passenger seat as I took another turn. Just then, I thought I saw her taillights through the rain. I squinted, trying to focus on the red lights. Adrian cried in the seat next to me as she dialed number after number on her phone. We were almost to the lighthouse when I clearly made out taillights in front of us. I found her, or so I had hoped. Finally, Adrian had gotten a hold of my sister, who had left the Prices' house early to take a late shift at the hospital. I distinctly heard their conversation as Adrian relayed the situation into her cell. For a moment, Adrian grew silent then said she'd meet her at the lighthouse. I guess Adrian knew where Caelyn was going too.

The car in front of us came into focus as they turned the corner before the lighthouse at full speed. With the conditions, the car seemed to lose control and fishtailed. I slowed down in preparation for the turn and held my breath. Then, before my own eyes, the car flipped twice. It stopped and hit the guard rail to its right, but the old rail provided no cushion. It broke easily, sending the car over the edge. Adrian shrieked, and I panicked. I put the car in park and ran into the freezing rain. The guard rail separated the road from a small cliff which expanded to the ocean. When I got to the edge, I barely made out the car sinking into the water, a Ford Edge. Caelyn's Ford Edge.

I turned around and yelled back at Adrian, "Call the police! Call the police! It's Caelyn's car." I turned back to the car in the water and heard Adrian frantically call the 911 dispatcher. A shiver overcame my body and rain continued to pour overhead. I stood helpless as I watched Caelyn's car sink more and more into the cold Atlantic. The worst possible thoughts crossed my mind: Caelyn was trapped, she was dead, she was unconscious, this was it.

I slipped off my shoes and walked over to the edge of the road. I turned back to Adrian, "I'm going to get her," I yelled through the pouring rain. The rain pelted my skin as I planned my next step. I looked back at the water but before I could jump, Adrian grabbed hold of my arm.

"Liam, you'll kill yourself. Are you crazy?" she said through her tears. *Yes,* I answered in my head. If I didn't jump in right now, I'd lose her for good.

"She'll die if I don't help her. I'm going." I jerked away from her and jumped over the edge and into the water.

My arms flung in the air as I dropped into the stormy Atlantic. As soon as my body entered the water, I felt the cold, familiar sting from last night. I surfaced and sucked in the cold air, gasping at the shock to my system. I willed every bone in my body to move and put one arm in front of the other. It was like a swim race, only I wasn't racing the clock to beat an opponent. I was racing the clock of death or hypothermia, and time was running out.

I swam to the driver's side of the car and saw Caelyn sitting helplessly. Her head hung low with her arms limp by her sides. I frantically hit the window, no response. *Think Liam, think,* I thought. I pushed aside my fears whether she was dead or unconscious and tried to open the door. *The car doors must be locked or jammed,* I concluded. I quickly assessed my options, but had to hurry since the water continued to fill up the car. I hung onto the car as a huge wave crashed into the frame. I blindly reached for the back door to test the locks once more. No luck. I racked my brain as the side mirror disappeared under the water. The window was next since it was sinking at an incline, nose first.

My first thought was to find something to break the window, but I didn't know what to use. Then, I remembered I was wearing a belt. I quickly released it from my waist, almost dropping it in the process. Strategically using the metal buckle, I hit the window as hard as I could. I continued this motion until I felt a searing pain surge up my wrist to my arm.

The window was halfway under the water now, and I started to panic. Another wave crashed into the frame, and I had an idea. I raced back to the edge where I had jumped in, hoping to find a small rock. I figured a rock would have better impact on the glass. I grabbed the first rock I saw and swam back to the car. Now, the window was almost completely under. *Shit, shit, shit.* Waves came at the car, splashing my face and stinging my eyes.

I stopped at the back seat passenger's window and threw the rock as hard as I could. The glass cracked, but didn't break. The rock bounced from the glass and whacked me right in the head. I desperately grasped for the rock that was beginning to sink, pushing through the pain. I had bigger issues to deal with and knew I was running out of time. I found the rock, threw it at the window one last time, and the glass shattered.

Water flooded into the back seat as I pulled myself through the window, ripping my clothes and skin with shards of glass. I climbed

to the front of the car and assessed that the water was up to the
bottom of the steering wheel and rising quickly thanks to the huge
hole in the window. Caelyn's head hung to the side, motionless, but
I saw shallow breaths raising in her chest. Water continued to flood
in while I reached for the seat buckle. Although I was thankful she
wore it, I grew pissed that it wasn't releasing. I pushed down as hard
as I could and yanked on the strap. It flung up releasing her from its
hold. My head spun, and I blinked aside the dots framing my vision.

Water continued to flood in through the bottom and the back
seat. I evaluated the options to get out, but the water was almost
up to the ceiling. I was running out of time but was more afraid
I wouldn't be able to get her out. How long did I have until she
needed to breathe? Clouds formed in front as I breathed in and out
of my mouth. I shivered at the temperature and more dots clouded
my vision.

I shook my head and focused on her slumped body in front of
me. I climbed to the back seat and blindly reached for her body.
I successfully pulled her upper half through the middle until she
cleared entirely. I tried to keep her head above the water as I
thought about how we were getting out the window. I carefully
went first, still feeling the shards of glass dig into my sweater and
skin.

Holding onto her I grabbed her hands and pulled her through
the window. We were out. We were finally out. The car continued
to sink under and with it went Caelyn. I grasped for her hands and
tried to pull her up, but something prevented her from moving.
Without thinking, I ducked under the water and opened my eyes. I
reached for her legs to find that one of her shoes had caught in the
glass. Midway through releasing her shoe, I had to come up for air.
I broke the surface, gasped for air, and retreated down. I got the left
foot free but the right foot had been pierced by some glass. In one

quick motion, with adrenaline pumping, I pulled her foot out of the glass's grasp and surfaced.

I tugged Caelyn by her back and swam to the edge where I jumped. My vision started to give way for good, but I focused on the outline of a rock formation in front of me. I was so close to getting us both out of here. Waves harshly crashed against the drop off, and I did my best not to get thrown into them. My adrenaline faltered and the dots returned.

"We're getting out of here C. I promise. I'm trying the best I can." The clouds coming from my mouth were unmistakable. It was absolutely freezing, and I couldn't believe the shock hadn't hit Caelyn. "Please stay with me," I begged.

From here it was going to be difficult getting out. I couldn't see five feet in front of me and had no way of knowing how to get up to the road. I checked Caelyn's face and her lips looked purple. I was afraid her body was in shock or that she was dying of hypothermia. Again, I tried to look and see if I could get us out of the water. The rain poured and poured, and I was almost out of options when I saw a light shine down to the water. I looked up and through the rain I saw what looked like people standing up on the edge.

"Sir, please wait right there. We are going to lower a harness down to you," a man yelled out. I treaded water, trying to keep Caelyn's head above it. The man returned with a rope with a canvas triangle at the end of it. They lowered it, and I slid on first. Then, I pulled Caelyn to my chest and cradled her body. I yelled up that we were ready and inch by inch, foot by foot, we were brought level with the road. First, I passed Caelyn to our rescuers. I held hold of her hand for as long as I could until they pulled her away from me. She was as cold as ice.

"Please, please take care of her," I said, out of breath. The air was so cold and the rain continued to pelt my body. The men said a few words to one another and put us on stretchers. I tried to keep an eye on her, but a group of men rolled her in another direction. I laid back and tried to steady my breathing. Just then, I began to feel a sharp pain in my chest along with my head. The bright, flash of red and blue lights did not help.

"We have two coming from the scene. One, a female, is unconscious but breathing. Hypothermia is an issue right now. The other, a male, has several lesions on the torso and head. Needing immediate medical attention. A few minutes out." I believed a man was speaking into his shoulder as he said those words. *Was he talking about me?*

No longer feeling the adrenaline coursing through my body, I let out a painful scream. It felt as if someone was repeatedly stabbing me. The rain continued to pour as my stretcher was loaded into a box. My head began to spin, and I felt my eyes roll to the back of my head.

"We're losing him."

Those were the last words I heard before blackness overcame me.

My eyes opened to a stark white room. My mom and dad sat at the end of my bed talking with another man and woman. Slowly, I came to and immediately tried to get my mom's attention. She gasped when she saw me lift my right arm. I dropped it to the mattress, realizing I was in excruciating pain.

"You're finally awake," my mom said, crying with joy.

"Mom, I'm fine," I said groggily. I looked around again and realized the other figures were not people I recognized. They had on blue and black police uniforms. What was going on? Why was I here?

"Well you've been in and out for two days Liam, we didn't know when you would wake up," she cried, but looked relieved that I was awake. She kissed my hands, and I smiled at her groggily. I felt extremely weak but was happy to see her and my dad with me right now. "Do you think you could answer a few questions for these two officers? If you can't yet, please don't worry."

"I'll try my best," I admitted. I slowly sat up in bed as the two of them introduced themselves.

"Mr. Carter, do you recognize this car?" The man held a picture of a Ford Edge. I tried to rack my brain, thinking about where I had seen that car before.

"I know it's a Ford Edge, am I supposed to see it as anything else?" I questioned. My mom stayed silent next to me, and my dad started to nervously pace the room.

"Why don't we look at the next picture we have?" I nodded my head. "Do you recognize who this is?" The woman held up a picture of a stunning girl with light brown, wavy hair. Her eyes were a piercing sea green color that were perfectly separated by a freckle-adorned nose. Her lips were a light shade of pink and she smiled a wide grin. She was absolutely beautiful, but I didn't recognize her.

"She's beautiful, but no I don't know who that is," I admitted. The officers looked to be upset, and I noticed that my parents showed the same emotion. Was I supposed to know who that was? "Wait, can I see that picture again?" The officer nodded. For a moment, the group looked hopeful, but I still didn't recognize the girl in the picture. "I'm sorry I really don't know who that is," I said, shaking my head.

What was going on?

My mom started to cry and the officers told me that they would be back later today or tomorrow to ask some more questions. I was very confused why they showed me two very different pictures and what they could have meant. When the officers left the room, my parents and I were left alone. I was about to ask them what was going on when there was a knock at the door. My mother sat straight up while my dad opened it. A tall man I did not recognize stood in the entrance and shook my father's hand. My mother got up and gave him a hug. Without another word, the three of them stepped into the hallway. Thankfully, there was a window right by the door that I could watch through. My dad was talking to the man and my mother couldn't help but cry. I was unable to make out the conversation, but the mysterious man began to cry as well. I felt as if I intruded on their moment, so I looked away.

My room was barren with a few cards and a couch with a blanket and pillow. I figured my mom and dad had been alternating who stayed with me if I had been here for two days. I looked up at my monitors and then followed the IVs to their location on my arms. My hand was heavily bandaged and my arms had a few scrapes. What did I do to my hand? I wanted to try and take off the bandage so I could investigate further, but my parents and another new face entered the room.

"Liam, how are you doing?" A man in a white coat asked me. His eyes looked to be darkly rimmed, probably from lack of sleep.

"I'm fine I guess. But I am so confused." I tried to make light of the situation and laughed, but it only caused my head to throb. I reached up to touch my head but felt a heavy bandage. Great, more bandages and still no explanation.

"I had a feeling," the doctor said. He retracted to the hallway and passed a few words on to the nurses in the hallway. He returned swiftly. "Liam, I am going to take you to get further CT scans of your head. I want to see if there was permanent damage from your trauma." He scribbled on a clipboard and put the board at the foot of my bed. "I can share more information with you and your parents after I get your results."

"Alright then," I said going with the flow. What trauma though? What happened?

The next few hours were tedious and agonizingly painful. My head throbbed constantly, and I just wanted to close my eyes and take a nap. The machines were loud and ginormous, but I followed the orders given to me by the doctors and nurses. Countless needles were pricked into my arms and fingers before each scan which made me anxious for my results. The pictures and brief explanations were foreign to me, and my throbbing head made the images and words blur together. I started to get frustrated because I understood nothing. After what seemed like hours, I returned to my room and was told to rest up until my results came in from the lab. I had no problem falling asleep with the beeping machines in the background.

I finally came to and noticed that my throat felt a little scratchy. I looked around the room for my Styrofoam cup but it was too far away. After several failed attempts, I gave up and just laid in my bed. My eyes wandered around the room to the open doorway, but I didn't see anyone outside. Finally, I decided to push the "call nurse" button and a short woman in her mid-sixties came in.

"What can I do for you, hon?" she asked sweetly.

"I'm not sure where my parents are, but can I go for a walk? I feel so cramped laying in this bed," I told her. I was afraid she was going to tell me no, and I really needed to stretch my legs. It was agonizing to lay here because I had so many unanswered questions. No, that would not do for me.

"Sure thing," she nodded her head and smiled at me. "Just give me a minute darlin'."

She left the room and returned moments later. She helped me sit up and moved my IV to a portable stand that I could wheel around. She tied my gown tighter and waited by my side while I stood. My legs were a little wobbly at first, but I was soon able to walk at a slow, easy pace. We walked down the hall past several rooms. I could make out several TVs through the open doors, but besides that the hallway was empty and quiet. My nurse stayed by my side the entire time, ready to grab hold of me if I went down. She didn't try to make small talk with me, and I gladly accepted the silence.

We came to the end of the hallway and turned right. There were two other people in this hallway and one was rolled in a wheelchair. The further we walked, the closer we got to the person in the wheelchair and the nurse accompanying them. It was a girl about my age and her hair framed her expressionless face. We were about to cross paths when she finally looked up at me. Her green eyes were the first thing I saw, and I was blinded by her natural beauty. She had a few scratches on her face and her leg and right foot were heavily bandaged. I tried not to stare, but it was hard not to. I felt like I recognized her, but I couldn't put my finger on it.

We stared at one another, caught in a trance. She had little color in her face and her eyes looked swollen. But man, those green eyes were vibrant and full of life. She smiled a full smile which caught me off guard at first. After a few seconds, I returned the smile the best I could. This smile was friendly and it made my heart pull in my chest.

Just then I had a flashback. I sat in my car and heard someone crying beside me. I squinted through the rain that pelted the windshield. The wipers were on the highest setting, and I still couldn't see anything in front of me. Finally, I saw bright red taillights ahead. As soon as I passed the girl, the memory faded. I couldn't recall when that happened or who was in the car with me. There were several missing pieces to complete the picture. I wanted to know more. Quickly, I turned my head around and the girl was already looking at me. She smiled again and waved.

I raised my bandaged hand to wave back and the motion sent my mind back to another memory. My hand connected with something hard and a horrific pain shot up my arm. I was still trying to use my hand even though the pain got worse. My hand connected with a hard surface and went right through. The pain in my hand shifted to my head simultaneously. *Did something come back and hit my head?* I peered through the dark and my hand was stinging and bleeding profusely. I dropped it and brought it back up to my face. It was clean. *How could my hand be clean? It was just covered in blood.* Then, I felt the cold water surround me.

I was brought back to reality and the girl was nowhere in sight. "Are you alright?" the short nurse asked me repeatedly. What had just happened? Was that me in real life or a dream? Did I watch a movie the other night?

"Yeah, I think so," I stammered. I felt lightheaded and extreme fatigue set in. "Can we go back to the room? I'm not feeling so well anymore."

"Of course." We returned to the room and I fell asleep as soon as my head hit the pillow. Who knew taking such a short walk would wear me out like that?

While I was sleeping, I dreamed of witnessing a terrible car wreck. A driver lost control during a bad storm which caused their car to flip twice before plummeting into the ocean. My role in the dream switched from the witness to the hero in a matter of seconds. I had a strong feeling I needed to save the driver, no matter the cost. The water was brisk and in no way refreshing. It was dark and little light shone on the sinking car. After several failed attempts to get into the car, I finally broke the window and my hand in the process. Water pooled into the back of the car, a Ford Edge to be exact. Then, without thinking, I maneuvered my way to the front to save the driver.

The person's face was blurry, but I knew it was a girl. Her features looked purple and blue and her skin was ice cold. Finally, I got her out of the seatbelt's hold before facing a bigger issue. How was I going to get myself and this girl out when the car was almost completely underwater? Then I had an idea, and it was the only option.

I climbed to the back and pulled her along with me. I tried to get us out of the window I had broken minutes earlier. Ultimately, she got stuck, and I knew I was hurting her but I didn't know how else to save her. I wondered why I was saving this woman, but then that feeling returned. I had a strong sense to not leave her behind. I used every ounce of energy left in me to swim to the side where paramedics waited to lift us out. When they dropped the line, I secured the both of us in the harness and was pulled to the top.

As soon as we got to the top the paramedics tried to separate us, and I held onto her, crying. My tears mixed with the rain that continued to pour. There was something wrong because she wasn't waking up. I screamed her name over and over, but she couldn't hear me. Her face came into focus and her brown hair was pressed to the sides of her face. I shouted her name, but I couldn't make it out in the dream.

Abruptly, I woke up from the dream, sobbing uncontrollably. I tried to get out of bed but the cords held me in place. Footsteps ran to the side of my bed, but my eyes weren't focusing. I felt a pressure in my arm and a calming sense overcame my body. I fell asleep as quickly as I woke up.

Seventeen

Caelyn

The doctors kept me in the hospital for two weeks to ensure I was healthy enough to leave after surgery and recovery. My parents never left my side during my stay and helped me piece together information from the night of the wreck, details of the wreck, and life after. As much as it pained them to tell me about William and Adrian, I had them tell me all the details so I wouldn't forget. The more I heard, the angrier I got towards them both. My parents claimed they were at the hospital for four straight days, taking breaks to shower and eat, because they were worried about me. I told them I didn't believe them and never wanted to see either of them again. Surprisingly enough, my parents didn't argue with me and told Adrian and William I wasn't ready for visitors. I didn't think I would ever be ready to see them after what they did to me.

The wreck was harder for me to hear about, but I asked my mom to relay the details three times a day so I wouldn't forget. I knew my car laid at the bottom of the Atlantic and Liam had somehow saved me from the sinking car. When I first heard that Liam pulled me out, I felt nothing but anger towards him. I still remembered what he did before I wrecked my car. Then, after two days of hearing the story over and over, my anger turned into sadness. We found out that Liam was close to dying that night and suffered from a broken hand, many lesions over his body, and severe amnesia. The worst part of it all was that he didn't know who I was, and the doctors were afraid his memory would never return.

Yeah, that's what I said. He didn't know who I was. If that wasn't the hardest thing to swallow, I didn't know what was. There was one day while my parents had gone down to the cafeteria to eat with Paul and Lisa, and I had insisted I would be fine without them, mostly because I needed a break. They were hovering nonstop after the wreck and that was partly because it reminded them of four years ago. It was also because I had no one else to turn to this time.

Anyway, they left and I wasted no time in calling a nurse so I could go on a walk, or for me, a wheelchair ride. My foot had been penetrated by glass when Liam pulled me out of the car, and the doctor wanted the stitches to have two weeks to heal before I put my weight on it. My nurse helped me sit in the chair and she took me out into the hallway. We went around the whole floor twice and on our way back to my room, I heard a pair of footsteps in front of me. I looked up immediately and saw Liam. There he was, standing right in front of me and it was like seeing a ghost.

He made no effort to run over to me, nor did he offer one of his famous smiles I loved. At this point, I had just found out that Liam didn't know who I was that morning. I had been in tears since Paul and Lisa told my parents and me. They told me he didn't recognize my picture and didn't ask about me, so that was why he hadn't come to see me. I kicked myself for staying angry at him for looking after me. I kicked myself knowing the last moments spent with him were nothing but a mix of bad, embarrassing memories. I held onto the hope that he would remember soon because the doctor didn't want to rule it out quite yet. However, when he saw me, I saw no semblance of recognition.

I cried myself to sleep that night and woke up crying the next morning. My mom held me and tried to soothe my worries, but it wasn't working. Over the course of the next two weeks, I tried to visit him, but was put on strict orders that I couldn't leave my room. Plus, the nurses were afraid if he saw a random girl sitting in his room he might freak out. I understood, but it broke my heart that I couldn't help him like he helped me four years ago. I wanted to be the first face he saw when he woke up. I wanted to comfort him when he was in pain. I wanted to tell him I was sorry for everything. I hoped that he would come back to me, but I reminded myself it was only wishful thinking.

The two weeks in the hospital were brutal, but I finally went home to my house in the Cape. My doctor advised not returning to campus because he was afraid it would be too overwhelming. My parents and I agreed, and I planned to take alternative finals from home and take the next semester off. I asked if I could go back to therapy as soon as possible and my parents agreed wholeheartedly. It broke my heart calling Bonnie and telling her the news. Of course she was supportive, and even offered to come visit over winter break. I told her we'd have to see because I just wasn't ready to see people. I was in a lot of pain physically and emotionally.

At home I refused to eat for the first few days, and I called the Carters as often as I could to get an update on Liam. They reminded me they didn't know when he would be released, and if he would get his memories back. It was hard to hear, but I appreciated their honesty. Lisa and Paul continued to check in on me too when Liam was finally released to come home. We met up for coffee, lunch, and walks when the doctor cleared me for physical activity. We tried to steer the topic of conversation away from Liam for my sake. They asked me how physical therapy was going, my plans for my semester off, and more. It was nice staying in contact with them, but hard knowing Liam wasn't the same.

This meant I was stuck at home most days wallowing in my own self-pity, wishing he remembered who I was. I wanted him to remember that night and everything he had confessed to me. I wanted him to remember our friendship and the memories we shared. But as the weeks went by, I didn't know if that future would ever be clear to him. A small part of me thought that if he saw me then maybe he would remember or maybe we could start over. I didn't care; I just wanted him to come back to me.

A few months later...

It was late March and I had been going to therapy for four months, trying to piece together my new normal. I got back into running around town, but couldn't bring myself to pass the lighthouse yet. It's the little steps, my therapist taught me. My mom also set up a time to have my sister come over and talk things over. I had been preparing for this meeting for a while and felt ready to face her. I was less angry at the situation and her, but still questioned why and how it happened.

"Mom," I screamed from the couch in the living room. There was no answer. "Mom!" I screamed again. I heard her run down the stairs into the joint kitchen and living room.

"What? What's wrong?" she asked me, scared and out of breath.

"I wanted to remind you that Adrian and William are coming over right now to get some of her stuff and talk." I stared at her and gave her a nervous laugh.

"Caelyn," my mom said as she sat next to me on the couch. "Honey, you're ready. I know how hard it's been for you to get to this place, but it will be good for the two of you to talk." She smoothed my short hair. I chose to cut it off a month ago to change some things up.

"I know, I'm just a little nervous I think," I admitted. I took a deep breath and looked her in the eyes. "Is it okay if I'm still angry?" I asked. Tears welled up in my eyes and she sighed seeing the pain rise again.

"Of course." She gave me a hug and held me for a few moments. "Unfortunately, this is a new normal for us all." She shrugged her shoulders. My mom was alluding to the fact that Adrian was almost five months pregnant with William's child. "It's weird to think about I know, I still struggle some days," she chuckled.

"How do you do it?" I asked honestly.

"She's still my daughter," she said matter-of-factly. "That means she's still your sister. Also, we can't change what happened in the past, all we can do is look forward."

She had a good way of putting it and I tried to use some of my mom's positivity to fuel my own. Just then the door opened and I heard Adrian and William walk into the foyer. *Here goes nothing.* I mentally prepared myself to stay calm.

"Hello?" Adrian called out.

"In here," I yelled from my spot on the couch.

"Caelyn?" my sister's voice rang down the hallway. She appeared in front of me with William tailing behind her.

"Hey," I said, letting out a big breath.

"I'm just going to go grab some of your things," William said, pointing over his shoulder. He left after Adrian nodded her head in appreciation. I was thankful William gave us the space to talk.

"Can I sit?" she asked. I motioned towards the couch and Mom excused herself from the room. We sat in silence for what seemed like forever. Adrian's sad voice cut the tension. "I'm sorry Caelyn. I've practiced what I wanted to say to you when we finally got the chance to talk, but I'm at a loss for words right now." She looked down at her clasped hands. "I never wanted to hurt you. I never thought we would be in this situation, but fate kept pushing us together." She looked up at my calm exterior and continued, "I'm just not sure what I can say to make the situation better, except I'm sorry and I wish you hadn't been involved. I'm so sorry."

"Thank you for your apology," I said. We sat in silence as I processed her words. I still had so many questions, and I couldn't help but want the answers. "Can I ask you something?"

"Of course," she smiled.

"How did it happen?" She looked at me confused. I racked my brain for a different question. "Sorry, how did you two get close enough to develop a romantic relationship?"

"We were working long hours and collaborating on cases together," she said plainly. "After a while, we began opening up about some things, and I realized he was genuine, pretty inquisitive, and funny. I felt challenged and appreciated for my intelligence and character. I know that sounds ridiculous considering, but I just fell for him."

I nodded my head in understanding. "Okay, I understand."

"It's not right, I know. It doesn't make up for what we did to you, trust me. I was sick knowing we hurt you."

"Okay, then I have one more question," I said, staring right at her. My comment came off more harshly than I intended and I heard her gulp. "Why did you do this to me? Did I do something that made you want vengeance? Did *I* do something? Did you intentionally want to hurt me? Did William?" I asked the burning questions that had been heavy on my heart these past few months. Tears filled Adrian's eyes and she took a deep breath.

"To be candid, at first I did want to hurt you. I think I've always resented the relationship you and David had. You both got all the attention growing up, and I never felt included," she cried as she said these words. "Then David died and you got all the attention, like you were the only one to lose him. He was my brother too, Caelyn." She looked away from me, and I was beginning to understand why Adrian did it. I placed my hand over hers, and she looked at me surprised.

"I got all the attention, from Mom and Dad, Liam, Liam's family, everyone. Then, I started getting attention from William, and that made you angrier," I said, piecing everything together.

"Yes," she sobbed. "It's so terrible, I know. It's so unfair to you and wasn't your fault at all. It was just my way of understanding the situation, and I couldn't help but feel those feelings."

"I'm so sorry Adrian, I never wanted to undermine your feelings about David's death. I never wanted to make you angry. Hell, I never wanted all the attention on me after David died," I said crying alongside her. We sat and cried together for a few minutes before Adrian composed herself.

"But it happened, and I think I need to work through some of those feelings on my own," she said, wiping the tears from her eyes. "Caelyn, after I realized what I was doing, I tried to stop and tell you. But by then, I knew I had developed real feelings for William and couldn't walk away." She continued wiping at her eyes and looked up at the ceiling. "Do you ever think you could forgive me?"

I took a moment to think over her question. I wanted to forgive her, but I didn't think it would be in this moment. I felt the pain she caused me rise in my chest and counted to five. I closed my eyes, focused on my breathing, and told the truth. "I want to, but I can't forgive you yet. I'm really working on it, but I don't want to rush into something I'm not ready for. Does that make sense?" I asked. I waited patiently for her response. These past few months proved particularly challenging when it came to working on myself. I had been so selfish before and still struggled with putting my thoughts and feeling above others. However, in this situation, I knew I wasn't ready. I also knew that if I forgave her too soon, I would ruin our future relationship.

"I understand and completely agree. I want you to take your time. Please know, that I am willing to do anything to help our relationship. I want to gain your trust back," she said honestly. Her kind eyes stared deeply into my own. "I want you to be a part of my child's life in whatever way you think you can be. But I also understand if it's too hard and if you can't make that work."

"I would love to be a part of their life, Adrian."

The conversation went better than I had hoped, and I appreciated how honest we were able to be to each other. Of course, it was hard to hear some of her answers, but I felt better knowing how and why things happened the way they did. Although our relationship wasn't completely healed, today's conversation helped us move forward and away from the past. We said our goodbyes and planned to meet up for coffee next week. I was looking forward to the endless opportunities we would have to strengthen our relationship.

I sat at the dinner table that night, telling my parents the progress Adrian and I made this afternoon. They were ecstatic that the conversation had been helpful for both of us, but still had their reservations about William. Ultimately, my mom and dad reminded themselves he was the father of their first grandchild so they needed to move past the obvious animosity. My mom switched the topic of conversation and the air seemed to escape the room.

"Lisa called me before dinner," she commented as she took a bite of food. I stopped chewing and stared at my plate.

"What did she have to say?" my dad asked, taking a long drink of his wine. I heard the unease in his voice.

"They just got back from their vacation this morning," she said matter-of-factly. I knew exactly what vacation she was talking about. About a month ago, Lisa and Paul told my mom they were taking Liam on a much-needed break to Florida to see Paul's parents. They left in early February and hadn't said when they'd come back up to the Cape. It was odd timing with everything going on, but they insisted it was for the best.

"How was it?" my dad asked hesitantly. I felt both sets of eyes land on me as I continued to stare at my plate.

"Good. She said it was just what they needed," she chirped. I knew why they suddenly left and why they were gone for a month. The doctor thought it would be stressful on Liam when he returned to his house across the street from the girl he saw in the hospital. Thinking about the details made me uncomfortable, and I wanted to excuse myself from the table.

"Can I please be excused?" I asked quietly. I looked up at my parents through tear-filled eyes.

"Caelyn, I'm sorry," my mom started.

"It's fine Mom," I replied. "I'm glad they had a good trip, really I am. I just don't want to talk about Liam right now." I held the tears back for as long as I could. When the first tear fell, I pushed back from the table and retreated upstairs.

I cried myself to sleep that night, thinking of my unresolved feelings for Liam. I had made so much progress these past four months; I'd focused on improving myself mentally and working through the pent-up feelings I had since David died. I went to therapy, physical therapy, and even followed through with the assignments the doctors gave me. I was finally feeling somewhat normal again until my mom mentioned Liam's name. Regret filled my mind as I laid down that night.

The next morning, I woke up with a burst of energy and decided to take a run. I pulled on some leggings, a thick sweatshirt and socks, and ear warmers before heading down the stairs. I stopped by the mirror in the hallway and admired the suddenly confident woman staring back at me. My short hair sat naturally under the ear warmers and my normal coloring seemed to return to my face overnight. I knew today was going to be a good day.

"Caelyn, is that you?" my dad called from the kitchen. I walked down the hallway and stopped in front of them.

"I'm going to go on a run. I woke up full of energy and think today is the day I'm going to run by the lighthouse," I said, trying to smile. They both looked up from their coffee mugs and smiled from ear to ear.

"Sweetheart, that's wonderful news," my dad said encouragingly.

"I don't want to think about it too much, I just know I need to run with it," I said laughing at the unintended joke I made.

"I'm so proud of you," my mom said. "Go, go! We want to hear about it when you get back!"

I opened the front door and the Maine air smacked me right in the face. I took a deep breath in and looked across the street. The Carters' house looked dark in the sea of lit up homes around them. I dared a glance toward Liam's bedroom window, but the curtains were drawn. I pried my eyes away, and told myself to stop thinking about him.

I took off in a jog toward town and saw very few people out today, which was common for a Thursday morning. Traffic was slow so I decided to run along the edge of the road just like I did on Thanksgiving. I decided to take the same route Liam and I did that morning, passing the lighthouse once, only to return for a small break on my second loop. As I ran past the familiar sights, memories of Liam flooded my mind.

I replayed every single moment that Liam and I shared during my whole run. I remembered the first day David, Liam, and I played together in the grass outside our house. I remembered riding bikes down our street and then to the lighthouse. I remembered that those bike rides turned into runs. I remembered the countless summer vacations at the beach when the three of us would go crab hunting late at night or lay on the deck of dock at the Carters' lake house reciting every constellation we knew. I remembered seeing Liam swim for the first time my freshman year. I remembered him being by my side through David's funeral and the dark days that followed. I remembered him staying home from prom so that he could take care of me. I remembered the day he left for college and every time he came home for a holiday break or weekend surprise. I remembered when he saved me that night after the ball and how he took such great care of me after. I remembered the first time he told me he loved me. I remembered it all.

Once the memories played through, I racked my brain remembering every feature of Liam's. It had been four months since I last saw him, but the image was as clear as if I'd seen him yesterday. I saw him smiling ear to ear when we won our first swim meet this year. Gosh, that grin; I smiled just thinking about it. I saw him playing with his hair when he got tired or when he worried about something. His messy, brown hair was one of my favorite parts about him. I saw his chocolate brown eyes when I closed my own. Those eyes had stared into my own for as long as I could remember. I had memorized every feature of him, and I remembered it all. *How could he not remember?*

Then the tears came, and I couldn't stop them for the life of me. Thankfully, I had gotten to the lighthouse for my break as the sun rose into the sky. I brushed the tears off my cheeks and took a seat on the all-too-familiar bench looking out at the ocean. I sat in a comfortable silence and took in the beautiful, calm scene around me. Just then, an empty feeling set in my chest, and I wished I had someone to share this moment with.

"Beautiful, isn't it?" a deeper voice said from behind me. I jumped even though I recognized it. I was afraid to turn around. I didn't know if I was ready to face the truth of this new reality. "You see, I remember coming here almost every day in the summers when I was younger. At first, I would ride my bike down here all the time, and then I started including this in my running routes. It's one of my all-time favorite spots in the whole Cape," the man said with a sigh as he looked out at the sunset. "I love it here, don't you?" he asked me. My heart skipped a beat with every word he spoke. I still didn't speak, for I was frozen in thought.

Silence filled the air around us for a few minutes as we looked out at the ocean. My heart rate increased, but I couldn't will myself to turn and look at him. He moved to take a seat next to me on the bench, and I inhaled. I was too nervous and afraid to face him right now. He sat enjoying the view as I was mentally freaking out. I thought today was going to be a good day when I woke up with that burst of energy. I didn't realize it would be the first day that I saw him since everything changed. This was where he saved me, hours after he told me my boyfriend was cheating on me, and minutes after he said he loved me.

I'm not sure if fate was on my side or not, but it was too much of a coincidence that we both were here right now. But then I remembered the scary truth; he didn't know who I was. I half expected him to reach his hand out and introduce himself, but that didn't happen either. He sat in silence and just stared at the sea.

My heart beat fast as I thought about what to say to him. I wanted to reach over and grab his hand or touch his cheek. I wanted to hug him and never let go. I wanted to apologize for everything and tell him I loved him, but I couldn't do that either. The tears started again, and I was afraid he noticed my breakdown. Embarrassed, I reached up to wipe the fallen tears off my face.

"I like the haircut," he said softly. I almost didn't hear him, he spoke that softly.

"What?" I said suddenly. I looked at him in disbelief.

"I like the haircut," he said again, eyes still on the ocean. My mouth opened and shut about ten times as I sat there thinking about what to say. There was no way he knew I got a haircut if he didn't remember who I was. I allowed myself to believe that maybe he knew. I looked at him and studied his calm expression. Could it be true? "It's rude to stare. You do know that right?" he laughed and looked at me. "It's also rude to not say thank you when someone compliments you, Caelyn."

"I'm sorry," I stammered and looked away at the water. *Wait. Did he just say my name?* I turned to look at him again. "What did you just call me?"

"Caelyn." All he said was my name, and I stared at him in shock.

"Wait, how do you know my name?" I asked, feeling my stomach flip. He looked out at the water once more and spoke.

"Caelyn Faith Price. Daughter of Steve and Beth Price. Your sister's name is Adrian and your late brother was David. Born February eleventh, which means I missed your twentieth birthday." He sounded sad, but spoke again. "You are one of the sweetest, most stubborn girls I have ever met. You're not afraid to test the limits and have proven time and time again that you will prevail, no matter the situation." He smiled his infamous grin. "Just look at you. Nothing keeps you down, even the death of your brother and my best friend. You are so strong and I hope to one day match that strength." He looked over at me and searched my features. "I fell in love with you many years ago and finally built up the courage to tell you four months ago. Your brother was the only soul that knew how I felt four years ago. I couldn't imagine pursuing my feelings after he passed away, but I so regret not telling you sooner." He closed his eyes and I noticed he was crying. "You make me feel alive. With every touch we share, I can feel the electricity and passion. I'm not sure if you feel it too, but to me it's undeniable. Now, in all the good, you still manage to scare the hell out of me. I've almost lost you three times. One, four years ago this past October. Two, this past Thanksgiving when I watched your car dive into the Atlantic Ocean. And three, when I woke up and had no idea who you were." His eyes focused on my own, and I was lost listening to his velvety voice. I held my breath awaiting his next words. I had to hear him say it. "Caelyn, I remember. I remember," he said softly as I began to cry. I smiled through the tears and he pulled me close. My head buried into his chest and my arms wrapped around his neck. I pulled away, looked straight into his eyes, and couldn't wait any longer. I placed both hands on either side of his face and pulled him to me as our lips met. His hands pressed flatly against my back as he pulled me to him. One hand moved to the side of my cheek as another slid into my hair and cradled the back of my neck. His lips were warm, and I'd never felt more alive. This kiss sent shockwaves throughout my whole body.

He pulled away and looked me in the eyes, "Caelyn, my love for you has always led me back to you." His eyes were on me and only me. "I couldn't erase you from my mind, even if I tried. I love you now and forever."

"What took you so long?" I closed the space between us and kissed him again.

"Does that mean you love me too?" he said, smiling against my lips.

"Yes!" I laughed and looked in his chocolate brown eyes. "I love you Liam Carter, always have and always will."

We sat on our bench, remembering it all.

Acknowledgments

I would personally like to thank all those involved in helping me reach this goal. With their support, I pushed through many road blocks. Let me tell you, there were quite a few. It was wonderful knowing I had an army of supporters willing to talk through ideas and helping with inspiration. Above all, I want to thank my "super" fans. I'm eternally grateful for each of you, and without you, this novel would've never been completed.

Remembering was inspired by those around me and those I have crossed paths with to write every page. As my mom said to me when she finished reading, "H, you included so many things from your life. The pie flavors, dates, and character personalities". These characters I've created became a part of who I am, and I'm sad to see it come to an end. I have loved this process and the many years it took me to create.

I'm unbelievably humbled by the reviews I have received from my "super" fans. It has been such a wild ride writing *Remembering*, and I'm excited to finally share it with other readers. I hope you enjoyed the book as much as I enjoyed writing it.

A very special thanks to:

My editor, Dominic Wakeford- thank you for believing in my work and being patient with me during this process. As a new writer, you made this process so easy and enjoyable. I have grown from your edits and suggestions, and I'm grateful for your help along the way. Thank you for your time and energy spent on *Remembering* and pushing the book that much further. I could not have done this without you!

My super fans, K.S., B.H., N.B., H.S., J.P., M.H., M.B., and E.B. who convinced me, through many meetings, that I could make it to the end. Your unbounded love and support helped me start and finish this novel with my whole heart involved. You all are the best fans I could have ever asked for. Thank you for falling in love with my characters and this story.

A huge overseas confidant, K.J.- I cannot express how much I appreciate you and what you've contributed to *Remembering*. Your feedback helped me see the work from a different perspective, which greatly impacted the story line. Thank you for sharing your laughs and shedding tears when I needed it most.

My mom, dad, and family members- who blindly encouraged and lent a helping hand even when I wouldn't share my plans. I looked to you for emotional support when doubt plagued my mind, and I am forever grateful to share my work with you. You all kept me going and even gave me tough criticism so I could push to the end.

A large thank you goes out to my readers. It has been such a blessing growing with this novel, and I am so ecstatic that I can share a piece of my heart with you all. I had a blast creating and going on this unforgettable journey with these characters throughout these pages.

I'll leave you with three things:

- Remember to cherish every moment because you may not live to see tomorrow.

- Remember to never take the people around you for granted.
- Remember to push towards your dreams even when others cloud you with doubt.

All my thanks and love,
H.B. Louise

Follow the Author

https://www.booksbyhb.com
https://twitter.com/booksbyhb
https://www.instagram.com/booksbyhb

CPSIA information can be obtained
at www.ICGtesting.com
Printed in the USA
JSHW021530211220
10439JS00003B/13